Beyond the Two Doors

Also by Collette O'Mahony

In Quest of Love
A guide to inner harmony
And wellbeing in relationships

The Soul in Words
A Collection of Poetry & Verse

Matrix of Light
The story of a soul seeking to remember its light origin by
taking a series of journeys to the earth plane

www.colletteomahony.com

Beyond the Two Doors

A journey through time to discover our
Spiritual Ancestry

Collette O'Mahony

STARLIGHT
Publications

BEYOND THE TWO DOORS
Copyright © 2022 by Collette O'Mahony

Cover design: Collette O'Mahony

Published by Starlight Publications 2022

Collette O'Mahony asserts the moral right to
be identified as the author of this work.

All the characters in this book are fictitious and any
resemblance to actual persons, living or dead, is
purely coincidental.

ISBN: 978-1-9160079-3-2

Starlight Publications
United Kingdom and Ireland

www.colletteomahony.com

CONTENTS

In the universe,
There are things that are known,
And things that are unknown,
And in between there are doors.

William Blake

.

PROLOGUE

*A*t the dawning of my lifetime, I wandered along a path leading to two doors. Being unborn to human form, I was curious about a state of duality. I wondered if I could enter both doorways simultaneously. There was a shift in my energy with and two distinct energy fields emerged before me; one was luminous, filled with particles of colour, the other was glowing with inner heat. I beheld the beauty of both energy fields and considered the possibility of entering the two doors to experience what lay beyond. With a strong curiosity, I observed the doors opening to allow the energy fields to the other side. The energies separated and moved through each doorway to experience a beautiful dream in the realm beyond. Through them, I would know what it felt like to live in a world of form.

A sharp sensation in my energy field alerted me that there was an imbalance within. I summoned my power to restore equilibrium. Soon after, both aspects of my energy field returned through the doorways. First, the light energy came, followed by the warm energy. As the energies merged with mine, their separate experiences flooded my awareness with vivid imagery. The light energy had experienced life in a masculine form and the warm energy experienced life in a feminine form. Within their experience, they encountered the construct of time and its building blocks of past, present, and

3

future. For the separated energies, the experience had lasted for over eighty years, a year being one full revolution of the sun. They lived separate lives for some of these years until the time came for the feminine to return. The masculine followed an inner calling that led him to her in her last hours in the world of form.

It occurred to me I was the intuitive signal that the totality of our energy field. They were free to make individual choices in the world of form, but awareness of their truth was only known through the third and unifying aspect, which remained beyond the two doors. In true union, there was no dependency on each other to fulfil expectations. Trust was placed on the unifying energy that dwells beyond the two doors. Holding to this truth, the earthbound relationship between the dual energies was free from fear and acted only from love.

One thing was clear: both energies wished to return to the dream of form and time on Earth. Both energies moved within me, desiring further experience in the world of duality. I entered an altered state of consciousness. My energies were playfully sparking off one another in a dance of light and love. There were images of vast emerald forests and rich golden sunsets, and with every image, there was an accompanying wave of warmth. The dual energies within me were revealing glimpses of the world beyond the two doors, and the sensations they evoked. The light energy within me held the visions, and the warm energy held the response. It was a beautiful flow of synchronicity flowing throughout our being. I knew I wanted a conscious awareness of this world in physical form. As soon as I held this idea in my awareness, I found myself once again at the two doors. A flutter of anticipation swelled within me, and both energies emerged as a sparkling light and warm glow. I felt something else well up inside me, something previously unknown to me, trepidation about what might happen beyond the two doors.

What if both energies did not find each other in the world of duality? Would I become unconscious, leaving both energies to their fate in a perpetual human state? It was crucial to have a plan in place. As I pondered the situation, a series of images flashed before me. The first image showed three interconnecting spirals to indicate our unity. Then I saw a vivid image of several humans separated by a dream, an illusion that only life on earth was real. Their evolutionary process would be to awaken from the dream of separateness. In the crowd of faces, I eventually beheld two energy fields calling to me. My dual energy was awake and ready to merge in the core of our being. Their human manifestations had finally traced their human ancestors back to their spiritual ancestry, and to the entrance of the two doors.

I was satisfied that the plan for both energy fields was firmly in place. They were ready to return to take part in the evolutionary process on earth. I felt both energy fields move towards the two doors. Before they entered through the doorways, I pulled both energy fields close, reminding them of our unity. The power of love moved through them and flowed like a ribbon of light from one to the other, joining them to the core of my being. I knew love would lead them back to the birth of their creation.

1

Gloucestershire, England. Present day.

Clara tread lightly past the rows of computers and filing cabinets to reach the door leading down the stone steps to the archives. She didn't want to alert Mrs Gregg that she was on her way to the vault. She had twenty minutes before the security guard did his rounds and locked up for the evening. It was eerie and quiet in the underground vault, almost as though the written word had died on the lips of their authors. She braved the literary ghosts and made her way towards the section dedicated to the Celts. She required documentary evidence to link the Celts to Eurasia. She had heard from a colleague that there were secret files in the archives on digs conducted in Siberia and Mongolia. Her thesis was based on the Celts and their spiritual beliefs. She posited that their customs and rituals originated in central Asia. Clara held down a part-time job at the Cheltenham Municipal Library while she completed her studies. Ten years after getting her first degree, Clara had resumed her studies. During those ten years, she got married and moved to Cambridge to work as a research assistant. She put her ambitions on hold to support her husband in his full-time studies. They separated two years ago and Clara returned to

Gloucestershire to take up her studies once again. She was completing a research PhD in history and ancient civilisations.

The archives comprised of rows and rows of dusty volumes of books no longer relevant to today's reader. At one end of the cavernous vault, there was a section of special historical and scientific interest. It was among these documents and books that Clara first noticed historical references to the customs and spiritual practices of the Celts. She chose the Celts as her main topic of study because of her background. Her mother was Irish and her father was Welsh. However, she and her brother grew up in Gloucestershire. She considered herself to be an English Celt.

Clara listened for a sound coming from the stairs that lead to the library. It was quiet. She could lose her job if Mrs Gregg found out she was down in the vault unsupervised. She put the thought to the back of her mind and concentrated on the task at hand, nimbly leafing through files until she found documents on digs in Mongolia. Clara took photos of relevant sections, breaking another rule of the library. Something caught her eye among the papers. It was a black-and-white photo of mummified remains. The human remains seemed to be partly obscured by a thick layer of permafrost. She could just make out an elaborate neck piece studded with gems, but it was difficult to discern what type of stones in the black-and-white photo. She inspected the elaborate collar; the stones weren't dark enough to be obsidian. She turned over the photo. There was tiny handwriting on the back describing the mummy. She took a photo of the back to help enlarge the writing. Clara felt a rush of adrenaline; who was this mummy and where was it discovered? She recovered her senses and quickly flipped through the documents to look for the answer, but footsteps at the top of the stairs stopped her in her tracks. Hastily, she returned the photo and documents to where she had found them. She hurried towards the literary section dealing with the Middle Ages. Pulling on protective gloves, she made a fuss of putting back a large volume of poetry just as her supervisor approached. Mrs Gregg, looking suspicious, reminded Clara that it was forbidden to enter the archives without a senior librarian. Clara's voice sounded like a whisper in the vault's labyrinth; 'A student inquired about further reading material on Chaucer.'

Mrs Gregg stared at Clara for a few moments before giving voice to her disapproval. 'All relevant works of Chaucer are in the main library.'

Clara stepped back towards the spiral steps, offering a meek apology, hastily making her way back up to the main library.

On the bus ride home, she took out her phone and scrolled through photos of the documents. She zoomed in on the writing on the back of the mummy's photograph. It read "Female mummy with jade neck adornment inlaid with gold and mother-of-pearl". There was nothing else, no date, no location, and no name or reference to the photographer. She stared out the window of the bus. Through the droplets of rain and the twinkling lights of Cheltenham, Clara wondered who the woman was staring out at her across the millennia.

The morning lectures dragged on interminably until finally the bell, and Clara's stomach, told her it was lunchtime. She quickly ate her packed lunch before heading to the university library to research the mysterious Jade Mummy. She found nothing to suggest that a similar mummy existed in the British Isles. She extended her search to Europe and Eurasia. Nothing turned up fitting the description. She opened her laptop and typed in 'mummy', 'jade necklace' and 'Celtic' in the search engine, but nothing matched her search. She pondered for a few moments and thought that her next step would be to trace the person who took the original photo. The colouring suggested it was developed seventy or maybe eighty years ago. There was no way to be sure without getting the photo from the archives. The documents were marked 'sensitive' which meant she needed permission to access them. If she asked permission from Mrs Gregg, she would know that Clara had been snooping through the sensitive documents. She was caught between a rock and a hard place. She needed access to the documents, but she also needed her job. A bad reference from the library could jeopardise her chances of getting a position as curator in a museum when she had completed her PhD.

The following morning, after attending a lecture on Celtic artefacts, she asked the professor if she knew of any jade artefacts found at Celtic sites. Professor Calder looked pensive for a while almost as if she was accessing the vast vault of her knowledge. Always curious about new discoveries, she asked Clara in what context had she come across the artefact? Clara, not wanting to divulge too much, said she saw a photo of a mummified woman wearing a jade neckpiece in a Celtic book at the library. The professor couldn't explain why it appeared on a Celt and wondered if the photo may be fake. She added that she associated jade with the Mayan culture.

Clara searched for evidence linking the Celts to Mongolia or Siberia, but if her professor was correct, the photograph seemed to point towards the Mayan people of South America. The jewellery seemed to support that theory, but why was it archived with Celtic documentation? The library had very little on Mayan culture except for publications in the main library. The only explanation must be that the photo was misplaced and it ended up with Celtic documents by mistake. Clara hadn't time to chase false avenues; she must follow the path where the archaeological evidence pointed. She put the image of the Jade Mummy out of her mind and concentrated on the other documents. The small looped handwriting wasn't easy to understand, but luckily there was a typed document giving a synopsis of the contents. According to the synopsis, a team of archaeologists and historians set off in 1936 to follow in the footsteps of Johann Ramsauer, who one century earlier had discovered a large Celtic prehistoric cemetery near Hallstatt in Austria. During his explorations, Ramsauer found evidence of their way of life perfectly preserved in the salt mines where they worked, giving archaeologists new insight into tools and weapons used by the Celts. Similar weaponry was later discovered with a mummified warrior in the mountains between Russia and Mongolia in the early 1920s. A group of Russians on a mountain climbing expedition on Mount Belukha in the Altay Mountains came across it when they camped nearby. A decade later, a team of British archaeologists travelled to Mongolia to explore the Altay Mountains for ancient burial sites known as Kurgans. Frustratingly, there was nothing more about the expedition, leaving Clara with no further clues. She felt in her bones she was onto something, that the team of archaeologists must have made some discoveries that corresponded to her thesis. Perhaps the explorers on that expedition discovered evidence that Celtic tribes originated in the central European Steppes. It was entirely probable that they merged their customs and beliefs with the early settlers of Western Europe. She focused on the screenshots of the handwritten notes accompanying the black-and-white photo of the Jade Mummy. On the notes clipped to the front of the file, the name 'David Perry' was typed, with 'Cheltenham' written underneath. His documents were donated to the museum a few years before his death in 1985. According to his notes, the team discovered pottery, weaponry and tools which suggested a link to Neolithic people of central Asia. Clara felt as if this man had foreshadowed her, making a discovery about the origin of Celtic tribes. Maybe he had also been looking to fill in the gaps about the spiritual ancestry of the Celts. She squinted at the tiny handwritten notes on her phone. She enlarged it on the screen, but it was still difficult to decipher. In the footnotes to the page there was even smaller writing, when enlarged to the maximum it just produced a series of loops and squiggles. However, something caught her eye, the word Jade' in block letters and beside it was the word 'Princess' or 'Priestess'.

Clara sat back and took a deep breath. This man took may have taken this photo on his expedition in the nineteen-thirties. She needed to speak to the person who donated the papers. Hopefully, they were still alive. She typed in a search for David Perry and the word archaeologist. A faded photo showed a man in his mid-thirties, and then a later image possibly taken twenty years later. There was no mention of relatives or personal information. Clara scrolled down and found his name on a list of countries where he went on archaeological digs; Austria, Germany, France, Hungary, Siberia, Mongolia and Kazakhstan. Clara wondered if the mummy was photographed in one of these other countries. She would need to find publications on the digs to be sure. An online search yielded no books or papers published by David Perry. She scrolled through her photos of the documents and enlarged the attached legal document pinned to the front of the file. It was signed by Tom Perry, and below the signature was written 'son' and a telephone number. Finally, she had a lead.

Clara stood up and stretched, she stepped onto the balcony off her bedroom. The sky was clear and full of stars; she breathed in the cool night air. Something stirred inside her, another pulse urging her to solve the mystery of the Jade Mummy. She resolved to find the son of David Perry, and maybe he could shed some light on his father's explorations, and the location of the Jade Mummy.

Tom Perry was well wrapped up as he stood by the Neptune Fountain waiting for the young archaeology student who had shown interest in his father's papers. He was now in his seventy-eighth year, and the February sunshine did little to keep him warm. He pulled up the fur collar of his winter coat to his chin, hoping he would not have to wait much longer. Tom pulled a photo out of his coat pocket. He looked at the wistful eyes of his father gazing into an unknown space. It was taken a few years before he died. He spent his final years in full-time care. His father had a troubled past. Tom recalled the time when his father attempted to jump off a bridge into the River Severn. A truck driver, who saw him climb onto the bridge, rescued him. After that, his father seemed to disappear into a distant place within where he couldn't be reached. He was no longer the man Tom had known as a child.

The voice of a young woman interrupted Tom's memories. He removed his glove and shook hands with Clara. They strolled down the Promenade towards a coffee shop she recommended. As they walked past the rows of regency buildings, Tom inquired what her interest in his father was. He stated clearly that he didn't wish to divulge any personal details about his father, but he would offer any insights about his work. Clara sensed he was protective of his father's legacy, and she needed to tread carefully. She began by asking him why he donated his father's papers to the Municipal Library. They took a seat in the easy chairs in the café window. Tom Perry stirred his coffee and stared outside at pedestrians walking up and down the promenade. He was in no hurry to answer her question. He was a deep, thoughtful man who took time speaking and asking questions in turn. He asked how Clara had acquired access to papers marked 'sensitive'. He was aware incidents from his father's past had cast a shadow over his earlier work and because of that his notes were not given validity for use in research. Clara reddened and Tom smiled despite himself. Clara confessed and told him she wasn't supposed to be in the archives of the library without supervision. She divulged her passionate interest in the Celts and how she had overheard talk about original documents in the archives pertaining to an early twentieth century expedition. She had hoped to discover material to help her with her thesis. Tom recognised an earnest interest in her chosen area of study. He asked what aroused her interest in his father's notes. Clara told him all her ideas and thoughts about the Celtic transmigration and her puzzlement about the photo of the Jade Mummy. Tom relaxed, he was certain she wasn't poking into his father's private affairs. She just wanted to do justice to the Celts in her thesis. He liked her, and he decided to help if he could.

Clara showed Tom Perry a screenshot of the Jade Mummy, but he was unable to throw any light on it. Clara detected a slight hesitation when he spoke about the photo. He looked like he was trying to access some past memories. She encouraged him by asking why he donated the notes and photograph to the library. He pushed away his coffee cup and leaned closer. In almost a whisper, he said that his father's state of mind in later years had led Tom to gather up personal effects belonging to the family. He kept all his expedition notes and photos at the house until his father decided what he wanted to do with them. Tom told Clara that he asked his father if he wanted to donate his work to the city museum. His father took a few days to ponder on it. Before agreeing to the idea, he gripped Tom's arm and told him to remove any photographs from the collection. Tom went through his files and removed all the photos as requested. He returned them in a large box to his father's cottage near his own house. He told Clara he never intended to include any of his father's photos with the documents, but somehow one must have got mixed up in the paperwork. Clara felt a rush of excitement. The photos of David Perry's adventures must be still in Tom's possession. However, her hopes were dashed when Tom explained that his father's house had caught fire a year or so later when he was burning personal items. Tom saw the flames from the window of his house and managed to rescue his father, but everything in the house was destroyed by fire and fumes.

Clara sat back and sighed. She would never discover what other objects David Perry had found with the Jade Mummy, or where it was located. Tom said he was sorry he couldn't help her any further, but his father didn't say much about his work. He stood up to leave and Clara thanked him. She gave him her phone number in case he remembered anything else that could help her. As they left the café she asked if his father had a peaceful death. Tom scratched his chin and reflected on that day thirty-three years ago. He had left the care home around eight that night. The nurse who was on night duty administered his father's prescribed medication before bedtime. She was new to the care home, and she later told Tom they had chatted for a little while before he went to sleep. When she did her rounds in the early morning, she found he had passed away peacefully in his sleep. The doctors said his heart just stopped, almost as if he had willed it to. Clara felt goose bumps all over. She stumbled as Tom finished the account of his father's death. He caught her by the arm to steady her. She assured him she was fine, just a little dizzy. He walked with her a little way towards the library to make sure she had sufficiently recovered her balance. He turned back towards the car, his mind full of memories of his late father.

Clara was glad to reach home after the late opening hours at the library. It was nine-thirty. She pondered her reaction to Tom Perry's account of his father's death. Perhaps it evoked feelings of grief around her own father's death a few years earlier, she thought. She partially closed her eyes and saw the face of David Perry. It was the image from the photo Tom had shown her earlier. He had said his father had disappeared into a distant place within. Clara wondered what mysterious place his soul had wandered to.

Clara ran a bath, relaxing in the warm fragrance of lavender and patchouli. She felt the tension drain from her body as she sponged her skin. She closed her eyes and relaxed in the warm water. A vision sprung up behind her tired eyes of a young nurse walking towards the large red brick building pointed with Bath stone. It was so clear, Clara felt like she could reach out her hand and touch the stone. The nurse wore a navy gabardine coat over a white nurse's uniform. She climbed a flight of stairs to a galleried landing covered with portraits in gilt frames. There were black and white group photographs with typed inscriptions. The nurse removed her coat and placed it in a small cupboard on the landing. There was a warmth and friendliness to her as she opened a door and stood by the bedside of an elderly gentleman. He was reading a book with a Celtic symbol on the front cover. The nurse prepared his medicine as he continued reading. His eyes were light brown and full of life. The nurse offered him pills, and he put down his book and looked up at the nurse. Clara was startled momentarily, as he seemed to look directly at her. He spoke to her, but she couldn't understand what he was saying.

Clara sat bolt upright in the bath. The vision vanished. The bath felt icy cold on her skin. She felt as if she was buried in snow and ice. Shivering, she stepped out of the bath and wrapped herself in her warm towelled robe. She pulled the cord for the light switch. She sat on the edge of the bath and watched the swirling movement of the water rushing down the plughole. She wished she could unplug her thoughts and fears as easily. Something strange was happening to her. She had a hunch it involved David Perry and the mysterious Jade Mummy.

2

I am looking at the two doors, portals into worlds unreachable to me except through my dual aspects of masculine and feminine energy. The journey beyond the two doors begins with both energies manifesting simultaneously in the world of form. They must find each other through the source of their unity, which lies on the other side of the doors. I feel love emanating to bathe both aspects in a warm glow. They are on a journey to lead them back to the dawning of their lifetime.

It was a glorious spring Saturday, and it seemed to Clara a shame to go to lectures when she would rather go for a ramble in the countryside. She couldn't remember the last time she awoke feeling so refreshed. She sat down to read her text messages and emails while rubbing a tingling sensation on her forehead. She had the feeling she had walked through cobwebs. She brushed back her hair from her face and tied it in a neat ponytail. She opened a text from her friend Imogen who asked if she was free for lunch. Imogen was doing a PhD in classical literature. Like Clara, she was in her early thirties and recently divorced. They met the first week at university and formed a friendship based on their mutual interests and experiences. Imogen was studying

Greek and Latin, as well as the influence of the early Greek literature on modern-day life. Clara admired Imogen's dedication especially since she had to juggle parenting responsibilities with her ex.

Clara finished her coffee and left for her morning lecture on campus, yawning her way through most of it. She was lost in a trance of ancient symbols and tantalising glimpses of a people living deep in the mountains. The lunchtime bell rang, startling her. She looked at her notebook and she realised she had taken very few notes from the lecture, which had focused on the anatomy of ancient animals found in caves of the British Isles. She noticed a doodle she drew while daydreaming. She had repeated the symbol several times on the page. It was three interconnecting spirals, a triskele in Celtic symbology. She snapped her notebook shut and gathered up her books to meet Imogen in the dining hall. Her friend's beaming smile greeted her across the cafeteria.

Imogen picked up a plate of pasta salad and went to join her friend. Imogen's expressive nature entertained Clara as she acted out her son's tantrum when he was told he couldn't have a smartphone. When she asked him what a seven-year-old wanted a smartphone for, he told her he needed it to play video games. Clara had met both of Imogen's children, and they were animated and funny, like their mother. Her ex-husband had the children on Saturdays, and so Imogen was free for the afternoon. They finished their lunch and chatted about their essays and upcoming exams. Imogen focused intently when Clara confided in her about the papers she had photographed in the library, intrigued by her friend's discovery of a mummy in an old black-and-white photo. She thought there must be a way to gain access to the documents without causing trouble for Clara. Clara explained she had very little time alone with the documents and she took just a few hurried screenshots of the photo and some handwritten pages. She needed access to the complete works of David Perry to find clues to the whereabouts of the Jade Mummy. Any written evidence would help progress her thesis to link the Celts with Eurasia. Imogen looked thoughtful and drummed her fingers on the table. She told Clara that in her research on Greek civilisation, she recalled the Greeks came into contact with the Celts near modern-day Marseille in the 6th century BCE. Many myths were created about the origin of the Celts. Legend had it that Hercules roamed Western Europe and fathered the nation of the Galatis (France), and the ancient Greeks had two names for the Celts: Keltai and Galatae, names derived from the Celtic language meaning valiant. Later, in the fourth century BCE, the Celts appeared on Greek battlegrounds and were known for their heroism and bravery.

Clara knew most of her friend's research already from reading references to the Celts in ancient Greek and Roman literature. It placed the Celts in Central Europe and France from the sixth century BCE. But it was the journey up to that time that concerned Clara. Where did they come from before this? Imogen offered to help by masquerading as an Oxford Professor to gain access to the Celtic archives of the library, half joking, half in earnest. Clara laughed at her enthusiastic offer, but she knew Mrs Gregg would spot a fake a mile off.

Clara gave her friend a warm hug and left to spend her afternoon in the hills near her home. There was a hill fort she was drawn to on the way home. She got off the bus and made her way up the hill towards the cluster of trees at the top. There were far-reaching views of the surrounding countryside and way beyond to the Welsh mountains. The Ancients certainly knew where to place their settlements, thought Clara. They were a beacon in the landscape that was easily navigable, and also provided optimum viewpoints to spot a hostile approach. She sat in the centre of the ancient fort and watched the evening sun light up the mountains in Wales to the west. She remembered her Welsh Grandparents and happy days she spent on their farm in Monmouthshire. She felt truly alive when she visited ancient dwelling sites, as though their energy imbibed her spirit with spaciousness and wonder. She walked around the circular earthworks and imagined what it must have been like for ancient dwellers of this land. Clara wasn't naïve about the hardships and brutality that occurred among the Celts. Evidence of ritual sacrifice had been discovered in several Celtic settlements. Later, during the first century BCE, many bloody battles had been fought with the Romans during their occupation. They saw the Celts as barbaric savages who needed civilising. The Romans conquered most of England and Wales but failed to subdue the tribes of Scotland, opting instead to build a wall named after the emperor Hadrian to keep the Highlanders out. In Roman Britain, Ireland was known as Hibernia, the place of winter. Like Scotland, The Celtic tribes of Ireland remained free of Roman domination.

As Clara pondered on the ancient dwellers of the British Isles, the sun began its descent on the south-western horizon, leaving a trail of pink, purples and amber hues. It was a scene that remained unchanged for millennia, allowing her to touch the ancient world through the veil of dusk. She carefully made her way down from the hilltop fort to the footpath where she reached a village at the foot of the hill. From there, she took a bus to Tewkesbury.

Every summer, during her childhood Clara and her family spent two weeks of the school holidays with her Irish grandparents in County Meath. When she and her brother Cormac were older, they were allowed to sail across the Irish Sea on a passenger ferry where their Grandparents eagerly awaited them. Her Grandfather was a wonderful storyteller, regaling tales to them of Irish myths and legends. Clara recalled his sing-song voice as he told them about the skilled warrior, Fionn Mac Cumhaill and his band of warriors known as the Fianna. He told stories of their brave and heroic deeds in ancient Ireland. To this day, the legend of the Tuatha Dé Danann, the original dwellers on the island, still intrigued her. According to folklore, the mythical Tuatha Dé Danann descended on a cloud to occupy the island. Clara wondered if this mystical tribe of gods were seafaring people from another land, bringing new spiritual beliefs and farming practices. When Irish people converted to Christianity, the pantheon of Celtic gods was shunned in favour of monotheism, and the Tuatha Dé Danann passed into folklore and myth.

Several books lined the shelves in Clara's small two-bed house. Many more books were in storage at her mother's house in Lyme Regis. When Clara's father died three years earlier, her mother decided that their house in the Cotswolds was too big to maintain on her own. The Cotswolds were a highly sought-after area, and she sold the five-bedroom house for a large sum. With the proceeds, she purchased a three-bed cottage in the coastal town of Lyme Regis. She was a thirty-minute drive from her sister who lived in Devon. Orla Lewis gave two-hundred and fifty thousand pounds to both her children, enabling Clara to buy a small mews house on the outskirts of Tewkesbury. The timing couldn't have been better as she had just left Cambridge and the home she shared with Charles. Charles was now a professor of Economics in Cambridge, and he vacated the house a year ago to live on campus. When their house was sold, Clara received a small sum once mortgage payments and solicitors' fees were deducted.

Clara picked up the phone and called her mum. She realised it was almost over a week since they had spoken. Orla sounded happier than she had in months. She told Clara she had gained a new housemate called Rufus. Puzzled, Clara was about to ask who he was when she heard a dog barking in the background. Orla had taken in a rescue dog that was found wandering the cliffs near the town. Since no one had claimed him at the Rescue Centre, she was now housemate to a two-year-old sheepdog cross. She paused and laughed, 'Sorry dear, I'm so preoccupied with my new furry friend, I haven't asked how you are.'

Clara smiled; she was gladdened by her mother's new found enthusiasm. 'I'm very well, and very happy to hear about your new housemate. I do have a favour to ask. Could you look through my books and see if there is a book on Celtic mythology? Granddad gave it to me for my twelfth birthday. It should be in one of the storage boxes in the spare room.'

Orla walked upstairs with the phone pressed to her ear while Clara told her the label that should be on the box. Orla searched through the pile of books until she found the colourful hardcover book. Flicking through the pages she smiled. It reminded her of her father's passion for Celtic mythology, something he had passed on to his granddaughter. She told Clara she would post it after the weekend. They made arrangements for Clara to visit Lyme Regis at Easter Break before hanging up.

Clara opened her balcony door to let the cool night air refresh her. Her thoughts wandered to the Jade Mummy and David Perry's notes. She wondered if his research could substantiate her theory that the Celts originally came from Central Asia to create new settlements across Europe and the British Isles. Without facts to back up her theory, it was all just conjecture and this wouldn't secure her a research PhD. If she could find evidence of David Perry's trip to Mongolia, she might have a lead. She picked up her phone to call Tom Perry when she realised it was after ten. She would call him in the morning and ask him if he had any recollection of the date of his father's trip to Asia.

Tom Perry was quiet for a few moments. Clara wondered if he had been cut off. Then she heard an intake of breath and realised he was just taking his time to answer. He said he was about twelve years old when his father returned from a ten-month expedition in Mongolia. As Tom recalled, it was a few years after the Second World War, possibly '48 or '49. His father served in a regiment in Yorkshire during the war. He hadn't been called up for active service because he was colour-blind, or at least that's what Tom had been told. Clara asked if he could remember any unusual artefacts or photos that his father brought home from the expedition. Again, there was a long pause on the phone. Eventually, Tom replied his father came home a different man. A few months in Eurasia had altered him much more than the war. Clara gently probed further and asked how his father had changed in his opinion. There was another pause before he said, 'He seemed distant, abstract from his surroundings. I believe he never truly returned from Mongolia.'

Afterwards, Clara pondered her conversation with Tom Perry. It was very mysterious what happened to his father. When was the photo of the Jade Mummy taken? Did it belong to his 1936 excavation in Austria, or from his Siberian expedition twelve years later? She needed an expert to look at the photo to know definitively when it was taken. She used the search engine on her phone to find professional photographers. Perhaps one of them could help her.

Clara stood outside the shop front that was given on Philip Jones' website. One of the bullet points read 'specialist in early photography'. A small bell tinkled when she opened the door and it almost felt like walking back in time. An assistant glanced up from her smartphone and continued scrolling through her newsfeed. Clara took a few moments to look at the old black-and-white photos on the wall. There were street scenes of Cheltenham, Gloucester and Tewkesbury, all taken in the 1920s and 1930s. The signature was F. Jones. 'My grandfather, Frank Jones,' a voice said, startling her from her thoughts.

Clara turned to see a tall man smiling down at her. Introducing herself, she told him she had an appointment. He nodded politely and invited her into his office as his shop assistant ignored them both and continued on her phone. She must be a relative, Clara thought.

Philip Jones looked at the photo of the Jade Mummy on Clara's phone. She enlarged it to give him more detail. He said that he couldn't be certain without the original photograph, but the photographer may have used a 35mm Leica camera. Philip said they were a popular make with travellers during the 1930s and '40's because they were light and easy to carry. In order to know when the photograph was developed, he would need to see the actual photo. Clara thanked him and left his office to pay the assistant who wore too much kohl and had an affected look of boredom. Philip Jones came out behind her and made a gesture to put her money away. He added that if she managed to get access to the original photo, he would test it for her. Clara thanked him and stepped out of the old-world shop onto the streets of twenty-first-century Tewkesbury. Although, with its black and white timber-framed buildings, one would be forgiven for thinking they had stepped into the seventeenth century.

Clara hurried to the bus stop to make her lecture in Cheltenham in half an hour, but by the time the bus reached the campus, she was already fifteen minutes late. She switched off her phone and slipped into the lecture hall quietly to see a large image of the Amesbury man projected onto a large white screen. This was the bronze-age archer discovered in Wiltshire in 2002; carbon testing proved that he had originated from central Europe. Clara opened her notebook and absent-mindedly wrote notes and dates. She glanced up when she heard the loud click as another image was projected on the screen. The professor called it the 'Siberian Ice Maiden'. Clara shifted in her seat as goose bumps rose on her arms and a tremor of excitement rushed through her. She heard of the Siberian Ice Maiden, but little was known about the discovery because the Russian team who discovered her in the 1990s kept it from international news. The professor passed out notes, which Clara eagerly took as they passed through the rows of students. The notes stated she lived in the Eurasian Steppes around fifth century BCE and was identified by archaeologists, as a member of the Pazyryk culture that lived in Mongolia, Siberia and Kazakhstan in the first millennium BCE. Clara listened intently as her professor explained the Pazyryk were Eurasian nomads during the Iron Age. The mummy had been found on a plateau of the Altay Mountains near the border with China. The Ice Maiden's chamber contained her coffin, made of a solid larch wood tree trunk and decorated with deer figures. Also, two small wooden tables used to serve food and drink. Animal meat and a beverage had been placed on the tables served in a horn cup to sustain her on her journey. She was between 20 and 30 years old at the time of her death. A shaft dug into the burial mound showed the grave had been robbed. Water and snow had seeped into the burial chamber. The water froze and formed an ice block within the chamber which never fully thawed because of the cold climate on the plateau. The contents of the burial chamber remained frozen for almost two-and-a-half millennia until the Russian excavation in 1993.

Clara squinted as the lights came on after the lecture. She sat in her seat writing furiously, trying to get down every detail of the Ice Maiden. She was still in her seat when the professor came up the steps on his way out of the hall. He stopped to ask her about her curious interest in the Ice Maiden. Clara replied she was looking for a link between the Celts of central Europe and the Stone Age people of Eurasia. Professor Roberts pulled some notes from his briefcase and flipped through them until he reached the relevant page. He showed Clara a reconstruction of the Ice Maiden's face created using her skull, with measurements taken from the skulls, facial features, and skin thickness of present-day inhabitants of the Altay Mountains. The artist who created the reconstruction had said that the Ice Maiden was an example of a Caucasian race without typical Mongolian features. Clara's mind was on overdrive. Perhaps her ancestors were the first tribes to cross the Eurasian Steppes to the Black Sea and up the river Danube into central and

Western Europe. Her instincts told her she was on the right track. Professor Roberts, seeing the look on her face, told her to be sure of her facts before committing anything to paper. It was wise, he said, to follow the evidence rather than jump to conclusions. Clara thanked him for his advice as she gathered up her papers into her satchel. She looked at the large face of the clock above the lectern; she had ten minutes to reach the Municipal Library for her afternoon shift.

3

I have seen beyond the two doors into the physical world of duality. Both aspects of my consciousness experience it differently. When the human mind allows the cosmic mind to shine through, the perfect plan unfolds in the world of form. The mind gives human beings free will to conceive and create a world separate from the cosmos, and each other. It is their choice to create a world of unity, or separation. When both energy fields fall out of synchronicity in human form, they find that life becomes a revolving door. As one enters, the other leaves to avoid further polarisation of the spiritual self. Once they feel the truth of their origin, the spirit lost inside the dream becomes restless and seeks a way to return to the truth.

Clara took a deep breath as she approached Mrs Gregg. She decided the Celtic files in the archives were far too important to allow her fear of the stern supervisor to thwart her research. She began by explaining the theme of her thesis and her need to find evidence of Celtic origins in Europe. The senior librarian continued to stare at her over the rims of her spectacles. Clara, determined to speak up, continued while glancing sideways at the archives, giving the older lady a clue what she wanted. Mrs Gregg remained mute, almost as if she enjoyed seeing her squirm.

'Is it possible to look through the archived material marked as *sensitive*?' Clara flinched under the haughty stare coming from the woman before her. Mrs Gregg looked solemn for a few moments and wrinkled her brow, giving Clara a sinking feeling that she was going to be fired on the spot.

Mrs Gregg shuffled some papers on her desk before speaking. 'Since it is to aid your PhD, I'll allow it, but with strict supervision and with certain conditions.' Clara held her breath. 'I will accompany you, but under no circumstances are you to photocopy or screenshot any documents marked "sensitive". You may, however, take notes,' concluded Mrs Gregg.

She pencilled in a time in her notebook when she and Clara could visit the archives before snapping it closed, showing the end of their conversation. It was scheduled for three days' time, one hour before Clara's next shift at the library.

Clara filled the intervening time with research into the Siberian Ice Maiden, the Scythians and Pazyryk tribes of the Eurasia. She looked up any information on the current people of the Altay Mountains that stretched across Mongolia, Siberia, and Kazakhstan. Her research yielded some interesting findings. The local people believed that the mythical kingdom of Shambhala was located at Mount Belukha, the highest peak of the Altays. The eight-petal lotus blossom surrounded by a chain of snow-capped mountains in

Buddhist texts represented the fabled utopia of Shambhala. Clara rubbed her brow. She needed to focus on the theme of her thesis, rather than getting drawn into several streams of thought. She made a list of the reasons tribes of Eurasia would migrate westwards to central Europe. Perhaps drought, famine, or natural disasters such as earthquakes or climate change had pushed them out of their native lands. There might have been ethnic or spiritual differences, a caste system that caused some Pazyryk tribe to head west. She pulled out her lecture notes on the Siberian Ice Maiden. The Professor said that there were also three horses buried with the Ice Maiden. They were all buried with their heads facing east as seen in other Pazyryk burials. One theory was that she was a priestess, based upon the items found in the burial chamber. Her preserved skin had a tattoo of a deer-like animal on one of her shoulders, and another on her wrist and thumb. Her remains were now in the national museum of Gorno-Altaysk in the Altay Republic. Clara wished she could go back in time and speak to her, find out what her life was like, what her spiritual beliefs were. Momentarily, she felt herself on the back of a galloping horse, its mane flowing as it cantered through the foothills of snow-capped peaks, her hair flowing behind her and freedom pervading her senses.

Clara blinked a few times and looked around. Her visions were becoming more frequent, only now she was remembering them clearly. Perhaps Charles was right when he said living with her was like living with two people. Who was this other person who lived within her? Logic returned and Clara shelved her visionary occupant for the more serious task of researching her thesis. She jotted down some notes about the Maiden's position in the tomb, sketching an outline of the burial mound, or kurgans as described by the Russian archaeologists. A kurgan was like a tumulus, a burial mound or barrow, filled with smaller sediment and covered with a pile of rocks. The mound of the Ice Maiden's kurgan covered a chamber which contained the wooden coffin, with her accompanying grave goods. Clara looked at her sketch; she had drawn a long barrow. It was like the West Kennet Long Barrow in Wiltshire; a style of burial used in Europe from the fifth to the fourth millennium BCE. Was it possible that the Pazyryk had introduced this type of burial to Celtic culture? Clara scribbled down ideas as they came to her. She would sift through facts and conjecture later. As she flipped through her notes, the word 'priestess' stood out. David Perry had written priestess on the back of the photo of the Jade Mummy, and there were many similarities between the two mummies. The Siberian Ice Maiden was documented, albeit sketchily, and could be correlated to her theory that Celtic tribes originated in Eurasia. She could also include their spiritual influences on Celtic practices and traditions. She realised she didn't need to go through the archives at the library for further evidence, but on the other hand she wanted to satisfy her curiosity about David Perry's Jade Mummy.

Clara followed Mrs Gregg down the spiral stairs into the archives, glad of her woolly cowl neck sweater. It was clear who was in charge as the older lady pulled out some files from the section on European Celtic Archaeology. Clara noticed she had excluded David Perry's file. She hesitated a few moments, unsure whether to ask for the file. Doing so would be admitting that she had already rifled through the files unsupervised. Instead, she opted for a meeker request, 'Are these all the files related to archaeological digs in the twentieth century?'

Mrs Gregg looked hesitant for a moment. 'I've included all the files whose provenance is not in doubt,' she replied curtly.

Clara pressed a little further, asking, 'Is it possible to see all the files?' She hesitated before adding, 'please?'

'You must be careful using material that isn't authenticated by the library or the museum. It could cast doubt on your research and affect your results,' said Mrs Gregg, sounding like her first-grade teacher.

Clara nodded to show she was aware of the implications. Mrs Gregg pulled out David Perry's file from a bottom drawer and reiterated her rules that no copies could be made of any document. Clara took out her notebook and pen and got to work. She had fifty minutes before her shift started upstairs in the library.

It wasn't easy to decipher David Perry's small handwriting and his notes were not in chronological order. There were some diagrams and hastily sketched maps on the back of some of his notes. He had written factual information about the trip to Austria in 1937. There were black lines drawn through some of his writing that seemed to be done at a later date. Clara held the document up to the light and deciphered the word 'Nazis', written in capital letters. Of course, thought Clara, he was in Austria before the occupation of Hungary and Austria by Nazi Germany. The notes contained a few more references to the Nazis and his concern about the Jewish population across Europe. Several pages had blacked-out sections suggesting that David Perry's notes contained sensitive information. Perhaps, thought Clara, this was one reason the files were kept secret. Yet according to Tom Perry, his father's mental health prevented his work from being authenticated by the History Museum and Municipal Library. As Clara flipped through the notes from the expedition to the Altay Mountains, the photo of the Jade Mummy fell out from between the pages she had hastily put it the previous week. Once again, it transfixed her. She peered closely at the neck piece. It was difficult to tell by the dark grey shade of the photo if it was jade. To her untrained eye, it looked a few shades darker, perhaps even dark blue. She turned her attention to a page of David Perry's handwriting, but from what she could tell, he was in a hurry when he wrote it. She scanned the pages and saw a tiny sketch of a burial mound, not unlike the one she had sketched of the kurgans on the Altay plateau. She could just make out some of his scrawled handwriting. This has to be from his trip to Mongolia, thought Clara, but frustratingly, no dates were given. Again, the words 'Priestess' and 'Barrow' were written in capital letters. Perhaps one kurgan contained the Jade Mummy, she thought, but where was it now? Surely the Russians would have discovered the Jade Mummy by now, particularly after the excavation of the Siberian Ice Maiden at Mount Belukha. From David Perry's map, it seemed as though he discovered the Jade Mummy a few hundred miles east of Mount Belukha. Clara had a dozen questions about David Perry's discovery spinning in her head when she noticed a few lines of poetry written under a sketch of the Jade Mummy. She wondered if he composed it, or was it lines of a poem he recalled from the past. Maybe the lines came to him as he pondered the life of the Priestess who lived a few millennia previously in the Mongolian wilderness. The tenderness expressed in the lines moved her to tears. Dabbing her eyes with a tissue, she scribbled down the lines in her notebook. Mrs Gregg called her name and said they had five minutes left. Hastily, she copied David Perry's sketch of the burial mounds and his rough map of the surrounding terrain, making a few final notes. Oddly enough, it was the few lines of poetry that gave her a deeper insight into the man behind the explorer. Mrs Gregg approached just as she was gathering all the documents to replace them in the folder. She thanked her and made her way up to the library to begin her afternoon shift.

A small package was waiting for Clara when she returned home. Opening it, she found the cherished childhood book her grandfather had given her with a note enclosed from her mother. The thought of her grandfather brought memories and stories tumbling back into her mind, visits to the Hill of Tara and Newgrange burial chamber. The legend of Dagda, a chief druid of the Tuatha Dé Danann, who was said to have control over life and death intrigued her. Folklore pointed to Newgrange as the dwelling place of the Tuatha Dé Danann, the pantheon of gods in Celtic mythology. The entrance to the Newgrange passage tomb was aligned with the rising sun on the winter solstice. For a few days around mid-winter, the first rays of the sun shone through a roof box lighting up inner chamber. Dating back to 3200 BCE, it was older than the stone circle at Stonehenge and the pyramids in Egypt. Clara flipped the pages of the storybook, illustrated with colourful drawings of heroes and legends. The Irish were skilled storytellers and knew how to embellish the facts, yet perhaps a modicum of truth survived in the telling and retelling of the Tuatha Dé Danann legend. Early references to them were made by monks and scribes who modified the stories, handed down for generations, to accommodate the dominion of Christian faith. In some texts, the Tuatha Dé Danann were even described as angels who fell to earth. Clara wondered about the passage from fact to legend and legend to myth. As a child, she had felt that the druids and chieftains came alive in the stories her grandfather told her. She thought Newgrange was a place of wonder, a portal into a parallel world where myth was just a word for an alternative reality that people were not yet ready to accept. When she picked up the envelope, a photo fell out of her and Cormac in front of the entrance stone to Newgrange burial chamber. The large stone was engraved with interconnecting spirals. It was taken twenty-one years ago when she was twelve years old. As she put the photo into the book, she smiled at the memory. She read the enclosed note her mother had written and smiled at her news. She had secured a part-time position in a care home on the Dorset coast. She placed the book and letter to one side and concentrated on her thesis, but fatigue got the better of her and she dozed off surrounded by books and papers.

The thud of an encyclopaedia on the floor woke her with a start. She reached for the woollen throw on the back of the couch and pulled it over her. She had been dreaming about the passageway in Newgrange and she could feel the light of the morning sun making her feel transparent. Rays of light fanned out from her and illuminated the burial chamber. Clara blinked, placing her hands on her chest to prove she still existed. She had never been to Newgrange at the winter solstice, only during the summer holidays. She threw off the woollen throw and picked up a crumpled piece of paper that fell to the floor. It was the poem from David Perry's file:

Even now, when I say your name,
It leaves my mouth in slow motion
Escaping my lips like a winged prayer,
A hymn before the altar of love.

Clara wearily climbed into bed. As soon as she closed her eyes to sleep, she saw the face of David Perry in front of her. There was something so familiar about the way he looked at her. His eyes were timeless, beckoning her to another world, another time, another place, and for the first time since she had come across his papers, Clara felt disturbed. Why did this man enthral her so, and what message was he trying to convey to her? She turned off the lamp and pulled the bed cover over her head. She was too tired to play games with the ghosts in her head.

4

When the soul begins to wake up it looks to the outer world for answers, leading it on a parallel path to the inner journey. The soul's primordial urge is to trace its lineage back to the cosmic self. Lifetime after lifetime on earth, both energies seek the truth, and each other. The symbol of the three interconnecting spirals shows that unity is the truth. By following the signs, the spell of separation is broken.

Altay Mountains, 1948

David Perry and his colleagues carried on despite freezing conditions in the Mongolian border regions. Their local guide indicated they were close to the plateau where the burial site was located. Nervous anticipation of what they were about to discover shot like bolts through David's veins, sparking an adrenaline rush propelling him onward and upwards to the plateau.

They were lucky to secure the services of a guide. Local people were less than friendly towards outsiders, and when they heard three foreigners making inquiries how to reach the plateau that bordered Russia and China, they shrugged and walked away. One of David's companions knew enough Russian to hold a basic conversation. He also had a smattering of the local Altai language. Through his concerted effort, Dr John Biddulph eventually found a Russian guide to take them up the mountains on three conditions. First, they must set off ahead of him where he would meet them at an allocated point. Second, they could never breathe a word to anyone about his involvement in the expedition, and third, he required payment upfront. As they were running out of options, Biddulph agreed to the conditions. David Perry and the third member of the group, Professor Tony Higgins, had an uneasy feeling about the agreement.

It was nearing sunset when their guide led them to a crevice in the rock face to camp for the night. Just above them was the coveted plateau. They rolled out their ground mats and sleeping bags before grabbing their torches to make their way towards the high mounds on the plateau. Estimating they had about one hour of daylight left, they went in three separate directions to check out the burial mounds, known locally as kurgans, which made up the long barrow. The guide remained behind at the campsite, wanting nothing to do with disturbing the dead. Tony Higgins, David's colleague from the Austrian expedition, went to the kurgan at the far left of the plateau; John Biddulph went to investigate the mound next to it. David, who would not be rushed, stood back and closed his eyes for a moment. Something drew him towards the far right of the barrow. He looked down at his feet moving through the thick snow, feeling as though he were walking in another person's shoes. Reaching the kurgan, he hesitated, unsure how to proceed. He wasn't a religious man, but he felt compelled to pray for permission to enter the sacred space of these ancient mountain dwellers. Perhaps the superstitions of the local people had got to him. Maybe they were right in their warning about disturbing the dead. That was exactly what it felt like to David Perry, that he was about to wake the dead.

His hand clasped the strap of his Leica camera hanging loosely from his neck as he moved hesitantly towards the kurgan. There were piles of small stones on top of the mound. A shaft on one side of the kurgan indicated that someone else had discovered the burial site. David scrambled atop the pile of stones, shifting his weight to get a better look inside the shaft and shining his torch into the opening. He could just make out human remains. He eased himself into the opening of the shaft onto a narrow ledge of rock. Underneath the first layer of stone, there were skeletal remains of a large animal, possibly a horse. Rain and snow which had seeped through the shaft froze the human remains in a layer of permafrost. David carefully threaded his way down the narrow passage to get a closer look at the mummified remains. The grave had certainly been looted because there were no valuable items or artefacts with the body except a partially decomposed wooden object which could have been a staff or walking stick. There was an alabaster vessel which only survived pillage because its handle was hooked onto the hand of the deceased. He moved the torch across the body to inspect the unusual markings circling the remaining frozen flesh on the arms; they looked like tattoos of animals. The clothing seemed to be ceremonial, robes with fibres of red and gold showing that the man was of high standing in the community, possibly a priest. David was certain the mummy was a male from the width of the pelvis and partial stubble on the face still intact from its frozen entombment. A mark on the upper arm suggested that some kind of arm cuff had fallen off the mummy and it was looted along with the rest of the contents several centuries earlier. David looked up through the opening of the chamber. The light was fading fast. He would continue his appraisal of the tomb at first light.

His colleagues met him at the campsite when they had completed their first impression of the site. The three of them agreed that the site had most likely been discovered and looted for valuables perhaps just decades after the burials, partially preserving the flesh in permafrost. The people who lived there must have fled the area, leaving the tombs of their dead vulnerable to pillage and plunder. They were probably opened by nomadic herdsmen who grazed sheep there in the summer.

David observed their guide shifting uneasily by the campfire. He exchanged glances with John Biddulph. Something was amiss, but Biddulph shrugged and whispered to David that locals were superstitious about the dead. David wasn't so sure it was as simple as that. Something else was on the Russian guide's mind. David drew a rough map of the area and scribbled down a few directions to the plateau in case their guide disappeared during the night. Later that night, David remained alert until he heard loud snoring from their guide's sleeping bag. He relaxed and drifted into a deep sleep where dreams transported him inside the kurgan on the plateau where he was looking down on his own half-frozen, wasted body. David woke, fearful someone was choking him. He felt around in the dark for his water bottle. His eyes adjusted to the darkness where he just about made out the outline of the guide, and his two companions asleep in their sleeping bags. Exhaustion got the better of him, and he fell back to sleep until once again he found himself inside the kurgan. He was dressed in robes to perform a burial ritual over his father. He spoke in an ancient language and said, 'Look for her. She is waiting. I shall guide you to her and tell no one of her resting place. Find her and she will lead you back to the dawning of your lifetime.'

The priest continued through a subterranean network of caves deep in the mountains. There was a fungus tipped torch lighting up the cavernous space. He pulled it from its hook and proceeded through the underground maze. Turquoise water shimmered in the light, alabaster jars and ornately carved animals surrounded a deep pool. He was in a temple, a place of healing. Tranquillity seeped from the walls, filling him with a blissful sense of peace. A young woman sat on the edge of the pool, filling an alabaster jug. She motioned him to come closer. She spoke in the same ancient language, 'You will find me here. I am ready to return.' Her image shimmered for a few moments before fading completely.

David Perry woke with a start. It was so vivid that he felt that this vision was real, and his current life was the dream.

Everything he believed was turned upside down. He knew he had to find the Priestess. He quickly wrote down fragments of the dream he remembered. He wrote a note for his companions to say he would be back by nightfall before packing a bag to go and find her. She was close by. He sensed it, perhaps two or three hundred feet down the slope from here. He set off with the light of the waning moon as its light glistened on freshly fallen snow, lighting a path to his ethereal Priestess.

John Biddulph wiped his eyes and peered out the narrow crevice. He saw David's note on the ground where he had been sleeping. He roused Higgins from his sleep. Something was amiss. Perry didn't say why he had sneaked off in the night. Biddulph noticed their guide was still asleep. He went over to wake him, but instead he found tufts of dried grass stuffed inside his sleeping bag. Something is wrong, thought John Biddulph. Had the guide had accompanied David Perry on a secret mission? He felt the ground beneath the guide's sleeping bag and it was stone cold. The guide had left hours before David Perry, his sleeping bag still had some warmth. He left less than an hour ago whereas the guide let at least two hours earlier.

He looked at Tony Higgins and said, 'Something or someone must have spooked the guide.'

'Maybe Perry realised he had abandoned us,' reasoned Higgins. 'He is most likely tracking him.'

'But surely he would have woken us if he knew our guide had left us here,' reasoned Biddulph. 'And besides, the guide's sleeping bag was undisturbed until I discovered it was full of grass.'

Higgins admitted that he had a point. They briefly discussed if they should follow him. Given that his note did not indicate that he was in trouble, they decided to wait for him to return. They must proceed with the task they had come here to do, to piece together evidence about the ancient tribe who lived in the Altay Mountains. They would document and gather whatever artefacts that remained. As both men emerged from the small cave into a cold Siberian air, another surprise awaited them on the plateau. A group of Russian soldiers armed with rifles were inspecting the snow-covered mounds. They pointed the rifles at the two British explorers and without explanation, they marched them down the slopes of the mountain. Dr Biddulph tried speaking to them in Russian, but they ignored his questions. One soldier asked, 'Where is the other man?'

John Biddulph knew he was referring to David Perry. Higgins and Biddulph exchanged a look, realising the Russian guide had sold them out to the authorities.

The soldier shouted at them again, 'Where is the other man?'

Higgins shrugged and got the butt of a rifle in his right temple for his troubles, making him fall back into the snow. Red blood stains trickled onto the surface and they held Biddulph back when he tried to help his colleague to his feet. Realising the gravity of their situation, he pulled out David Perry's note from his coat pocket and handed it to the soldier. Two of the soldiers helped Higgins to his feet, and he nodded to Biddulph to show he was okay. By nightfall, the soldiers threw them in a small cell in the village of Tiungar, deep in the Russian state of Altai.

David Perry was in a rapturous frame of mind as he descended the mountain to find the subterranean cave system that he saw in his dream. He didn't stop to think about the consequences of his solo adventure into the inhospitable mountains, so buoyed was he by the excitement of making a life-changing discovery. There were several legends about a mythical kingdom in these mountains, some claiming it was the location of the mythical Shambhala. Was he about to discover the Utopian legend? Snow was falling hard again, and the wind was rising. David stopped for a moment and surveyed the blank white wilderness. He wanted to pursue his Priestess but his mountaineering instincts came to the fore. He carved out a hole for shelter where the snow gathered beneath a high boulder. It would protect him from the worst of the blizzard. He waited several hours until the snowfall abated. With three hours of daylight left, there wasn't enough time to return to camp. David pressed onward, hoping to reach the underground caves before nightfall. With every difficult step in deep snow, he became increasingly agitated with the battle raging in his mind. The tantalising glimpses of a forgotten world shown to him in his dream were replaced by an inner critic that took the voice of his father. It warned him of impending doom. The adrenaline rush from the dream had given him momentum to begin the journey to the subterranean caves, but his logical mind had caught up and was berating his carelessness. David wanted to beat his head against a rock torn as he was in opposing directions by his feuding inner dialogue. His energy levels were dipping from anxiety and frustration. Stopping for a few moments, he took a drink from his hip flask and a few bites from a protein bar. He took some deep breaths to slow his heart rate before looking at the sketch he had made of their location. They had begun their trek from the southern slopes of the Altay Mountains in Mongolia. One issue with getting a local guide, besides the spiritual beliefs, was that the plateau was in the Altai region of Russia. It wasn't safe to cross into Russia during post-war times and that's why they hoped a Russian guide would be an advantage. The guide had told them on their ascent that the plateau was part of a region that was disputed between the USSR and China.

David wondered what country he was in now. He could be standing in Russia, Mongolia or China. He looked at the golden light fringing the clouds on the western horizon. There was another hour before nightfall. David figured he was heading due south because that morning he was facing the light of the sun, and now the sun was setting to his right. He took out a pencil and wrote the directions, finally working out that he was in Mongolia, close to the Chinese border.

Part of David Perry's brain was frantically working out a route back to his companions on the plateau but with every step in the opposite direction, something else seemed to lead him further away. It was a momentous struggle within him as he grappled with the thought that something or someone else possessed him. The rising snow hampered his movements, and he needed to find shelter for the night. Exposure on the lofty peaks meant certain death. He wasn't a religious man, but he prayed to whoever was listening to find him shelter from the elements. Tears rolled down his face at the thought he may never see his young son again, all because he was stupid enough to follow a dream. He had heard mountaineering colleagues say that high altitude caused hallucinations and altered states of consciousness. Perhaps the vision he had the night before was just an hallucination. Had he had put his life at risk on a fool's errand? He screamed out to the white wilderness, a primal roar full of pain and suffering. He could no longer distinguish between reality and illusion. A high rise of snow on a nearby ridge caught his eye. He stumbled his way towards the mound, and with his gloved hands, he brushed the snow from the south face of the mound to reveal a shepherd's hut. He opened the door and fell to his knees with relief and gratitude. There was just enough dried grass and twigs to make a small fire. There were a few rotting wooden laths stacked up against the wall. It was enough to warm him and dry his clothes. He melted some snow in his tin cup over the fire and threw in some leaves of tea. He took a protein bar and sugary snack from his backpack. He would have to ration his food, not knowing how long it would take to reach a village in the valleys below. Exhausted, he collapsed on the ground and angled his feet towards the fire. His big toe was blue from the cold conditions. David knew he was perilously close to frostbite. Once he had warmed up, he pulled up his heavy coat to cover him and closed his tired eyes. The last image he saw before drifting off to sleep was the Priestess. She smiled at him, and told him she was watching over him.

Early the following morning, David was ready to continue his search for the underground caves. He pushed open the door of the hut against the snowdrift that accumulated overnight. The sky was startlingly blue, and the sunlight and brightness of the snow hurt his eyes. He put on his shades and headed south. His mind was quieter, exhausted by the constant tirade of his inner critic. He felt a sense of surrender and peace. It was essential that the busy mind quieten down, because something told him that his subconscious was the key to finding the caves. He reached a small plateau about one-hour south of the shepherd's hut. He noted the landmark and figured it would take six hours in good conditions back to the camp on the plateau. There were slight mounds to the east of the smaller plateau. David's heart beat faster. Could it be a kurgan? He brushed the snow from the top of the mound to reveal a pile of small stones laid on top of some bigger rocks. He was sure it was a burial chamber. A feeling of elation flowed through him, heating him from within. He pulled back some small stones, but unlike the kurgan with the mummified priest, there was no shaft leading into the burial chamber. This was good news, showing that the chamber was undisturbed but it also meant more work for David to gain access to it. Luckily, it was still early in the day and there were hours of daylight left. Carefully he removed the stones, placing them in a mound beside the kurgan. After a couple of hours, he saw an opening into the chamber. He worked quickly to make an entrance big enough to lower inside. He flashed his torch around the upper chamber. Similar to the other kurgan, it contained animal bones and a wooden table. He had to squeeze through the small opening to gain access to the lower chamber. He shone the torch around the wooden interior in amazement. It was full of objects; polished jugs, wooden carvings and alabaster urns. Water had seeped into the floor of the chamber over several centuries and covered it in a thick layer of permafrost. Within the frost, there were human remains. David Perry went to take a closer look. He pulled a pick-axe from his backpack and carefully dug around the remains. The body had partially decomposed, but the freezing conditions preserved some flesh and hair. The mummy was that of a young woman, perhaps twenty-five years old. She was laid out in a semi-foetal position facing east. Gold armlets were circling each arm. The arm facing upwards was mostly bone where it lay above the permafrost. David took out his camera to take photos of the chamber but the flash didn't seem to work, perhaps because of the cold. He shone his torch on the mummy, just making out tattoos on the upper arm similar to what he discovered on the priest in the other kurgan. He took a deep intake of breath almost afraid to move. He had found the Priestess.

He propped the torch in place to shine the light onto the mummy so he could take a photo. A wave of sadness overcame him and he sobbed uncontrollably. He asked the Priest from the dream to help him and almost immediately, a feeling of calm came over him like a shield. He crouched over the mummy and touched her hair. Around her neck was a collar, usually worn by high priestesses of the Pazyryk culture. He placed his hands about a foot above the mummy moving them up and down the length of her body. A deep primal sound emitted from his lips. He was chanting something in an ancient tongue. David felt powerless and powerful all at once. He seemed powerless to control his movements, yet powerful as he carried out the movements of the Priest. He was performing a rite of passage for the human remains who had once been a rare and powerful being. David struggled to use his logical mind to regain control of his body, but the Priest was too powerful and continued the ritual over the body of the Priestess. He watched the Priest's movements through a lens of ubiquity. He watched as his hand picked up a sharp stone to etch three interconnecting spirals on the wall. In a moment of clarity, David realised that the Priest and Priestess were two spirals of one unit. He became aware of two doors, and the passage he had come through at the dawning of his lifetime.

5

Pure joy fills my being when I emerge fully conscious in the world of form. It allows me to have a fully immersive experience through the five bodily senses. The aftermath of such revelations has a profound effect upon mind, body and spirit in the human being. They may experience shock and disbelief at the emergence of their true unmanifest being. When they try to return to this state of bliss through the process of thought, it evades them. Thought is the very action that keeps the doors to Reality firmly closed.

Clara waited for Tom Perry by the entrance to Montpellier Gardens. It was a frosty morning, and she was wondering if he'd even show up. Reluctantly, he had agreed to see her, although he maintained he had nothing much to offer about his father's expeditions. After thirty minutes and about to make her way down the Promenade, she saw him crossing the road, coming from the direction of Charlton Kings. When he reached her, he apologised for his tardiness but offered no reason for why he was late. Clara turned to walk to the coffee shop where they had met previously, relieved that he had come. Tom linked her arm and gently steered her in the direction of the Rotunda, which housed the upmarket brasserie, The Ivy. Clara rarely came here unless it was for a special treat. The price was above her student budget. It was lunchtime and there was a queue of people hoping to find a table at short notice. The head waiter spotted Tom Perry and beckoned him to a table under a large mural of Cheltenham's famous festival, the National Hunt. Clara didn't take Tom Perry for a regular of The Ivy, but it was obvious they knew him well there. As Clara took in her surroundings, Tom came straight to the point and asked the purpose of their meeting. By now, she was aware of his direct manner. She asked him if he knew how much time his father spent in Mongolia during the 1948 expedition to the Altay Mountains. Tom was tense and played with the buttons on the cuff of his jacket. Clara realised her questions were evoking uncomfortable memories for him. 'I'm very sorry for intruding into your past like this. Please forgive my insensitivity.'

Tom looked off into the distance with a slightly glazed look. Clara noticed there was deep sadness etched in the lines of his face. Her questions brought up unresolved feelings that he had tried hard to forget. He raised his hand to his mouth and cleared his throat. 'My father left for a three-month expedition early 1948. He returned ten months later much altered by his experience.'

Clara nodded as he spoke about the effect of his father's absence, and how for a time he was presumed dead. Deciding not to probe further into his past, Clara asked just one more question, 'Where is your father buried?' She wanted to visit his grave and pay her respects.

'My father was cremated. We placed a small portion of his ashes in the family burial plot in Charlton Kings,' replied Tom.

'Where are the rest of his ashes?' asked Clara, feeling a sense of intrigue.

'I scattered them near Newgrange in Ireland, according to his wishes,' Tom replied.

Clara's mouth fell open. Nothing could have shocked her more. She expected that the rest of David Perry's ashes were in Mongolia, or perhaps China. Never in a million years did she expect Tom to say Newgrange. There was a slightly bemused smile on Tom's face. He enjoyed the shock on her face as she struggled to find a response. She regained her composure and asked, 'Does your family originate from Ireland?'

Tom shook his head. As far as he knew, there were no family links to Ireland. His father had visited Ireland only once in his lifetime as far as he knew. Clara said she couldn't think of a more peaceful resting place than the ancient landscape that shaped her childhood. Tom offered more information when he heard the genuine emotion in Clara's voice.

'Eight months after my father passed away, I took his ashes to Newgrange as he had requested. My family and I took a two-week holiday to tour the West of Ireland. It was shortly before the children were due back in school after the summer holidays,' he smiled as he recalled the memory. 'We stopped in Newgrange on the way back to the car ferry in Dublin, and I scattered my father's ashes in the river Boyne.'

Clara told him that the river Boyne flowed through her grandparents' farm in County Meath. She had spent every summer of her childhood there. Tom reflected that there were no coincidences in life. He wrote the location of his father's tomb in Charlton Kings on a napkin. He passed it to Clara before requesting the bill from the server. As they stood outside the restaurant, he gave her a warm smile. Something in her manner affected him. She possessed a timeless quality, almost as if she had stepped out of another era. He walked along Montpellier Terrace towards his car, and he wondered how long he had left before he also joined the family vault at Charlton Kings.

Piles of books greeted Clara when she reached the storeroom of the municipal library. Each book needed to be tagged, stamped and allocated to the relevant section. She hung up her coat and got to work. Robbie, a young philosophy student working part-time at the library, joined her. They attached different coloured post-it notes to each book according to its category. The stack of books in the history category was piling up fast. Robbie lamented the lack of philosophical publications in the library, his specialist area. He showed a book to Clara, unsure if it belonged in the historical or autobiographical section. She opened the book to read the inside cover sleeve. It was written by a historian at the British Museum, first published in 1975 and reprinted in 1994. She thought it was odd that it was included it with the pile of new edition books that she and Robbie were sorting through.

'Do you know where these books came from?' Clara wondered. Robbie looked at the label on his inventory sheet, 'They were donated by a bookshop clearing out old stock.'

Clara snapped the book closed. It looked an interesting read, but she had several more books to get through before the library closed at seven. She wrote the author's name on her checklist, *Dr John Biddulph.* She glanced at the high pile of books to be stacked in the history section and she decided to put it on the autobiography pile.

Heavy rain pounded the streets of Cheltenham and brought late evening traffic to a standstill. Clara looked out the bus window at pedestrians sidestepping each other to avoid a clash of umbrellas. Some covered their heads while getting splashed by the traffic. It was times like this she missed the convenience of having her car, but until she completed her studies, it was an extra expense she couldn't afford. Road works on the A4019 added to the delay, and the bus had to reroute through the city centre, adding to the congestion. The extra delay would cut at least an hour off the study time she had set aside for her thesis. At this rate, she would be lucky to reach home by eight-thirty pm. The bus turned onto Malvern Road. As they passed Christchurch, Clara noticed a beautiful Victorian red brick building set back from the road. She swivelled around in her seat to catch another look as the bus drove past; she was sure it was like the nursing home she had seen in her dream. The narrow-arched windows edged with Bath stone and ornate pitched portico looked identical to the entrance she had seen the nurse walk through. It didn't look like it was used as a nursing home any more. As she noted the location in her diary, she felt a tickle on her forehead, a sensation that was happening regularly to her. She quickly admonished herself. She needed to prioritise her time and her thesis was her foremost priority. She needed to drop any extraneous research about David Perry and his explorations. She simply hadn't time for it.

Clara worked late into the night on her thesis, editing and rewriting sections where she ruled out links to Celtic spiritual beliefs. One thing she was sure of, that deities were the glue of most ancient belief systems, from the Greeks to Egyptians, to the Romans and the Celts. Most times, the priests were more powerful than the Kings, Emperors and Pharaohs. She wondered had this caused the downfall of the Celts. Had the druids exerted too much power over the Chieftains and struck fear into the heart of the people? Too often, those in authority underestimated the power of the people until they rose against them. It was a precept that was as true today as it was then. Perhaps the concept of one God, under which every man was equal, appealed to the Celtic tribes oppressed by their masters. Although most Britons converted to Christianity during the Roman occupation in the first century CE, they reverted to their pagan beliefs when they left a few centuries later.

The Irish, who were never conquered by Rome, converted to Christianity around the sixth and seventh centuries CE. Their mass conversion may have had more to do with equal rights rather than an apocalyptic awakening to Christianity. Monastic scribes recorded certain aspects of life in the British Isles before Christianity, but mostly the Celts were portrayed as a barbaric pagan race who needed saving from their destructive ways. Tantalising evidence of a sophisticated and spiritually tuned race came from the few legacies they left behind on the ancient landscape. Stonehenge and Avebury in Wiltshire, the Ring of Brodgar in Orkney and Newgrange in Ireland, were but a few of the well-known monuments left behind by Celtic ancestors. The Celts comprised several tribes across the British Isles and Europe, united by a similar belief system overseen by the druids, who travelled extensively to burial sites and places of worship. Clara proposed in her thesis that a geological catastrophe, such as ongoing earthquakes in central Asia in the fifth and fourth Millennium BCE, started the migration of several nomadic tribes into Europe. They brought with them their culture and spiritual beliefs influencing the customs of the early Celts. She tapped her pen on the table; she needed more geological evidence about seismic activity in Asia during that period to support her theory.

Clara made a note to call her father's brother Arthur, a professor of geophysics at Bangor University in Wales. Arthur Lewis helped Clara to secure her first archaeological dig at a hill fort in rural Herefordshire four years earlier. She closed her laptop, put away her notebooks and called it a night. She had another long day ahead, two morning lectures at the campus in Gloucester, and then a five-hour shift in the library until seven in the evening.

The visiting professor from Oxford University was a highly regarded archaeologist. He was part of the team who unearthed a Roman gravestone in nearby Cirencester, with an inscription that read *Bodicacia.* It caused widespread anticipation among the public and archaeologists alike. Could it be the final resting place of Boudica, the Celtic warrior queen?

Boudica, the heroic queen of the Icini Celts, led a revolt against the Romans in 60 CE. Had she won, perhaps Celtic beliefs and spiritual practices would have survived, but the occupying forces of the Roman Empire eventually quashed her heroic uprising. Boudica passed into legend as a rare breed, a female warrior. However, the remains at Cirencester turned out to be that of a twenty-seven-year-old male, and so the last resting place of Boudica remained a mystery.

Dr Ian Gardiner, the visiting professor, knew how to weave suspense and history with archaeological facts, a gift which landed him a job as a presenter of historical documentaries on television. Clara glanced around the auditorium. Students from all faculties came to hear him speak, leaving standing room only at the back of the hall. He told the story of how the Icini Celts, led by Boudica, razed the Roman garrison of Camulodunom to the ground. This was her revenge for both her daughters, raped by Roman soldiers. He presented slides of Roman remains found in Camulodunom, now Colchester in Essex. In the excavation, they found evidence of Roman dwellings burnt to the ground by Boudica and her army as they bore down on the garrison. The Romans hurriedly buried their treasured possessions, hoping to retrieve them at a later date, but alas, that day never came.

Archaeologists discovered their treasures several centuries later. Dr Gardiner quoted passages from the classical historian Tacitus, citing the success of the Celtic attack on the fact that Roman legions were absent. The Roman general Paulinus had left Camulodunom to lead an attack on the island of Anglesey off the Welsh coast, known to be the stronghold of the priests of Celtic society, the Druids.

Until the mention of the druids, Clara had been doodling in her notebook. She was mildly entertained, but she was already aware of the history that Dr Gardiner presented in his lecture. The mention of the Druids stirred her interest, and she began taking notes of dates and locations given by the visiting professor. According to historical evidence, the Romans saw the Druids as a dangerous element in Celtic society. They were the keepers of sacred knowledge, wisdom and history, binding the tribes together through shared beliefs. They were the ones who chose leaders and kings and decided the rules of Celtic society.

Clara wondered if it was merely coincidence that the professor was voicing the theories that she had written in her thesis the night before. The Druids were an enigmatic and mysterious part of Celtic tradition but remained elusive. According to Dr Gardiner's research, the Druids must have had an adept understanding of the Cosmos and their place in it to plan the rotation of feasts such as Bealtaine and Samhain. Then Neolithic and early Bronze Age settlers required an intimate knowledge of the seasons and astronomy to build structures such as Stonehenge and

Avebury. Clara agreed with his summation. Planning a structure like Stonehenge, or Newgrange, required an exact knowledge of the solstice and the directional movement of the sun, moon, and stars. The Roman legion's attack on the Druids in Anglesey was a tactic to annihilate an ancient culture. The Romans believed that whoever controlled the religion controlled the people, and so they set about converting the people of Britannia to their beliefs.

Clara ran to the bus station to make the one-thirty bus to Cheltenham. She had to be at the library at two. She was already a few minutes late. Robbie was already stacking books they had categorised the previous day on the library shelves. She went to the storeroom and loaded a pile of books from the history section onto a trolley and went to find a new home for them on the library shelves. Mrs Gregg was meticulously sifting through Robbie's pile of books, double-checking to see if he had assigned them to their correct section. He looked down the aisle at Clara and raised his eyebrow, while Mrs Gregg leaned over his trolley, picking up book after book for inspection. Clara smiled at Robbie's feigned look of interest in her comments. Clara started stacking books in the history section when she spotted Mrs Gregg heading her way. Her eagle eye spotted a few titles assigned to the wrong category. Among them was the book Clara had placed in the autobiography pile. Mrs Gregg asked her to put it in the History section. Clara was about to confess that it was she who put it in the wrong category when she noticed Robbie wave at her and put his finger on his lips, gesturing to her to keep quiet. He had already owned to the offence that upset Mrs Gregg's obsessive tendencies. Clara waited while the senior librarian conducted a thorough search of the books in her trolley until finally, she was told to proceed.

Clara's thoughts wandered to the lecture at the Gloucester campus that morning. Dr Gardiner made some valid and interesting points about Celts and the Druids as power brokers of society. He had woven a vivid human story of the traumatic events that caused violent clashes between the Celts and their oppressors, the Romans. Clara searched through the classical history books to find some works by *Tacitus,* whom Dr Gardiner had quoted in his lecture. She found his book '*The Annals*' and flicked through the pages which contained a history of the Roman Empire in the first century CE. Clara had already exceeded her book limit in the library so she made a note to withdraw the book when she returned her current reading material. She glanced at the clock. It was almost six. She still had to bring the book inventory to the office to be added to the library database. She hurriedly placed the last of the books on the shelf.

The disputed autobiography that Mrs Gregg placed in her trolley was the last book to place on the shelf. Clara absently wondered why this book seemed to attract her attention. She opened the book and inside there were some nice glossy photos of artefacts at the British Museum, photos of expeditions, text outlining discoveries and their importance in history. Clara was about to snap the book shut when something caught her eye. It was a grainy black-and-white photo of three men dressed in 1940's hiking gear. She read the caption; *Left to Right, Professor Tony Higgins, Dr John Biddulph and the Hon. George D. Perry Esq*. Clara stared at the page as if some further clues should jump out at her. Who was George D. Perry, she wondered, and was he related to David Perry. It looked like him in the grainy reproduction. She went to the desk to withdraw the book from the library until she realised that she had exceeded her limit. She glanced at the clock, thirty minutes until closing time. She placed the book on the shelf and hurried to the office with a list of titles for the database.

Road works were still in place on the A4019. The bus took the same detour down Malvern Road as the previous evening. Clara watched out for the red brick building. The bus slowed down at the pedestrian crossing before the entrance, giving her enough time to read the gold plaque on the pillar; *Kendall, Hargreaves & Associates*. She jotted down the name in her notebook. She took out her smartphone and typed in the name. They were a firm of architects who were in business since 1996. She wrote their contact details in the margin of her notes. Perhaps someone there could tell her about the previous occupier of the building. She stared at the blank space in the search engine; she wanted to type in George D. Perry, but something held her back. She wanted to know more about him, but she didn't have the time to chase leads that were unrelated to her thesis. She put her phone back in her pocket. It could wait. She had enough work on her plate.

When she reached home, Clara took out her laptop and got to work. She had many new ideas she wanted to write after the morning lecture. She popped a ready meal in the microwave and paused from her writing just long enough to eat it. Clara tried to push aside any thoughts about the photo in David Biddulph's book, or how it related to David Perry. After another hour on her laptop, she realised *it* was all she could think about. She opened a new search engine page and typed in 'Hon. George D. Perry'. An image popped up on her screen. There was no mistaking his eyes. It was David Perry staring out at her from the 1940s with the caption; *Right Honourable George David Hargreaves Perry; younger son of Viscount Maybury, Charlton Kings, Gloucestershire.*

Clara stared at the screen. This man was an enigma that trailed her and she had a feeling his legacy held some promise for her. She reached for her handbag and pulled out the folded napkin Tom Perry had given her at lunch a few days before. '*All Saints' Church, Charlton Kings*'.

Clara recognised the name. It was the church on the Maybury Estate. As a child, she went to the estate with her family. The annual May Day celebrations were famous for their pageantry. Whenever she caught the smell of freshly cut grass, it transported her to her childhood days at Maybury estate.

6

---

*A*n inordinate amount of human energy is given to avoidance; avoidance of truth, avoidance of love, and avoidance of reality. That which is seen, is mistaken for reality. That which is unseen is dismissed as fantasy. The world of duality is a continuous loop of birth and death.

The clarity David Perry received when he was in the burial chamber with the Jade Priestess soon faded. He knew his colleagues would have growing concerns about his safety. He emerged from the burial chamber during mid-afternoon and replaced all the stones that he had removed from the kurgan. His war training in the Yorkshire countryside served him well. He had learned how to rebuild damaged dry stone walls as part of a defence strategy.

He made his way back through the snow to the shepherd's hut he slept in the previous night. He lit a small fire and pulled his coat up around his shivering body, allowing the day's events to filter through his mind. He had worked up a sweat from physical exertion at the kurgan. The moisture had frozen on his clothes during his trek to the hut. The fire blazed up, and he was grateful to the shepherd who placed dry firewood in the hut. As the heat slowly thawed his cold body, he closed his eyes and focused on breathing. A Buddhist monk he met a few years earlier in the Himalayan kingdom of Sikkim had taught him how to generate heat in the body. He felt his wrist to check his pulse. It had returned to normal. He was certain that some mystical force had led him to the burial chamber. It wasn't a coincidence that he found the Priestess. He had seen no evidence of an opening beneath the chamber and there was nothing to suggest that the cavernous temple in his vision existed there. Somehow, he felt he had completed whatever task was required of him, at least for the present. He felt inside the pocket of his padded coat, to retrieve the memento he had taken from the kurgan. He stared at the dried lock of hair that he had taken from the Jade Mummy. Wrapping it carefully, he returned it to the inside pocket of his coat. Perhaps it would make a good talisman and return him safely to his companions.

At dawn, David Perry began his ascent to re-join Biddulph and Higgins on the plateau by the burial mounds. He had been gone two days now, and he expected to meet a mixture of anger and relief when he reunited with his friends. The warmth of the sun made the trek northwards easier, and he covered ground quickly. Feeling inside his pocket for the lock of hair, he was reassured he wasn't going mad, despite the inner critic that berated him for leaving the expedition in the first place. However, he had found the mummy. It was evidence of the Priestess in his vision, which was enough to help him trust his intuition. He had a sense that the Priest and Priestess were accompanying him. They too were travelling in time to some unknown destination, and when the time was right, this destination would be revealed to him. David focused as he began the steep ascent onto the plateau. In one hour, he would reach the others.

David stood on the plateau and looked all around in every direction. There was no sign of his colleagues. Puzzled, he made for the campsite where they had planned to stay at least four nights. Perhaps they left a clue to their whereabouts. It was unlikely that both of them would leave the site if extra supplies were needed. As he turned towards the site where they camped, David spotted something fluttering in the wind. A red flag was blowing on a kurgan and as David walked towards it his blood turned cold. It was the unmistakable symbol of a hammer and sickle. The Russian authorities had found them. A hundred thoughts ran through his mind at once. He must reach the village before nightfall to find out the whereabouts of Higgins and Biddulph.

It was a torturous descent to the small Mongolian village. His mind in turmoil, he slipped and tumbled down the mountain. He got to his feet and took a deep breath, remembering to calm his mind and proceed cautiously. His friends' lives may depend upon it. He saw lights twinkling in the valley below as he approached the village. A goat herder stood on a boulder calling his flock from the pasture below. He watched David curiously while tapping his stick like Morse code on the rocky ground. David stopped to ask if he was on the quickest trail into the village. The goat herder gestured and nodded towards the trail on the left. He was issuing some kind of warning, but David didn't understand the native dialect, he barely had enough Russian to get by. An older man appeared from the trees below the pasture, waving frantically at David and the goat herder. Unused to the local customs, David continued on the path to the village until he heard a distinctive call of 'wait' from the second man, who was by now nimbly climbing the steep trail. When he reached David, he wagged his finger while stopping to catch his breath. 'No, do not go to village, soldiers!'

'Do you know where my friends are?' David hoped he understood. He tried to throw out one or two words of Russian, but the man gestured for him to speak slowly. David tried again while accompanying his words with movements, as if he were playing an absurd game of charades.

The man nodded and replied, 'Altai.'

David pointed up the mountains and said, 'Up there?'

The man shook his head, 'Tiungar.'

David hadn't heard of this place before. Pulling out a map from his rucksack, he spread it out on the ground and asked the man to point to Tiungar. The older man and the goat herder moved their heads from side to side as they studied the map, the latter looking bemused by the turn of events. David spotted *Tiungar* written in small writing beneath Russian letters. The town was in the Russian state of Altai. The soldiers had taken Biddulph and Higgins there, and left a patrol in the village to await his return. David was in a dilemma. If he went to ask about his colleagues, they would arrest him, and there would be no one to alert the Authorities in London. He and his colleagues could rot in a remote Russian prison. David thought for a moment; the only way he could help them was if he made it to the British consulate in Ulan Bator in Mongolia, a thousand miles away. There were no telephones or means of communication in this remote region. The older man gestured towards the trees, from where he emerged to warn David about the soldiers and said, 'Come!'

David had run out of options. He followed him. It was getting dark, and he needed to stay out of sight of the Russian patrol in the village. He followed the old man to his farmstead with a heavy heart and leaden feet. He needed sleep, and perhaps a solution would present itself in the morning.

David Perry spent a restless night in a hay barn along with two solidly built horses. He had to resolve two problems; first and most important was to alert the British Museum that Russian soldiers were holding both his colleagues captive, and second, he had to find a route back to Europe that didn't involve travelling through Russia.

The three of them had left Britain in March when they took a flight from RAF Northolt to Ankara in Turkey. As there was no airport in Ulan Bator, Mongolia's capital, they had to make a long arduous trip over land and sea to reach the Altay Mountains. From Ankara, they took a train to the Caspian Sea, where they crossed by boat to Kazakhstan. Kazakhstan was now part of the USSR, and post-war relations with Britain were tense and growing ever more problematic. Border control rigorously searched and questioned them on the USSR border before allowing them to proceed to Mongolia. David knew if he attempted to return through Kazakhstan, he would be arrested. Overland travel to the Mongolian capital, Ulan Bator, was risky and could take several days or, perhaps weeks. Even then, David would have to return overland through Mongolia and Kazakhstan to reach Europe. This ran a high risk of exposing him to the mercy of the Russian police. His only option to avoid Russian territory altogether was to head south to China and India. From Delhi, he could take a flight to London. Once he safely reached the first town with a cable network, he would send a telegram to the British Museum and British Foreign Office about his colleagues' arrest in the remote Russian region of Altai.

Following an intermittent night of sleep, David awoke to the fresh smell of bread close to where he had slept. The local farmer, or perhaps his wife, had left a package of food for him. He unfolded his map and, using his compass, set a course for Xinjiang Province on the south-western of the mountains. He left some American dollars as a way of thanking his host, who was probably far off in pasture with his herd. He set off on the long trek through the mountains.

Although it was summer in the Altay Mountains, the weather was unpredictable as David had experienced in the blizzard conditions a few days before. He needed stamina and good fortune to make it safely through the mountain pass into China. David had a sketchy knowledge of the political situation in China, but enough to know there was deep unrest between the Nationalist Government and the Communist Party. The political unrest in China might work to his advantage. They based most of the government troops to the east in Peking and Shanghai. To reach India, he would have to travel south through the western province of Xinjiang. He would cross the Indian border at Kashmir. Despite the treacherous and potentially dangerous journey ahead, David felt a tremor of excitement at the prospect of travelling through the ancient kingdoms along the Silk Road and through the mighty peaks of the Himalayas.

After three days trekking through mountains, David was unsure if he had crossed the Chinese border. For the fifth time that morning, he looked at his map and compass, trying to figure out his exact location. Fortunately, the Great Wall didn't extend to this region. It should be relatively easy to cross, but the downside was he had no way of knowing if he was safely out of Russian territory. He made good ground because of favourable weather. He wanted to reach the town of Altay in Xinjiang province. There he could send a telegram to the Foreign Office and the British Museum. So far, he had seen no border patrol, just the odd herder grazing their animals on the pastures. He continued in a south-westerly direction, hoping it would lead him to the plains of Xinjiang by morning. From there, he hoped to catch a ride to Altay.

By noon, David saw the plains of Xinjiang spread like a vast continent before him. He picked up a ride on a hay cart with a friendly farmer who nodded and smiled continuously before dropping him off at a small market village in the foothills of the mountains where he now stood with a sweeping view of the plains. David reached in his pocket for a notebook and sketched the terrain, marking in the meandering rivers and villages.

The locals in the market followed David down the street with rugs, metal buckets, straw baskets, hawking their wares in the hope of a sale. David bought a conical straw hat to keep the scorching sun off his face. Temperatures soared in the plains without the fresh breeze of the mountains. David felt relief to see a building that looked like a telephone exchange, but his relief soon turned to frustration when he realised the telephone was out of order. David asked the operator of the exchange if he had a telegraph machine. The man nodded eagerly and beckoned him into his office. David felt like a giant inside the tiny room. At six foot two inches, he was at least a foot taller than the operator. He took the sheet of proffered yellowed paper to write his message to both the British Museum and the Foreign Office marking it 'Urgent'. The operator typed each letter carefully into the telegraph machine, looking at David after each word to make sure it was correct. David felt a tremendous rush of relief that the message would reach London. It was eight days since Biddulph and Higgins had been arrested. He would place a call to London as soon as he located a working telephone. David asked the operator if there were any buses to the city of Altay. He shook his head and shouted something to a man waiting by the door. After some deliberation between the two, David was led to the town square.

David was unsure why he was there until thirty minutes later, a battered old vehicle belched its way towards the square coming to a halt in a haze of black fumes. The man spoke to the bus driver and nodded to David, who climbed on board amid the livestock, passengers, and sacks of grain. For the first ten minutes of the bus ride, all eyes were on him, and David smiled wryly, knowing that to the locals, he was the oddest creature on the bus. The chattering of the locals, squawking of chickens, and bleating of goats resumed until they reached the plains of Xinjiang three hours later. The bus driver pulled up at a drab concrete building with a rusty sign advertising toothpaste with the white smile covered in black marks. David's stomach felt sick from the constant rocking on the bus as it negotiated the hairpin bends leading down from the mountain. The foul-smelling animals on the bus hadn't helped his queasiness. He leaned against a wall to steady his quivering legs. A few minutes later, another bus pulled up and passengers from his bus clambered to get on board. The man who had sat beside him for the last hour of the journey pointed at the bus and said, 'Altay.' David took a deep breath and joined the hustle for another two-hour bus ride to Altay.

The sound of car horns and general bustle of life was a welcome contrast after several weeks of isolation in the mountains. David closed the window of his small rented room and wrote notes in his journal. There was a knock on the door as a young boy brought a bucket of warm water. For David, it was pure luxury to wash in warm water and lie on a mattress for the first time in weeks. He was asleep as soon as his head hit the pillow.

The city of Altay had poor road links to the rest of China due to its remote location near the Altay Mountains. There were no trains or regular bus links to Urumqi, the major city of Xinjiang Province. David purchased a map of the region in a grocery shop while asking for information about transport to Urumqi. There was no rail network in Western China. It would be a long and arduous journey to the Indian border. The fastest route to Delhi was through the Himalayan region of Kashmir in India. India had recently become an independent nation, free from British rule. The northern state of Punjab was split in two resulting in the death of millions when people at each side of the divide became displaced and homeless. The western region of Punjab was now called Pakistan, and it was seeking to include Kashmir in its territory.

David's uncle, his mother's brother Lord Hargreaves, was stationed in India for three years. He would leave once the British Raj handed full authority over to the newly formed government in Delhi. It was David's plan to reach his uncle in Delhi and secure a flight back to London.

David located a telephone exchange near the bus station in Altay. He asked the operator to place a call to London. After four failed attempts, a crackling noise revealed a faint male voice on the other end. David shouted his name into the receiver when the voice asked him to repeat his name. David had beads of sweat on his brow and his cheeks flushed with the stifling heat in the building. Trying a different approach, he shouted Dr John Biddulph's name into the receiver. Finally, the man said, 'Where are you?'

David shouted out the last known location of Dr John Biddulph and Professor Tony Higgins, and the town where they were held captive by the Russian authorities. There was a click, and the line went dead. David wanted to scream with frustration. He asked for the call to be put through again, but with no success. There was no way to know if the man at the British Museum had understood him. He asked the telephone exchange operator if there was a bus to Urumqi. He shook his head and said, 'No bus.'

David pulled out his newly purchased a map of the region and showed him where he wanted to go. The man pointed to *Karamay* and said, 'Here bus go.'

David felt relieved. From Karamay, he could travel to Urumqi. 'When will the next bus go to Karamay?' David asked the phone operator who was helping another customer. He shrugged and said, 'One, maybe two days.'

Two days later and still no bus had arrived to go to Karamay. David made inquiries at the local market asking if someone could take him to Karamay. A local trader who regularly visited Karamay agreed to take him. He held up four fingers, and David wasn't sure if he meant he was going in four days or four weeks. David repeated the word tomorrow, and the trader shook his head. When David produced ten American dollars and placed them on the counter and the man said, 'We go tomorrow.'

A beaten-up old truck pulled up outside David's lodgings at six in the morning. The journey was two hundred miles. Eventually, after ten hours on dirt tracks that passed for roads, David arrived in Karamay. The trader pointed David toward a boarding house, where he wearily dropped his bags on the scruffy sofa jammed up against the stairwell. A young woman took his money and handed him a key. David strapped on his backpack and climbed the stairs to find his room. His clothes were covered in dust from the long drive. He threw his bags on the floor and went down to fetch a bucket of warm water to wash off the grime. The smell of freshly cooked food wafted in the window from the street vendors below. Once he was dressed, he left his lodgings and followed the smell until he reached the market. He eagerly sampled the mouth-watering dishes. He had tasted nothing quite like it before. Not even the finest Chinese cuisine in London could compare with it. He savoured the sights, taste and smell of the Orient as he observed locals peddling their wares. A group of children playfully weaved through the stalls as they chased a stray cat. Babies were tucked up asleep in a tight sling on their mother's back, and men struck late evening bargains before carrying their merchandise home.

David felt that someone was observing him. Turning around, he saw a traveller in dark red robes smiling at him. David gestured at the stallholder for another plate of food and offered it to the traveller. The man in maroon robes came to sit beside him. It was difficult to put an age on him. He could be in his forties or fifties David thought. He was fit and agile, with a youthful demeanour. When he finished eating, he gave a slight nod of gratitude. David ordered two cups of tea. They each sat sipping their tea as if drinking oceans of traditions and beliefs that separated them. One by one, the stars came out. To David, the monk's calm presence was star-like, distant but true. The stallholder was closing up for the night, prompting them to move from their position. David pointed towards the boarding house. The monk bowed his head and walked into the night. David watched him leave a trail of calm amid the bustle of the closing market stalls. It was a valuable lesson he thought, to leave peace in your wake.

.

7

The memory of unity emerges from the breadth of time, propelling the soul to the brink of eternity and its home among the stars. Human life is a brief interlude in the vast consciousness of the universal mind.

The early winds of March blew through the streets of Cheltenham. Rain pelted against the pavements and Clara struggled to fold her umbrella, which was proving useless in the formidable gale force wind howling from the east. She backed her way into the revolving door of the library, glad to be out of the inclement weather. It was almost empty except for a few regulars using the computers. Richard, the supervisor that morning, whispered to her to take a seat and work on her thesis. He would call her if they needed her. Clara thanked him and sat at an empty table near the window. Opening her laptop, she pulled a notebook out of her bag. Looking around, she saw another few regulars coming in as she walked down the aisle to the history section. She pulled out Julius Caesar's *Gallic Wars* and a book by Tacitus called *Histories and Annals.* She glanced at a book to the left called *Celtic Calendar Year*, and she added it to her reading collection.

Tracing the spiritual beliefs and traditions of the Celts was proving to be a tricky task. They left tantalising glimpses of their cosmic knowledge and festivals based on lunar cycles. They had a high regard for the moon and the feminine principle it represented. The moon was seen as the queen of the night. Clara stared at a diagram of the Coligny Calendar in the book *Celtic Calendar Year*. The Coligny Calendar was the earliest known Celtic calendar, dating from the 1st century BCE. Each month began with a full moon, and there were thirteen months in each year. The Coligny calendar achieved a complex organisation of solar and lunar months, showing considerable sophistication and knowledge of the seasons and lunar cycles. March was known as Cutios, which translated as 'windy time'.

Weather patterns had changed little in two thousand years, Clara thought as she looked at the rain pelting against the window. She noted the four major festivals of the Celtic year, beginning with Samhain, which marked the start of winter. Next was Imbolc, or Brigid's Day, which the Celts celebrated in early spring. The third major festival was Beltaine, marking the beginning of summer, and finally, Lughnasadh, the harvest festival, celebrated in the first half of August. The names of three festivals gave their name to months of the year in the Gaelic language. Samhna was Gaelic for November, Beltaine was May, and Lunasa, the month of August. Several links to Celtic traditions could be found in the Gaelic language of Ireland and Scotland. Clara had learned some phrases from her grandmother, who spoke native Irish fluently. She came from Dingle in County Kerry, a Gaelic speaking region in south-west Ireland. Clara missed both her Irish grandparents. They had enriched her life beyond measure and ignited the Celtic fire within her.

Early Christian monks grafted Christianity onto the Celtic tree of Spiritualism by gradually superseding ancient customs with newer religious festivals. However, the roots of these festivals survived in the culture and language of the Gaels, the inheritors of Celtic traditions and beliefs. The importance of the winter solstice, evident in Newgrange and Stonehenge, ebbed as the tide of Christian fervency swept through the British Isles. In the modern world, the winter solstice, along with the birth of Christ, was lost in the wave of commercialism that accompanied the holiday season.

Clara lamented a lack of evidence from the Celts who were averse to keeping written records. It was impossible to know with any certainty the practices that led to the construction of stone circles and burial chambers. She cross-referenced her information with the classical histories of Tacitus and Julius Caesar. They gave little insight into Celtic ceremonies or the inner sanctum of the Druids, the Celtic priests. She turned her attention to transcripts of the Vedas, from Sanskrit to English. Clara saw similarities between the Vedic religion and the practices of the Druids. The origin of the Vedas could be traced back to 1500 BCE, when a large nomadic group known as the Aryans arrived in Northern India from central Asia. The hymns, myths, and prayers were transmitted orally over many generations before eventually being committed to writing. It was ancient texts such as the Vedas, and the hieroglyphic records of ancient Egyptians, that reminded Clara of the rich heritage and spiritual wisdom lost with the Druids. In Julius Caesar's book '*Gallic Wars*' there were several centres of learning already established in Britain when he crossed the English Channel from Gaul (France) in 55 BCE. Perhaps, thought Clara, these education centres included documented evidence of Celtic practices and spiritual beliefs. Alas, all was lost a hundred years later when the Roman general Paulinus killed all the Druids at Anglesey and destroyed their centres of learning. The Romans accused the Celts of barbaric practices and ritualistic sacrifices. They began a four-hundred-year campaign to wipe out all druidic practices and festivals to annihilate the spiritual origin of the Celts. This gave Rome total dominance over the people of Britannia. In the fifth century CE, Christianity swept across Ireland, gradually creating a hybrid race of Celtic-Christians. These replaced traditional festivals with Christian rites and ceremonies.

By lunchtime, Clara was pleased with her progress, adding another five pages to her thesis. She thanked Richard for allowing her the time to research. He smiled and said no problem. He had completed a history degree ten years previously, and he understood the time needed to dedicate to research. Clara had the afternoon free, but she stayed on at the library to continue her research and to avoid the inclement weather. She hoped to trace the stories of Fionn MacCumhaill and the Fianna to their Celtic origin. She pulled out the book her grandfather had given her many years before and leafed through the pages. Fionn MacCumhaill was a legendary Celtic hero and leader of the Fianna, a band of third-century warriors and hunters who protected Ireland from invasion. Stories of the Fianna that doubtlessly passed through storytelling from generation to generation were eventually put on paper in the 12th century CE as part of the Fenian cycle, a vital part of Irish folklore. According to legend, Fionn was a descendant of the Druids. One story tells how he became leader of the Fianna by slaying a ghostly figure haunting the place of the High Kings of Ireland. The High Kings lived at Tara in County Meath, and every Samhain (November), the phantom terrorised the people of Tara by playing music on his harp and sapping the strength of every warrior. Fionn, using a magic spear that granted him immunity to the music, killed the phantom. As a reward, he was made the leader of the Fianna. He replaced the previous leader, Goll, who had to swear fealty to him. Clara learned that the Fenian Cycle, the tales of Fionn MacCumhaill and the Fianna, were written by early medieval monks. The Irish tradition of storytelling had its roots in the past, stories recounted from one generation of Celts to the next, and it was from this source that Christian monks gathered their colourful tales. When committing the stories to paper, they created a fractured history of Ireland by casting ancient Celtic legends into a Christian mould. In doing so, they demoted the pantheon of gods, the Tuatha Dé Danann, to mortals, and rewrote the legacy of the Druids into a labyrinth of heroes and villains whose chief preoccupation was hunting. Clara wondered if it was possible to tell fact from fiction in a distilled monastic version of Celts who lived seven hundred years previously. However, it offered some insight into the storytelling of the Christian Celts and their folk heroes.

The wind died down and the rain finally stopped. The sun lit up the buildings across the street from the library. Clara returned the books she used for reference to the History Section. She found the book by Dr John Biddulph and signed it out at the desk. She walked out into the afternoon sunshine. It smelled fresh after the rain and she took a shortcut through the Imperial Gardens. She stopped to admire the beautifully proportioned Regency houses lining the square. Clara walked towards the bus stop to take the bus home. Instead, she looked at her watch and realised it was still office hours. Quickly, she turned on her heel and headed for Lansdown Crescent before she changed her mind. She speeded up trying not to think about where she was going until she came to the church on Malvern Road. She stopped for a moment to take in the large red brick building surrounded by iron railings. She clenched her fists and walked to the pedestrian crossing to reach the imposing entrance. The brass plaque on the pillar read '*Kendall, Hargreaves & Associates*' and was covered in droplets of rain.

There was a sign marked *Private* on an inner door of the ground floor. Another sign marked *Reception* had an arrow pointing up a flight of stairs. Clara gingerly made her way up the steps pausing to look at the old black and white photographs lining the walls, making it eerily like a flashback to her dream weeks before. The receptionist smiled and asked if she had an appointment. Clara explained to her she was a student of history who was researching different building styles in Cheltenham. She asked if there were any documents to help trace the occupants, or use of the building since its construction. The receptionist looked blank and pressed a button on her desk phone. Politely, she informed Clara that Mr Hargreaves would see her. Clara barely had time to gather her thoughts. She hadn't expected to be led into the boss's office. She entered a room with generous Georgian proportions, and behind an enormous mahogany desk sat Mr Hargreaves. He motioned her to take a seat while he finished jotting notes in his desk diary. Clara looked around, taking in the beautiful cornice and mouldings. She felt a chill move down her spine and it occurred to her that this was the room where David Perry drew his final breath. Mr Hargreaves asked how he could be of assistance. She continued with the story she gave the receptionist, telling him she was a student of history researching buildings in Cheltenham. He gazed steadily at her a few moments before giving a reply. Something in his manner reminded her of Tom Perry. He had an air of assurance and confidence. Clara could tell he was assessing her and how much information he was prepared to divulge.

'The building was constructed in 1833 as a town house for Viscount and Lady Maybury. It remained as a dwelling until the Second World War, when it became an infirmary for wounded soldiers. Post war, I think it was rented to a family for a number of years. It was turned into a private nursing home in the 1970's.'

Mr Hargreaves noticed a slight flush on Clara's face. She kept her head down and jotted a few notes on her notepad.

'What happened to the building after the nursing home closed?' Clara asked. 'Who owned it in the intervening years before your company acquired it?'

Mr Hargreaves replied evasively, 'It is still owned by the Maybury family.'

Clara sensed the exchange was coming to an end. She tried to press him for more information about the current owner but Mr Hargreaves smiled politely and said he had a meeting to attend. He looked at her with a studied air and she felt herself flinching under his scrutiny. She was no good at deception and she felt that he had seen right through her. She wrote some notes while thinking about what to say before he ended the interview.

'Do you know of the explorer David Perry?' It popped out before she realised what she was saying.

Mr Hargreaves' eyes opened wide and he said, 'Yes, I knew him. He was my grandfather. Now, you really must excuse me, I'm rather busy.'

Clara stepped out into the cool evening air and walked up Malvern Road towards the bus stop. She had so much to process. The building was identical to the one she saw in her dream. She was in awe of her intuitive powers. It was likely that David Perry moved there because his family owned the building. If David Perry was Mr Hargreaves grandfather, then that would make him either Tom Perry's son, or perhaps his cousin. Clara wondered if he was present when the family scattered David Perry's ashes at Newgrange. Clara wanted to turn back and ask him about it, but common sense prevailed. He had dismissed her pretty quickly when she asked about

David Perry. Besides, there was nothing he could say to alter the fact that David Perry was dead. She was chasing a ghost.

8

Often in dreams, the soul traverses time and moves mountains to return to the place where they broke loose among the stars. They see the echo of love shining in every awakened soul on the planet. While thought is mind in action, love is spirit in action.

The dirt track opened onto something that seemed more like a navigable roadway. It was almost nightfall as the truck pulled up on the outskirts of Urumqi in central Xinjiang Province. David paid the driver in dollars and headed for the centre of town. He came to a large building which looked like an administrative centre. David spoke a few words of Mandarin that he picked up from his driver to ask if he could use the telephone. He called his uncle's office in India. Robert Hargreaves' secretary answered the phone. There was a crackling noise until finally his uncle took the receiver. David heard the relief in his voice when he realised who was on the other end.

'Your mother has been beside herself with worry, David. She has called several times to ask me if I have any news of your whereabouts.' David was about to ask about his two colleagues, but Lord Hargreaves interrupted. There was a few seconds' delay in the connection. 'Your parents have been dreadfully worried since news reached them that your colleagues were arrested by Russians. They thought you were dead.'

David interjected quickly, 'I'm fine, really. Is anything being done to release Dr Biddulph and Professor Higgins?'

A crackling sound lasted for a few moments before Lord Hargreaves answered, 'A member of the British Foreign Office and a senior member of the British Museum are on their way to Novosibirsk in Russia. This is where they are detaining your colleagues. Relations between the USSR and Western Europe have worsened because of a blockade on Berlin by the Russians.'

Lord Hargreaves continued to outline the political situation until David cut across him and said he had to go. He realised it would take careful negotiating before Biddulph and Higgins could return home. David told his uncle that it was he who had sent a telegram to the Foreign Office and made a call to the British Museum. Lord Hargreaves' voice returned after a prolonged crackling, causing David to hold the receiver a few inches from his ear.

'To the best of my knowledge the British Foreign Office didn't receive a telegram. A call operator at the British Museum alerted them that they received news of the arrest from an anonymous caller.'

David realised despite the terrible connection in Karamay, the Foreign Office had received his message. His uncle's voice came booming through the receiver again. 'You can't return home through the USSR, my boy.'

David shouted, 'I know Uncle, I'm travelling through Xinjiang in China. I'm heading for the Indian border.'

Lord Hargreaves rambled on a little while thinking out loud. 'Terrible business, this partition. It's not safe to travel to western Kashmir. You'll need a guide to cross into India. Perhaps we can get you across through the Himalayas near Ladakh. If you make it to the border in the next six weeks, the Rohtang Pass will be open, but it closes again in September.'

David once again cut across his uncle's ramblings. 'Tell me where to head to, Uncle.'

David heard his uncle barking orders at someone in his office. 'I'll make arrangements for a guide to meet you in Yarkand, a town on the Silk Road between Khotan and Kashgar. He will get you safely into India. Now, I must call my sister to let her know you are safe.' There was a click, and the line went dead.

The Silk Road passed through Urumqi, and David marked out his journey to follow the ancient trading route westward. From Urumqi, he would travel to Kucha and on to Aksu, across the Northern fringes of the Taklamakan desert in the Tarim Basin. From there, he would head south-west on the Silk Route towards Yarkand where he would meet the guide his uncle had dispatched. The journey would take him through the ancient kingdoms and trading posts spanning western China. It had taken him thirty days to reach Urumqi, and he estimated it would take another five or six weeks to reach India. It was an epic journey through some very inhospitable terrain, and he needed to tread carefully through the southern region of Xinjiang, where warlords and bandits followed their self-made laws and justice.

To continue the journey west along the Silk Road, David needed to find transport from a merchant who knew the route. David recalled his history lessons, where he learned about the ancient Silk Road and the adventures of Marco Polo. To a young boy, the exoticism and mystery of the Orient were enchanting. He imagined the smells of spices and the gleam of precious jewels traded by merchants between East and West. The people in the kingdoms of Kucha and Khotan were said to originate from the Eurasian Steppes. David realised he was literally following their migration route from the Altay Mountains through Xinjiang Province. They spoke a language which related to Sanskrit, the ancient language used to record the first written texts of the Vedas. These texts originated from a group of nomads known as Aryans, who came from the European Steppes. For thousands of years, people had travelled along the route David was taking from the Altay Mountains into Xinjiang Province and through the ancient trading routes known as the Silk Road, connecting East and West.

David placed a scarf over his nose and mouth to keep from breathing the dusty air. His driver was taking the route through the Tarim Basin, between the Tien Shan Mountains to the north, and the Taklamakan desert to the south. Up ahead, a truck was pulled over on the side of the road. Quickly, the driver threw a baseball cap at David and motioned to him to pull it down to shade his face. David did as he was told. Just as they pulled up beside the parked vehicle, a man with a gun waved them over to the side. Another man was counting notes he had taken from the driver of the stationary truck. Warlords patrolled the route, extorting money from traders for taxes and protection money. The man looked at David and asked the driver who he was. David didn't understand the full conversation, but he held his breath while the driver negotiated a price for their onward journey to Kucha. There were raised voices between the gunman and the tax collector. In the rear-view mirror, David saw a convoy of trucks coming up behind. Many traders travelled in convoys to avoid paying extortionate rates to get to the Aksu region of Xinjiang. The man hurriedly took the money offered by David's driver and waved him on. David let out a sigh of relief. He thanked his lucky stars that the convoy came along. Given his driver's heated conversation with the bandits, he wasn't sure he'd make it out alive.

Three days after setting off from Urumqi, David arrived safely in Kucha. The discovery of ancient Sanskrit manuscripts in the Taklamakan desert at the end of the nineteenth century sparked several expeditions to the region. David had a vague knowledge of an expedition led from Britain by Aurel Stein, a Hungarian explorer, expert in Sanskrit and other Indo-European languages. He was credited with rediscovering the Silk Road. David, feeling exhausted after the journey, went in search of a room for the night. He stepped into the lobby of a boarding house where he noticed a western tourist standing at the desk waiting for his room key. He looked at David and nodded politely. The man introduced himself as Lorenzo De Campo. David shook his hand and gestured to the concierge for a room. Once he had the room key in his hand, he turned to the Italian. 'Please excuse me. It has been a long journey.'

Lorenzo shrugged and replied, 'I understand. But if you want some food later, you can find me up the street at the market.' He pointed left towards the square where the driver had dropped him off.

David wearily climbed the narrow stairway, ducking his head. He threw his bag and clothes on the floor and used a full bucket of tepid water to wash off the grime and dust. He lay on the bed for a few moments, drying quickly in the heat. The smell of food wafting through the window made him realise how hungry he was. He set off to join the Italian in the market. He could do with some company.

Lorenzo was an avid admirer of the thirteenth-century explorer Marco Polo. The thirteenth-century explorer set off from Lorenzo's home town of Venice, in search of ancient trade routes linking China to Constantinople and Venice. Lorenzo had reached Kucha several days previously, on his journey east toward Shangdu, once known as Xanadu, ancient capital of Kublai Khan's empire. David asked him about his journey so far. Lorenzo, a keen orator, was happy to oblige. Before entering Xinjiang, he had travelled through Kashmir. He warned David about the treacherous areas where the fighting erupted between the people in the newly formed country of Pakistan and the Indian state of Kashmir. Lorenzo followed the footsteps of his hero, Marco Polo, to cross the border at the ancient kingdom of Kashgar. From Kashgar, he travelled to Khotan, the next kingdom on the

Silk Road. He told David about the Uyghur people living in the region, still producing silks and carpets to trade across China. Lorenzo took a small pouch from the inside pocket of his khaki jacket. He produced a shiny stone amulet that he purchased in Khotan. David sat transfixed for a moment; it was identical to the stone in the Priestess' neck piece in the Altay Mountains.

'What is this stone?' he asked Lorenzo.

'This is the treasure that put Khotan on the map, and on the Silk Road,' Lorenzo beamed eagerly. 'It is jade. This jade is mined nearby in the Kunlun Mountains.'

Lorenzo continued to effuse about the history of the Tarim Basin and its kingdoms, but David's mind wandered to the subterranean world of the Priestess deep in the Altay Mountains.

Once they had finished their food, David and his new friend returned to their lodgings. Lorenzo asked him if he wanted to join him on a trip to Buddhist caves the following morning, explaining that it wasn't far off David's route to Khotan. The archaeologist in David was intrigued, and he agreed to leave with Lorenzo the following morning.

Kumtura Caves lay twenty miles west of Kucha. They were inhabited between the fourth and eleventh centuries CE. The grottoes were first chiselled out in the fourth century CE when Buddhism was brought from India to China. Lorenzo read aloud from his well-used guide book as he and David walked through the caves of the complex. The frescoes, with serene faces full of loving-kindness, represented the Buddha and the Bodhisattvas. David noticed severe damage caused to some frescoes on the walls of the caves. Lorenzo explained that, under the guise of preservation, an expedition from Berlin in 1901 had broken of large chunks of the frescoes and took them to Germany. David knew only too well the damage done to ancient monuments in the search for treasure and glorification. The Elgin marbles, now housed in the British Museum, were a case in point. As they wandered through the labyrinth of caves, he felt the sacredness associated with these Buddhist monks. Spirituality seemed to be a theme of his adventure so far; priests, priestesses, holy men and monks spreading a universal message of unity across the continents.

That night, David and Lorenzo set up camp near the caves. David slept poorly. Dreams of the Priestess unsettled him and he woke during the night in a fitful state. He lay there until dawn, not wanting to wake Lorenzo, who was snoring rhythmically. Eager to continue his travels towards Khotan, David dressed and was ready for his driver, who picked him up at the caves. He said goodbye to Lorenzo, and he set off with his driver just as the sun was rising over the Taklamakan desert. He was ready for the next chapter on his adventure.

His driver, who spoke a few words of English, told David it would take two days to reach Khotan. David was adjusted to the long road trips while drivers stopped to nap and refuel at intervals. The journey usually took twice the time that they said. He allowed four days to reach Khotan.

Buses in the Tarim Basin, comprising almost the entire area of southern Xinjiang, were infrequent and unreliable.

This was because of skirmishes and racketeering by local warlords. David sat in the back of the truck and tried to catch up on the sleep he missed the night before. The jolts from the bumpy ride didn't make it an easy journey, and by the time they made their first stop, he was feeling queasy. He felt his stomach wretch a few times before he finally heaved up its contents. He grabbed his water bottle and gargled, spitting it out on the dried ground. During July, temperatures soared past forty degrees Celsius. After a few hours' rest from the sapping heat, they resumed their journey to Khotan. David's thoughts turned to the jade amulet Lorenzo showed him and its similarity to the jade in the neckpiece worn by the mummy of the Priestess. It was a light pasty colour, unlike the darker jade from other regions in Asia. It most probably came from this region of China. Jade held significant spiritual properties for ancient tribes in Eurasia. Closing his eyes, he saw the Priestess performing a ritual in the cave of the Altay Mountains. Sometimes, he heard the Priest speaking to him, which caused him deep anxiety. He tried to blot it out, but it always found a way through to him. Lately, he had been so exhausted from the constant travelling his agitation had dissipated, until last night when the Priest's presence seemed stronger, as if he were inside the Buddhist caves. David pulled his cap down over his face to block out the bright sunlight. He was growing tired of the arid conditions and featureless terrain of the Taklamakan desert. He welcomed the prospect of reaching the Himalayas before he crossed the border to India.

When they finally reached Khotan, David was nauseous and had a fever. He didn't eat or sleep on the journey. The driver looked concerned and drove him to a lodging house, where he checked them both into a room. Dropping their bags in the room, he indicated for David to follow him. David followed him through a maze of alleyways. Feeling dizzy, he stopped to lean against a wall. The driver, who had already turned the corner to another street, came back and helped him the final few yards until they came to a tailor's shop. The tailor gave a jerk of his head towards the rear of the dilapidated building. The driver hooked David's arm around his neck and almost dragged him to a tiny room behind the tailor's shop. David hadn't the energy to protest and lay where his driver placed him, on a grass mat on the floor. An old man appeared above him, lighting some incense. He crouched on the floor next to David. He pulled a long needle from a wooden box, placing it in David's chest. He continued to place needles along his torso and around his head. David relaxed. The healer was performing the ancient Chinese practice of Acupuncture, that was said to transport life energy around the body. He closed his eyes, falling into deep relaxation. He felt detached from his body, free from the cares and worries of physical habitation. Two doors appeared before him, one opened, and he stepped into absolute bliss. Here, there were no divisions, just the joy of union, beyond the appearance of duality.

A gentle touch on his arm slowly reminded him he had a body in the physical world. Opening his eyes, he saw the old healer lean over him. He pulled David to a sitting position and offered him a drink of water. David never felt so alive. The dizziness and sickness had completely gone. He thanked the old man and went out front to the tailor's shop where his driver was waiting for him.

9

With every step the soul takes with presence, grace translates each movement into beauty. When the human and spirit merge in love, the entire world falls at their feet.

Cheltenham was busy preparing for the four-day horse racing festival that made it famous around the world. Every hotel and guesthouse was booked out months in advance. Accommodation was scarce as race goers filled up every spare room within a ten-mile radius. The Cheltenham races occurred during the week of St. Patrick's Day, Ireland's national holiday and the Irish were there in force for that week. Cheltenham echoed with laughter and joviality during this period on the racing calendar year.

John and Tilly Flaherty came to the races every year. This year, they had an extra reason to cheer. Their son Jack was riding in the prestigious Gold Cup race. They booked into Queen's Hotel in the town centre to celebrate Jack's special event. John Flaherty was Clara's uncle, her mother's eldest brother. He inherited the family farm near Newgrange in County Meath. Clara had booked her ticket well in advance to watch her cousin riding *'Kilcoole Lad'* in one of the biggest events of the racing calendar. She hadn't seen her relatives in almost three years. Her mother and aunt Deirdre were due to arrive the evening before the Gold Cup and were going to stay in her house in Tewkesbury. No doubt they would add volume to the crowd who were cheering for Jack. Clara smiled when she thought about how her younger cousin would be oblivious to any fuss. He was eight years her junior. Clara spent many Saturdays of her summer holidays in Ireland at Gymkhanas. She watched as Jack and his brother Gavin competed, picking up more rosettes and trophies to add to their collection.

Jack Flaherty had spent five years with a top horse trainer in County Meath honing his skills. It had paid dividends as next Friday he was riding the Stud's star mare in the Gold Cup. Jack would take it all in his stride. He was remarkably composed. Gavin, twenty-six, was two years older than Jack. He had a nasty fall when he was eighteen, putting an end to his dreams of becoming a professional jockey.

Clara made plans to meet her cousins, Jack and his sister Jenny in Cheltenham. Gavin was running the arm in Ireland and planned to fly over the night before the big race. Jenny was ten months younger than Clara and had always been more like a sister. They planned a night out when Jenny arrived. Clara was already dreading the hangover. It was going to be a busy week with all her relations coming to stay on various days.

Saturday morning, Clara dusted and vacuumed the house in anticipation of her visitors. When she was finished, it gleamed. The house hadn't looked so clean since she moved in. She had spent so many long winter evenings poring over texts and documents for her research that she barely had time to clean up after herself. It would be a welcome change to have fun and frivolity during race week she thought. By lunchtime, she was pleased with her efforts and decided to treat herself to coffee in Tewkesbury.

A couple were just leaving as Clara entered the little tea shop, leaving a table vacant by the window. Clara thought luck was on her side because it was her favourite place to sit and watch the world go by. She popped her coat and newspaper on the chair and went to order a strong coffee and homemade pie. Martha, the proprietor, had just baked a fresh tray of cookies. She popped one on a plate with the pie. Clara thanked her and nibbled on the sweet treats while watching people go by on the street. She watched as tourists stopped to look up at the ancient timber-framed buildings that characterised Tewkesbury while locals went hurriedly about their business. A familiar face caught her eye striding down the street. Philip Jones came to a halt and crossed the street to the tea shop. He glanced in the window and caught Clara staring at him. She flushed and dropped her head hoping he didn't recognise her. Clara saw him ducking his large frame to enter through the seventeenth-century doorway. He ordered a coffee and came striding over to Clara's table. He motioned to the chair opposite her, saying every seat was taken. The photographer tucked his long legs in the narrow space between the table and the bay window. Martha arrived with his flat white coffee. He took a sip and smiled at Clara.

'Have you located the original photo of the mummy yet?' He had remembered exactly who she was.

Clara shook her head and said, 'Unfortunately, it's off limits at the Municipal Library.'

'Such a shame,' replied Philip. 'It was an intriguing proposition.'

They chatted easily over their coffee and Clara realised how much she had missed having male company. As if picking up on her thoughts, Philip casually mentioned his recent divorce. She listened as he spoke about his ten-year-old son, who spent every second weekend with him. He asked if she was married. 'Soon to be divorced', Clara replied.

'Any children?' Philip raised a quizzical brow.

Feeling uncomfortable about where the conversation was heading, Clara shook her head and changed the subject to race week in Cheltenham. Philip showed interest especially when he heard Clara's cousin was riding in the Gold Cup. He told her he had corporate seats from a sponsor for the first day of racing on Tuesday and asked if she'd like to come along as his guest. Clara said that although it was tempting, she had two lectures Tuesday morning and to work in the library in the afternoon. Philip drained his coffee and shrugged. Clara, sensing his embarrassment, quickly added that maybe they could meet another time for coffee. He nodded, smiled and went to pay at the counter. She watched as he crossed the street in front of the café and walked back to his shop. For the first time since her divorce, she considered what it might be like to be in a relationship again.

Recently, she had been so preoccupied with her studies and the ghost of David Perry that she hadn't considered a new relationship. Perhaps it was time to date again. The image of David Perry seemed to flash before her eyes as if he stood outside Martha's tea shop looking in the window. She blinked a few times until she realised a man was standing outside reading the menu posted on the windowpane. She often imagined what David Perry was like when he was her age. Was he happy? Had he walked the same streets she now walked? Sometimes, she allowed her fancy to take flight, and she thought maybe they were meant to be together, but their timelines were out of sync. She felt a kindred spirit in him, as if he somehow lived in her soul, reminding her to connect to love. Clara blinked as the bright sun peeked over the rooftops opposite and shone directly into her eyes waking her from her dream world. She stood up and thanked Martha and left the café. She knew where she wanted to go next.

She waited at the bus stop for the bus to Charlton Kings. Hopefully, visiting David Perry's grave would bring closure to her fascination with him. She did not want to waste time on a ghost in the past. The bus route took her through Cheltenham on the way, passing the University campus. As the bus crawled through race week traffic, Clara noticed Cormac standing outside the gates of Francis Close Hall. She pressed the bell and got off the bus at the next stop. She waved down the street at her brother who came to greet her with a warm hug. She chided him for not telling her he was in town. He told her he had tried her phone but it went to voicemail. When he went to the library where Clara worked, a very prim and proper lady told him to try Francis Close Hall.

They cut across to the High Street and up the Promenade, weaving their way through the tourists and race goers that had descended on the town. All the cafes were full, so Cormac suggested they take a drive out to Winchcombe in the Cotswolds, the village where they had grown up. Clara told him that she had plans to meet Jack and Jenny in town at four. Cormac looked at his watch. They still had two hours.

Walking along Montpellier Terrace, they reached his car and set off for Winchcombe. They passed through Charlton Kings on the way and Clara thought her visit could wait for another time. As they drove past Maybury Estate, Cormac chuckled and asked Clara if she remembered the time she fell into the fountain. She remembered it well. She tripped and fell in because she was so engrossed in her candy floss. They both laughed as they recalled the dismayed look on passers-by. Clara was so embarrassed that she turned as pink as her candy floss.

'Are you staying in Cheltenham for the week?' Clara asked her brother.

'Unfortunately, no', Cormac replied. 'I have a business trip to Munich next weekend and try as I might, I can't get out of it.'

As they wound their way through the country lanes of the Cotswolds, Clara inquired about Maria, Cormac's girlfriend of two years.

'She's returned to Santiago,' Cormac replied tersely while shunting the gear stick into fifth and revving the engine unnecessarily. Clara sensed he didn't want to discuss it any further. Maria had wanted to return to her family in Chile for some time, and Cormac assumed she wanted him to come with her. From his pained expression, Clara realised Maria had decided not to include him in her plans. She quickly changed the subject, inquiring about his work and upcoming business trips. Cormac travelled every month to Italy and Spain for business meetings. He was an IT representative for a software company in London. He loved Italy the most, and Clara joked he must buy a holiday home there and make sure it had a spare room for her.

Cormac smiled and said, 'Of course, sis, you're the one woman I can always rely on.'

Clara wondered if it was bitterness or regret she detected in her brother's reply. He'd had his heart broken on a few occasions, and now, with Maria's departure, old wounds were resurfacing. Before meeting Maria, Cormac dated a girl for six years whom he met at Bath University. He took the break-up badly and left home for London. Clara thought that he and Maria would eventually tie the knot, although she didn't want to think about the possibility of her brother moving to Chile.

Cormac seemed to read her mind and said, 'You don't have to worry about me moving to South America. Maybe I'm just not destined for a great love in this lifetime.'

He gave her a side glance and switched on the radio, humming along to a tune on the golden hour. Clara wondered what if he was right. What if we are all destined for great love, but not in this lifetime? It would explain why we get our hearts broken over and over, just because we don't have the patience to see beyond our limited time frames to a bigger picture. Maybe, thought Clara, we need our hearts broken to discover what it's like to love ourselves, not by the reflected glory of another, but in our vulnerability. We try to divorce our pain by searching through a sea of faces to mend our inner heartache, but life's lesson is to accept our pain and marry the beauty within us. In that moment of clarity, Clara no longer wanted a permanent relationship for her brother. She wished he could discover his inner hero, a man to be proud of regardless of his relationship status.

They pulled up at the entrance to their childhood home, two miles outside Winchcombe. The honey-coloured stone, a trademark of Cotswold properties, gleamed in the afternoon sunlight. Cormac asked Clara if she'd like to pay a visit to the new owners, but she shook her head. They shared a glance that said the past belongs to the past.

Winchcombe, normally busy with tourists passing through the Cotswolds, was quiet that afternoon. A few of the locals recognised them and asked after their mother. Clara saw two of her school friends walking towards her on North Street chatting to each other while pushing buggies. There were exclamations all around when they looked up and saw Clara. She congratulated both mothers on their recent arrivals. After a discussion about choosing baby names and sleepless nights, they had exhausted the conversation. Clara said it was lovely to see them and hurried to catch up with Cormac. She spotted him up the street about to enter the Lion Inn. When she reached him, he was already ensconced watching a six nations rugby match on TV. It was Ireland v Wales. She pulled up a stool beside him and took a sidelong glance at her brother, who was engrossed in the game. The slight bend in his nose resulted from a scrum in underage rugby when he played with Gloucester Old Boys Rugby Club. Clara knew it would take a monumental effort to move him from the game. She looked at the clock above the fireplace; it was a quarter past three. She stepped outside to phone Jenny and tell her where she was. Jenny told her that Jack was on his way to pick her up at the train station. She said they would drive out to meet them in Winchcombe.

Just as the half-time whistle blew on the rugby match, Jack and Jenny arrived at the bar full of smiles and hugs for their cousins. With the arrival of Irish accents, the three Welshmen at the bar began a friendly rivalry. Cormac got a round of drinks at the bar while Jack grilled him about the first half of the match. Meanwhile, Jenny grilled Clara about her love life, dismissing Clara's protestations about her hectic study schedule. Jenny, not one to mince her words, said it was just an excuse to avoid a relationship. She saw Clara's neck and cheeks flush, and she immediately apologised for her insensitivity. Clara shook her head to convey she was fine, but she felt the sting of tears behind her eyes. Jenny's hands flew up to her face as she realised how her words had upset her cousin. Clara touched her arm to assure her she wasn't offended. Cormac and Jack returned from the bar, and the conversation turned to childhood escapades in County Meath. Cormac recalled a horse they nicknamed *Kick-Ass* because he threw each of them off during jump practice in the back paddock. The conversation ceased when the second-half began, with the Welshmen jeering when the green shirts emerged from the tunnel, Cormac and Jack grinned, raising their glasses, saying *'Slainte'*. With five minutes left, there was another 'try' conversion for Ireland. The Welshmen groaned and shouted at the men in red shirts, hoping they could hear their coaching skills in Dublin. Finally, when the whistle blew for full-time Jack, and Cormac punched the air, shaking hands with the Welshmen showing no hard feelings. Cormac explained to them he had divided loyalties, his father came from Wales, his mother was from Ireland, and he was an Englishman. One of the Welshmen recognised Jack and asked if he was a jockey. Cormac put his arm around his young cousin's shoulders and said, 'Only the best in the business.' Amid much back-slapping and jovial banter, they finally left the inn at six o'clock. Jack had to get back to Cheltenham to meet with his trainer. Cormac and Clara hugged him, and wished him the best of luck in the Gold Cup. Jack winked at them and said, 'Luck is for amateurs.'

Cormac wandered off to the fish and chip shop. He was ravenous after a few pints of ale. Clara drove him back to her house in Tewkesbury and made up the bed in the guest room. By nine o'clock Cormac was snoring in the armchair. Clara nudged him and he fell into bed, where he slept soundly until eight the following morning.

Clara wasn't feeling tired so she opened the library book by Dr John Biddulph entitled *'Museums, Mummies and the Mysterious Mountain'*. She flicked through the glossy pages until she found the photo of David Perry, together with the author and a man called Professor Tony Higgins. She looked up the index to find mention of Perry in the text and skipped to the pages. She read of their expedition to the Altay Mountains in 1948 that ended drastically with the arrest of Biddulph and Higgins. Dr Biddulph explained he wasn't allowed to disclose details of their detainment because of the Official Secrets Act, but he wrote that they were released into British Custody in August 1948, four months after their arrest.

Clara wondered what happened to David Perry during the time of their imprisonment after he had managed to evade capture. Enthralled, she continued reading Biddulph's account of the mysterious people living in the Altay Mountains. They had a high regard and reverence for Mount Belukha, the highest peak in the Altays, which they believed was home to a higher plane of existence. He referred to a discovery made by Russian archaeologists the year after his trip to the Altays, his veiled language left Clara in no doubt that the expedition with Perry and Higgins, led the Russian team to the ancient burial site. The site was discovered on the border between Mongolia and Russia. That explained their arrest, thought Clara. They were interfering with archaeological evidence on Russian soil. Biddulph made another brief reference to Perry alerting the British Museum leading to his and Higgins' eventual release. Dr Biddulph wrote that David Perry had escaped arrest and crossed the border into China, where he alerted the British Foreign

Office. Biddulph didn't mention how David Perry had made it back to England.

Clara was aware from her history classes that in the late 1940s, relations between the USSR and rest of Europe became icy, leading to decades of Cold War between East and West. She pulled out an atlas and looked at Russia and the countries that formerly comprised the USSR. David Perry must have to undertake an arduous journey to avoid the Eurasian territory that came under Soviet rule. She turned the page of the atlas to China. If he had escaped through China, as Biddulph had said, he must have crossed the vast province of Xinjiang into northern India. This was the most probable explanation of why Tom Perry didn't see his father for several months during 1948. He was on a monumental journey through western China and northern India to avoid being arrested by the Soviets. Clara's immediate reaction was to call Tom Perry and tell him what she had discovered about his father. On second thoughts she glanced at the time and realised it was late. Perhaps it was already too late for Tom Perry who had grown up several years ago, leaving the young boy awaiting his father's return with long forgotten hopes.

10

The wind of change blows through a soul ready to evolve. Like a ripening fruit, a change of season is necessary before it fulfils the promise of the seed that bore it. Consciousness is the fertile soil that nurtures the soul's fulfilment.

The town of Hotan was a bustling oasis town in the Tarim Basin. A lively mixture of people traded in silks, carpets and jade. David Perry wandered through the bazaars imagining a time when the ancient merchants of the Silk Road bought and sold goods there. The colourful town was a welcome sight amid the arid landscape of the Taklamakan desert. During the Silk Road era, the town was known as Khotan and provided a meeting place not only for the silk trade, but for people interested in an exchange of ideas such as philosophy, religion and culture.

David walked with his driver through the market stalls and noticed a red sandstone hill glinting in the morning sun. The driver followed his gaze and told him it was Cemetery Mountain, an ancient dwelling place of Buddhist monks. It was said to be the final dwelling place of the Chinese philosopher Lao Tzu. David showed he wished to go there.

He and his driver went back to the car and drove out of town to Cemetery Mountain.

Mazar Tagh, as it was called locally, was a unique structure jutting out of the Taklamakan desert. One side was red and the other white. It mirrored the differing cultures and religious beliefs that caused tension between the Uyghurs and the Muslims. The two faces of one town unable to find a middle ground to resolve their conflict. David looked up at the huge sandstone hill. He had a strange sense he had been here before. He felt a magnetic pull to the interior. Yusup, the Uyghur driver, told him about the Buddhist carvings inside that dated back two thousand years. David asked him to wait for him by the entrance to the cave. Yusup nodded, and he stood at the entrance, his face not betraying his concern as he observed a change come over David. It was said that people became possessed by spirits of the mountain.

The deeper he stepped into the mountain, the more David disappeared into another life. His personality diminished with every step, and it was the Priest from the Altay Mountains who entered the caves in Cemetery Mountain. He walked around the interior. At intervals, he pressed his hands against the cool stone walls. He found a narrow crevice in the stone and he squeezed through into a hollow chamber just big enough for two or three people. He began to chant and move his hands. It was like the ritual he performed on the Jade mummy in the Altay Mountains. The Priestess emerged before him and his chest seemed to crack open with a powerful energy charge. A white light emerged, uniting them as one, closing the portal of time.

David opened his eyes and peered through the narrow crack in the stone, wondering how on earth he had ended up in the cold antechamber. Even though he had lost nearly ten pounds during the trip, he had to force his body through the crack, scraping his knees and shoulder blades. A few tourists who were observing the Buddhist drawings looked up in amazement to see a white man emerge from the walls of the cave. David Perry realised he must look like a ghostly apparition.

Yusup was waiting for him near the entrance and held out his hand to stop David from stumbling. He helped him to a sandstone boulder jutting out of the arid ground. Yusup sat beside him, quietly waiting for him to recover. It was said that many people saw apparitions in the cave varying from the Buddha to Lao Tzu, who had once lived there. Legend had it that inside the cave, there was a portal to another world, a world of transcendence where only enlightened beings can enter. When David had sufficiently recovered, Yusup told him that the great master Lao Tzu had disappeared through a portal inside the cave two-and-a-half thousand years before. David didn't particularly believe in legends, but then something flashed before his eyes like a bright white light. He remembered the vision of the Priestess as her light entered his heart. He was clear about what had happened. The Priestess would remain with him until it was her time to enter human form again. He would die before she was reborn.

Yusup looked at David's ghostly pallor and offered him a drink of water. It was time to take him back to the healer for an acupuncture session. He had seen a transformation come over David's features when he entered the mountain. The man who entered the cave looked different to the man sitting before him now.

To appease Yusup, David went to another session of acupuncture the following morning. Yusup needed reassurance that David was well enough to travel on the next phase of the journey. David felt his thoughts evaporate with every needle placed along his spine, allowing for a natural flow of wisdom to replace his troubled mind. The healer began a light chanting, a sound David recognised from his experience at Cemetery Mountain. David tried to remember details of what happened to him in the mountain but thought evaded him. He relaxed and focused on the healer's chant until he felt himself drift off into a peaceful place. It was the same place he found during his visions in the Altay Mountains. An immense radiation emanated from him as he harnessed the power of the Priest and Priestess.

When he came to, the healer had already removed the needles and extinguished the incense. He was alone in the small room at the back of the tailor shop. He felt revived and full of energy. When the session was over, he and Yusup were leaving for Yarkand, a town halfway between Hotan and Kashgar. It was where Lord Hargreaves arranged for David to meet the guide who would take him to Delhi.

When David emerged, Yusup moved quickly to the vehicle. It was eight-thirty in the morning and he was eager to reach Yarkand before dark. At night, the road between Hotan and Kashgar was a treacherous place for travellers. In

July, sunset was at nine-thirty. Yusup estimated they needed at least twelve hours to reach the small town of Yarkand. To date, David had been travelling in Xinjiang for six weeks. Today was the twentieth of July, his fortieth birthday. He hadn't envisioned travelling on the Silk Road in China for his birthday. Instead he had planned to be with his son Tom, who by now was on summer break from school. David would miss Tom's entire summer holidays. He had promised they would go on a fishing trip to the Wye Valley and visit the ancient ruins of Tintern Abbey. He had wanted to take Tom on a hike along Offa's Dyke like he had done with his father when he was a boy. His thoughts turned to Gertrude, his wife. He realised he hadn't missed her, and he guessed she probably didn't miss him. Sentiment had disappeared from their marriage long ago.

David and Yusup drove with a small convoy of trucks along the Hotan to Kashgar route. Up ahead, they noticed four armed men stopping vehicles. They were envoys of the local warlord. Yusup threw a black and white check scarf at David. David used it to cover his head and shield his face. Yusup pulled over the truck and got out to join the other drivers. Amid raised voices and angry protestations, David guessed the drivers were refusing to pay the extortion rate. Suddenly, a shot pierced the sound of raised voices. Everything was deadly quiet and two more shots rang out in the blistering heat. Men began to scatter and take cover behind the vehicles. The bandits took off in a battered truck, leaving plumes of dust and exhaust fumes. Amid the confusion and shouting, David noticed a body on the ground with a dark stain on his chest. He ran to the scene where some of the other drivers stood around the body. Yusup was lying flat on his back as blood seeped from his shoulder to the dusty ground. A man felt his pulse and shook his head. He looked sombrely at David as the other drivers began moving away toward their trucks.

David shouted, 'We can't just leave him here!'

One driver gestured to Yusup's abandoned truck, 'You go, now. Not safe.'

David watched in disbelief as, one by one, all the trucks pulled away. Clearly, they expected more trouble and wanted to get as far away as possible. David dragged Yusup to the truck. He wasn't sure what to do next. He felt in Yusup's pockets for the keys of the truck. He almost leapt out of his skin when Yusup's fingers clenched his wrist. David had assumed he was already dead. He pressed his ear to Yusup's nostrils. He was barely breathing, but he was still alive. David knew what he had to do. He turned the truck back towards Hotan. If anyone could save Yusup, it was the old healer.

The two-hour journey back to Hotan seemed like an eternity. He stopped at intervals to check Yusup's pulse and pour drops of water into his dry mouth. David prayed that he would get him to the healer before it was too late. In the early afternoon, he pulled in by the alley leading to the tailor's shop. The tailor, ever vigilant, helped lift Yusup from the truck and into the room at the back of his shop. The healer opened the bloodstained shirt. The bullet had shattered his shoulder blade. The tailor disappeared leaving David alone with a feverish Yusup. He sponged his forehead with cold water. The healer returned moments later with a bucket of water and torn up clothes to bathe the wound. The healer gently turned him over on his stomach and placed a cushion beneath his head. He removed fragments of the bullet that were lodged in his shoulder. Placing acupuncture needles along his spine, the healer began the same chant David heard that morning. To David, that seemed like days ago, rather than hours. So much had happened in the meantime. He joined in with the healer's chant. A powerful vortex appeared to emerge and cocoon Yusup in light. The Priest was present and his healing powers were working to restore Yusup's life force.

Once Yusup's shoulder was bandaged and his breathing normal, the old healer motioned for David to follow him. They walked to a food stall where both men sat quietly drinking green tea. The healer looked into David's eyes and with one look he conveyed lifetimes of friendship. He was the Priest's old master and friend, serving humankind for millennia as a healer, philosopher and priest. Both men were guardians of the healing forces that gave life and restored life. They were gatekeepers who restored order when there was chaos. Chaos was splintered truth, fragments rearranged to distort reality. Humans could not see the mirror of their being with thoughts that trapped them in a world of death and decay. The constellation of truth was replaced by fallen stars who believed they were of the dust of the earth. Greed shattered the last vestige of unity known to man, and had found a host in the merchants who sought their fortune on the Silk Road.

Gatekeepers of the truth wore jade amulets to ward off greed because of its purity. It became tradition in Hotan to pass on a piece of jade from one generation to the next to help ward off evil. This tradition still survived in the region.

The old healer took a polished piece of jade from his pocket. It was intricately carved with symbols of animals that looked like deer. He took David's hand, placing the jade amulet in his palm. David felt power emanating from the stone. The healer said it would keep him safe for the rest of his travels.

Two days later, Yusup was sitting up and able take small bites of food. David knew he couldn't drive for several weeks, which would leave him and his family without income. David gave him some local currency to see him through the next few weeks. He put out his good arm to shake David's hand and thank him for saving his life.

Erkin, a relative of Yusup, stepped in as a replacement driver. David threw his bag into the back of the truck to take the first leg of the journey to Yarkand. He touched the jade amulet tucked inside the breast pocket, and he felt confident that they would get there safely. After the fracas that ended in Yusup getting shot, large convoys took to the road to show solidarity against the bandits. Drivers armed themselves with guns and knives against the predatory bandits who pounced like carrion crows on lone travellers. Erkin pulled up on the outskirts of Hotan to join a convoy due to set off at seven in the morning. By the time they pulled out, twenty vehicles had joined the convoy and were winding their way along the desert road from Hotan to Yarkand. The ride took longer because of the long caravan of traders. It would be nightfall by the time they reached Yarkand. David fought to stay awake to keep watch for bandits, but finally he succumbed to exhaustion. He saw the face of the Priestess, her gentle smile lulling him to sleep and bathing his spirit in her restorative powers.

Erkin jammed on the brakes and David woke with a start. Erkin raised his hand in apology. A young deer had leapt out in front of the truck. It was standing frozen on the road, afraid to move. David got out of the truck to take a closer look. Her frightened eyes reflected his own fears and he willed her to run to safety from the road traffic. She darted off through the scrub towards her herd further up the hill. Erkin restarted the engine and said they needed to press on to catch up with the convoy. David felt a stab of sadness. He was going to miss this land and the journey when it was over, and its effect on his blossoming soul.

11

Beyond flesh and bone lies the truth of self. Uncovering this treasure is the work of many lifetimes. Somewhere, between the shadow of separation and the spiral of karma, there is a door that leads us back to our essential being.

Clara and her mother strolled by the river Avon towards Tewkesbury locks. They were in good spirits, if bleary-eyed, after last night's Gold Cup party. Jack finished a respectable fifth in the prestigious race. Clara, her mother and her aunt Deirdre took a taxi back to Tewkesbury at two-thirty in the morning when the party was revving up to top gear. They stopped by Martha's tea shop to order breakfast and strong coffee. Orla chatted happily about her new job in an assisted living complex. She worked three days a week and was glad to use her nursing skills again. She had taken early retirement when Tony, Clara's father, was diagnosed with cancer so she was at home to take care of him. He passed away peacefully in his sleep eight months later, at age sixty-two. Three years on, Orla had etched out a new life on the south coast with the support of her sister and a new group of friends. Orla's phone buzzed. Deirdre sent a message to say she was finished shopping and was on her way to meet them for breakfast.

Martha seemed extra cheery when she arrived at the table with coffees and croissants. She told them she had picked the winner of the Gold Cup in the local business sweepstake.

Clara noticed a faraway look in her mother's eye. 'Are you okay, Mom?' she asked.

Orla patted her daughter on the hand and said, 'Ah, it's nothing, dear. I was thinking about my Mom and Dad after my chat with John last night. I still miss them, which is silly I know. They're dead nearly ten years now.'

Orla, Deirdre and their brother John, had been reminiscing about their childhood in county Meath. It had stirred up memories for Orla. Her father and mother died within four months of each other. The siblings believed their mother died of a broken heart soon after her beloved husband passed away. Although Orla was settled in England for almost forty years, she still remembered the sound of the Boyne as it flowed past the meadows in June and the resonance of her father's voice when he read to them at bedtime.

Orla asked Clara if she received the book on the *Fianna and other Celtic legends*. Clara nodded and thanked her mother.

Orla's eyes opened a fraction, as if she just remembered something. 'Oh, I almost forgot, I have some good news!'

Clara put down her coffee, bracing herself to hear her mother had met someone, but it was something else, something she never considered in her wildest dreams.

'Did you know your grandfather helped with the excavation at Newgrange in the 1960s?' Clara nodded and

121

Orla continued, 'Your uncle John received a letter from Heritage Ireland a few weeks ago. It said that in honour of the local men who contributed to the restoration of *Brú na Bóinne*, they were inviting two of their family members to enter the tomb in Newgrange on the days before and after the winter solstice.' Orla took in the incredulous look on her daughter's face. 'He asked me to go with him.'

As long as Clara could remember, she heard her Grandfather talk about the significance of the sunrise in Newgrange on the shortest day of the year. Only dignitaries, government representatives, and a few members of the public who applied through a lottery scheme were allowed into the tomb at sunrise on the winter solstice.

Orla couldn't hold the suspense any longer and blurted out, 'I want you to go in my place.'

Clara was dumbfounded. She opened her mouth to speak, but no words came out. Orla knew she couldn't have bestowed a greater gift on her daughter. The door of the cafe opened behind them. Deirdre stood at the table and when Clara looked up, she said, 'Clara, you look like you've seen a ghost.'

She sat in the spare seat, and Martha brought more coffee and croissants. The three women laughed as they recounted events of the previous day. Deirdre almost spit out her coffee when Orla reminded her how she was rescued by a ten-year-old when her heels stuck in the turf.

'He had no choice,' said Deirdre, choking back laughter 'I grabbed his arm as he was walking by. I think I frightened the poor fellow half to death.'

Finally, after much coffee and laughter, it was time for Deirdre and Orla to leave. Clara walked with them to Deirdre's car and they said their goodbyes. She promised to visit her aunt and young cousins the next time she was on the south coast.

Clara wondered what to do with her free afternoon. Part of her wanted to go back to bed and catch up on sleep, but it was a shame to waste a sunny afternoon. The number 41 bus drove past and before she knew it, she was on the bus to Cheltenham. She sent a message to Imogen asking to borrow her bicycle and half an hour later, she was cycling on a primrose lined country lane towards the Maybury estate. She locked the bike and propped it by the gate leading to All Saints' chapel. Daffodils nodded in the breeze, opening like a sea of yellow towards the double-arched door. Tombstones, crosses and various monuments kept the secrets of the dead. The inscriptions were long worn off by the elements. Tom's handwritten note hadn't specified the burial spot and so Clara searched among the gravestones for more recent engravings, but none had the inscription she was searching for. Clara followed the direction of the nodding daffodils to the door of the chapel. A woodpecker drumming out his territory on a nearby oak tree pierced the stillness. Clara turned the large wrought iron handle. The door made a creaking noise as she pushed it open. She stepped inside and took in her surroundings. There were two rows of pews at either side of a central aisle. Four stain glass windows denoted the seasons on the west side, with clear glass panes along the east side. Spiral stone steps led up to a raised pulpit, and there were two rows of wooden pews on either side of the altar. A round stain glass window above the altar flooded the chancel with rose light. Clara sat in the front pew, absorbing the quietness. There was something primordial about prayer, she thought, it gave a focal point to racing thoughts. She sat transfixed by the rays of sunlight showering the altar with drops of pure rose gold. It brought to her mind the lines from David Perry's poem:

Even now, when I say your name,
It leaves my mouth in slow motion,
Escaping my lips like a winged prayer,
A hymn before the altar of love.

Clara closed her eyes and felt a tear slide down her cheek. Something stirred within her, not just an emotion but another time, another woman. Had she lived many lifetimes inhabiting many bodies? Who was she beyond Clara and all the stories before this lifetime? She closed her eyes and saw a pair of dark almond-shaped eyes looking back at her. She felt serene and calm looking at her true reflection without the constriction of time. Her mind became a still pool and the image expanded to show a woman dressed from head to toe in a long ceremonial gown, it was tied at the waist with a twisted hemp rope. Around her neck was an ornate collar carved from jade. This was a rare and special woman who could move through time and space to heal souls lost in the darkness of dreams. Clara realised this special energy field must dwell within her. It was the archetypal feminine. She was a receptacle of truth. Clara had a choice to allow this energy to work through her or continue with the illusion of her conditioned self.

Clara gradually became aware of her surroundings again. The sun's rays shone through the stain glass windows to the west. She needed to return to Cheltenham before the sun set, there was no dynamo on Imogen's bike. She bowed her head before the altar and turned to walk down the aisle. As she approached the door, she saw a plaque to the right of the entrance with the name she was looking for. It was placed under two more commemorative stone plaques and directly above the Maybury crypt.

George David Hargreaves Perry
20th July 1908 – 15th January 1985
Beloved son of Lady Isabel and William Perry, the
Viscount Maybury

Clara stared at the date on the wall, taking in the dates. She was born on the twenty-fifth of August, the same year David Perry died. Surely, this was no coincidence. An invisible thread linked her to him. She could feel it. She unlocked the bicycle and rode towards Cheltenham. She hoped she would make it back to Imogen's before dark.

The brisk ride helped clear her head, and she pulled up at Imogen's just as the street lights were coming on. Imogen invited her to stay for supper. Clara welcomed the mayhem as Imogen's two children chased each other with light sabres.

Imogen said it was the latest craze after they watched a rerun of Star Wars on TV.

Imogen looked closely at Clara and asked, 'Are you feeling okay? You look tired?'

Clara glanced in the mirror above the fireplace. It was true. She did look pale, considering she had a vigorous cycle from Maybury. 'It must be all the late nights this week. My Irish cousins certainly know how to party.'

Imogen filled the kettle to make a strong cup of tea for her friend. 'Did you go anywhere nice this afternoon?'

Clara was about to tell her about her vision at All Saints' church when Imogen's youngest child, Lisa, ran in wailing. Her brother had knocked her over with his sabre. Imogen grabbed the light sabres and placed them out of reach on the kitchen cupboard. There was a chorus of protests which Imogen ignored and told them to sit quietly at the table until suppertime. Imogen apologised for the interruption and asked Clara to continue. She decided Imogen had enough to deal with and besides, she might think Clara was losing her mind.

After supper, Clara took the bus home to Tewksbury. She was exhausted from a roller coaster day, and she had very little sleep the night before. She switched on the television, but nothing caught her attention. Saturday evening programs comprised of game shows and reality TV, which didn't interest her. She picked up an old copy of the National Geographic magazine and flicked through it. An article caught her attention; it was about mummies discovered in Xinjiang's Tarim Basin. The article was called the Tocharian Mummies. The first mummy, discovered in 1989, was a white female with long blonde hair, preserved by the arid desert atmosphere of the Taklamakan desert. Archaeologists believed she was a sacrificial victim based on partially dismembered limbs and gouged out eyes. The Tocharian Mummies were of Indo-European origin and DNA testing dated them around 3000 BCE. Other mummies were of Eurasian origin, thought to be Siberian. Clara digested the information for a moment. This would tie in with her thesis. She opened a book on the ancient Silk Routes. The oasis kingdoms of south Xinjiang were where people of different cultures met to exchange cultural and spiritual beliefs. Clara grabbed her notebook and wrote furiously, focusing on the mummies of the Tarim Basin. She picked up the magazine to reread the article and she noticed a link between the Hallstatt Celtic community and the Tarim Basin. Woven material, identical to Celtic cloth, was found on the mummies definitively proving the Indo-European origins of the Tocharians. They had travelled from central Europe to the Silk Road towns of Xinjiang. The article mainly focused on the Tocharian mummies of European descent, but several mummies could be traced to native tribes that currently lived in Siberia and Mongolia.

From her vision earlier that day, she knew without a doubt that she wore a jade collar, identical to the one in David Perry's photograph. The city of Hotan was known for jade mines. Khotan, as it was historically known, became a major oasis town on the Silk Route. She felt certain that the Jade Mummy, who originated from the Altay Mountains of Siberia, had been to Khotan. The tribal people of the Altay

Mountains were renowned for their skills with horses. They may have traded horses in Khotan in exchange for silks, rugs and jade. They could have been responsible for introducing domesticated horses to Europe and southern Asia.

Clara imagined just how impressed travellers on the Silk Road would have been when they saw a pale Mongolian woman riding a muscular stallion. She would have commanded attention. Other travellers would be eager to learn the ways and traditions of her tribe. The early Celts may have learned about the tribes of Eurasia and their way of life on the Silk Road. Clara realised early cultures did not evolve in isolation as previously thought. A network of roads linked merchants seeking new treasures, philosophers seeking new ideas and healers seeking new cures. It all took place at the cultural confluence of East and West in the ancient kingdoms of Xinjiang.

Clara closed her notebook and the magazine. She hadn't intended to work on her thesis this weekend, but she had to follow the evidence. Her phone buzzed. It was a message from her mother to say she was home. Clara thought about the invitation to witness the winter solstice at Newgrange. It was the opportunity of a lifetime. The tomb in Newgrange was built around 3500 BCE. Around the time, several of the mummies in the Tarim Basin were frozen in time by the sands of the Taklamakan Desert. It was older than the Egyptian pyramids and Stonehenge. The tombs of Newgrange could have resulted from spiritual ideas learned in Western China from tribes of the Eurasian Steppes. Clara felt tingles of excitement. Maybe in another lifetime in

Khotan, she had sown the seeds that sprouted far away on islands off Western Europe.

12

The naked spirit, stripped of human plumage, ascends to higher realms of consciousness. He who is blinded by ego cannot know the summit of achievement until he discards the weight that ties him down. Thoughts saturated with fear and worry keeps the soul earthbound.

The innkeeper gave David the keys to his room. A petite woman balancing a young child on her hip appeared from a small office behind the reception desk and handed a note to the innkeeper. 'For you,' he grunted, using a grubby finger to push the note across the desk. Written on the note was a local phone number and the name *Arjun Sharma*. David pointed to the telephone behind the desk, showing he wanted to make a call. The innkeeper picked up the receiver and thrust it at David, mumbling something under his breath. Ignoring him, David dialled the number and after three rings, a man answered. 'Is this Arjun Sharma?' he asked.

'Mr Perry, your uncle sent me. I will pick you up at seven tomorrow morning.' The receiver went dead. He was not a member of the diplomatic service, David thought wryly.

Arjun Sharma was on time. A car and driver were parked outside the inn, ready to take David across the border to India. The border patrol that previously separated China and India had changed. It was now a crossing into the newly formed state of Pakistan. There were tensions at the border and diplomatic status no longer guaranteed safe entry. Arjun Sharma gave David official papers to cross the border while giving him an outline of the route. They would take the road to the Indus, and then follow the river to Ladakh. Their driver was from Pakistan, Arjun said that should allow for an easier crossing at the border. When they reached the town of Skardu, they would change drivers to continue the journey to Delhi.

Two hours into the journey, David saw the majestic peaks of the Himalayas rising like a diadem above the low-lying clouds of the plains. The roads grew steeper as the jeep winded its way into the foothills. By sunset, the pink hue of the Karakorum Mountains surrounded them and they stopped in a small mountain village to rest for the night.

By mid-afternoon the following day, they reached the border control between China and Pakistan. The driver handed over the papers. They asked David to step out of the car. The officer asked him routine questions in Urdu, which Arjun translated. The official seemed happy enough to stamp his passport and let him through. The snow line had receded on the mountain passes, allowing them to cover the distance to the town of Karimabad before nightfall. Tomorrow they would reach Skardu, where they would change driver on route to the Indian Border.

Tensions had escalated between India and Pakistan, countries that had coexisted as one nation less than a year before. Violent clashes broke out between Sikhs and Muslims in Kashmir, which claimed several lives. The fighting made it difficult to pass through Kashmir, India's most northerly state. Arjun Sharma had chosen a lesser-known route through Ladakh to avoid skirmishes. The journey between Leh and Manali could be treacherous in bad weather. The mountain pass only opened from July and September when the snows had melted. It would take at least a week to reach Delhi. It would be late August when they arrived in the capital city.

The British ruling class had to depart India by the end of August. The Viceroy had already left India, a country now torn apart by religious intolerance. David's uncle remained to oversee the exit of the old order. Lord Hargreaves had arranged a flight for David from Delhi to London.

The tension was palpable as they drove through Pakistan. David touched the jade amulet that the healer had given to him to help ease his mind. As they drove further south, they saw signs of the monsoon. Wisps of clouds shrouded the treetops. The driver only spoke to answer a direct question from Arjun. David caught him staring at him in the rear-view mirror and closed his eyes, finding his penetrating gaze unsettling. They descended from the high mountain pass to the foothills to Skardu. Poor visibility, occasional downpours and rock fall hampered their journey. Occasionally, when the mist cleared, the scenery was breathtaking. The lush surroundings were a welcome sight to David after the arid conditions of the Taklamakan Desert.

The Indus River widened into a tranquil lake surrounded by vibrant green hills and it was framed by the white peaks of the Karakorum Mountains. The peak of the world's second highest mountain, K2, was shrouded from view. Arjun led David to a guest house overlooking the river. The plan was to rest a night in Skardu before crossing the Indian border into Ladakh. David threw his backpack on the floor, gratefully taking a bucket of warm water from the owner. He felt refreshed after washing off the dust and grime of a week's travel.

The Indus River raged like a torrent as it carried meltwater from the large glaciers on K2. The raging waters seemed to harness the force dividing this land. With the stroke of a pen, hundreds of miles away in Delhi, the River Indus was cut like an umbilical cord. It had given its name to India and now it emptied its glacial meltwater in a country with a new name.

David lay on his bed and closed his eyes. The Priest stood before him, his hands raised in prayer, the sleeves of his long tunic fell back to reveal jade armlets on both his arms. His eyes were piercing like lightning rods. David opened his eyes and sat bolt upright, trying to adjust to the darkness of the room. He struck a match to see his watch face. It was two-thirty. He lay back on the hard mattress and began reciting a poem he learned when he was at school. It was something he did as a child when he was afraid of the dark.

'*Tiger tiger, burning bright...*' perhaps he was losing his mind, or maybe, he was possessed, '*...in the forests of the night.*'

A sharp rap on his door startled him. 'Who's there?' David asked croakily.

The alarm in Arjun's voice jolted him awake. 'Get dressed quickly, we have to leave immediately.'

David fumbled in the dark. Arjun came in and lit a candle while David quickly pulled on his trousers and shirt, stuffing his belongings into a bag. Arjun looked around to check the room was empty before shutting the door. A different driver pulled up at the entrance in a jeep. David jumped in the back. The driver was already moving before he had time to shut the door. When they were ten minutes on the road, Arjun finally spoke. 'We have received intelligence from a trusted source. Militants are on the way to kidnap you.'

David went pale. 'Why me?'

Arjun replied, 'Because of your connection to Lord Hargreaves.'

'But how did they know I was in Skardu?'

Arjun shrugged. 'Most likely there's an informant at the border police. We must keep driving until we reach the Indian border. They will certainly try to ambush you before you get to India.'

David gripped the jade amulet. In his dream, the Priest had tried to alert him. David took a deep breath. He felt confused. He wasn't sure who he was any more.

David slept until he heard raised voices between Arjun and the driver. The driver argued it was too dangerous to continue to the border. The militants would have men waiting to shoot them if necessary. Hemmed in by the great wall of the Himalayas, they were still a four-hour drive from the border. David tried to intervene between Arjun and the driver, but they ignored him. After much gesticulating and waving of arms, the driver got out of the jeep and Arjun slid in behind the wheel. He turned to David. 'Stay low and cover up.'

David lay on the back seat and pulled a blanket over his head. He remained that way for a few hours until the engine stopped. He peeked out from under the blanket. Dawn was breaking.

'We walk from here,' Arjun said matter-of-factly.

The vehicle was pulled up by an old shepherd's hut just below the snow line. Arjun pointed to some fallen branches, which he and David dragged down the hill to camouflage the jeep. David asked no questions. They took supplies from the jeep, strapping on their backpacks and they set off on foot for the Indian border. Both of them were silent for over an hour keenly listening for footsteps behind. Once Arjun was satisfied they weren't being followed, he said, 'I told the officer at the border checkpoint we were going to Kabul. I didn't mention we were going to Delhi. It was not the border guards who informed the militants of our whereabouts.'

David looked at Arjun closely and realised he knew the identity of the informant was. 'Who do you suspect?' David asked.

'The driver who took us to Skardu,' replied Arjun.

'And the driver who came last night...?' David trailed off.

'He is scared,' said Arjun, confirming David's suspicions. 'He knows something, but he won't talk.'

'Will he tell them where we are?' asked David. Arjun shook his head and fell silent.

David spent a month in the Cairngorms in Scotland to prepare him for the expedition to the Altay Mountains. Neither the Scottish Highlands, nor the Altays had prepared him for the high altitude of the Himalayas. His breathing was laboured and his muscles ached from the climb and lack of oxygen. Arjun was a natural in these conditions. He was raised among the high mountains of the Spiti district in southern Ladakh. Noticing David's struggle in the high altitude, he suggested they take a break. David threw down his pack and sat hunched over on a boulder, taking slow, deep breaths. Arjun observed him for a few moments before demonstrating how to breathe in high altitudes. He told him to quicken his intake of breath and release slowly with no gaps between the breaths. David sat upright and followed Arjun's lead. After a few minutes, he felt an exhilaration move through him. He had to remain focused on his breathing to survive in high altitudes. There was no room for worry or negativity of any kind. He looked around fully, taking in his surroundings. He looked at Arjun, sitting cross-legged on a boulder with Buddhist prayer beads in his hands, softly chanting, *'O Mani Padme Hum.'*

David assumed he was a Hindu from the red mark on his forehead, a symbol of marriage for Hindus. When they resumed their journey, David asked him about his beliefs and the tradition of his people. Arjun explained that the name *'Spiti'* meant middle, the land between India and Tibet. The people of Spiti inherited a mix of traditions from both countries. Their faith was Tibetan-Buddhism, and many of their traditions were Indian. At sixteen, he left his home in Spiti to find work in Shimla, the summer capital of the British Raj. He had a talent for picking up foreign languages, and soon became fluent in English. His linguistic talents and knowledge of local dialects brought him to the attention of the British Raj. After twenty years in their service, he must now embrace a new beginning. He told David that he purchased land near Manali, which he had planted with orchards. The climate in Manali was ideal for apple growing, a fruit that was in high demand in Delhi and Mumbai. His wife and two children had moved to the farm a few months previously. He told David their journey to India was his last mission for the British. When he reached Manali, he planned to live there permanently with his family.

The sun dipped below the western peaks. Darkness came quickly after sunset. Arjun pointed toward a rocky outcrop high above the Indus River where they could rest for the night. They Indus would lead them to Leh, the old summer capital of Ladakh. Leh became the primary town of Ladakh since the recent political redrawing of the border. Skardu, the previous capital, was apportioned to Pakistan. Arjun had chosen a difficult route through the mountains to avoid ambush. The militants would have patrols in the valley below, so it was best for them to stick to the peaks. Arjun and David had to follow the Indus to navigate their way to the Indian border. Militants would try to intercept them before they crossed over into India. They would use any means necessary to gain leverage against the British Raj to force them to hand over the entire province of Kashmir to Pakistan. Religious intolerance had cut a deep scar through the Indian nation.

David was unclear about the history of Northern India, but Arjun assured him that the religious divide was deep. As a member of the British aristocracy and nephew of Lord Hargreaves, David was a perfect kidnap victim to use as leverage.

The following morning, they set off at first light. They covered four kilometres before dawn. By Arjun's calculations, they were an eight or nine-hour trek from India. They veered to the east to avoid a direct approach to the official border control. There would be patrols waiting for them along the final ten kilometres of the approach.

By noon they had walked six hours, and David's legs were slowing down. They stopped for a moment, and Arjun took out his binoculars to survey their surroundings. In the valley below, he saw rooftops. A farmer was leading his goats to lower pasture. As he moved his viewer to the right, he caught a glint of sun reflecting on something, perhaps a mirror. He crouched down and signalled for David to do the same. Something wasn't right. David sensed the tautness in Arjun's body. They crept towards one of the large rocks that were a feature of the terrain. David gripped his jade amulet, asking for protection. He needed the courage of the Priest to get through this. Arjun gave a signal, crouching low, they descended the escarpment. David lost his footing as rock and stone gave way under his feet. Arjun helped him back to his feet, and they continued, slipping and sliding onto a path leading into the Indus Valley. David pulled out his compass and saw they were heading due east. They needed to turn south-east to cross the border. When finally, they stopped to catch a breath, David asked Arjun what he had seen.

'Three men are on the way up the mountain.' Arjun sounded out of breath. 'One had a rifle. I couldn't see if the others were armed.'

They resumed their trek and Arjun set a faster pace. David struggled to keep up with him. They walked swiftly without speaking for two hours, saving their breath for the gruelling pace. Finally, Arjun spotted a crevice where they could temporarily take shelter and take a ten-minute rest. He did a sweep of the area with his binoculars, but saw nothing unusual. The sun gleamed on wet slate roofs in the valley below. Arjun realised they were close to the border, and it gave him an idea. 'We will find a place to cross the border in this direction,' he said as he pointed east of the border control.

David looked out over the wilderness and wondered how they would know where the exact border was.

Arjun continued, 'If we try to cross at the official border control, the militants will wait for us at the Pakistan side. The only way we can avoid them is by crossing the Indian border a few miles east of here. Then we can approach the border control from the Indian side, which will give us protection.'

It seemed plausible to David, he certainly didn't want to fall into the hands of the militants, but he had some doubts. 'Won't there be high fencing for miles along the border?' he asked.

'The border only runs four miles in either direction. This is a new border, and they have not built a physical border. I know where we can cross.'

Arjun's last words seemed final, and David realised he had no option but to follow him. They walked well into the afternoon. David was despairing they would never reach India, when out of nowhere, they found themselves surrounded by a herd of goats. A local woman who made clicking noises as she drove the herd stopped in her tracks and looked at David in amazement. She had never seen a western man before. Arjun spoke the local dialect, and David saw her tired face break into a smile.

Arjun turned to David. An enormous smile took years off his troubled face. 'We are in India!'

Relief flooded David's body, and tears stung his eyes. Arjun raised a hand of warning. 'Still, we must reach the Indian police at the border.'

He continued speaking to the woman and David saw her pointing in the direction of the border checkpoint. She nodded and smiled at David. He bowed and said, 'Namaste Ji.'

When he turned to leave, Arjun had already walked at least thirty paces. As Arjun predicted, there was a vehicle a kilometre to the east of the border control, on the Pakistan side. David looked at the makeshift border fencing and knew it was not robust enough to stop the militants from crossing over and snatching him into the waiting car. He panicked and ran, but Arjun stopped him and pulled him to the ground. He hissed, 'Stay down. We will wait until the light fades.'

David looked up at the slightly pink tinted clouds and realised the sun had set. Darkness would descend soon. They waited until it was dark and crept on hands and knees along the barbed wire fence. When they came within five-hundred meters of the border police, Arjun flashed his torch as a distress signal. Through his binoculars, he saw two officers hop into a vehicle and drive towards their location. Arjun kept the flashlight on and told David to stay down. A noise rang out, and David saw the unmistakable flash of gunfire. He felt Arjun apply pressure on his back pressing him into the ground. The Indian police opened the windows and shot their rifles a few times. There was no response from the militants on the other side of the fence. An engine started up and tyres screeched as the car sped away. Arjun and David rolled over to a sitting position when the police told them to place their hands behind their heads. After an interrogation and an urgent call to Delhi, David and Arjun were released and taken by a police car to the hilltop town of Leh.

Three days later, David was on a flight from Delhi to London.

13

What is whole cannot be divided. It is only in the human mind that the dream of separation occurs. In Reality, there is no separation. Once the human mind awakes from the dream of separation, the doors of consciousness open and unity is realised.

Clara alighted at Axminster railway station where her mother was waiting to drive her to Lyme Regis. The sparkle of the sun on the sea greeted them as they reached the crest of the hill overlooking the town. Rows of magnolia trees and cherry blossom unfolded their petals like a kaleidoscope against the clear blue sky.

Easter was late this year and families had flocked to the small seaside town to throw off the long winter months and welcome the glory of longer days. Holidaymakers ambled along the seafront in shorts and tee-shirts, more out of wishful thinking than necessity. The Cobb, an old stone wall, gleamed like a sea creature curving between the harbour and sea. It carried a steady stream of people on its back to take in glorious views of Lyme Bay. A cool wind greeted Clara and Orla as they turned onto the promenade. They strolled passed the rows of brightly painted beach huts that framed a picture-postcard coastal scene. Vendors served up fish and chips, ice-cream cones and iced lollies to a queue of visitors. Seagulls circled overhead, perching on lampposts, ready to pounce on a fallen chip or an unguarded ice-cream cone. Colourful wind breakers lined the beach, protecting families from the sea breeze. Mother and daughter sat on a seafront bench while Rufus sniffed at every passing dog. Clara asked her mother if she was happy at her new job.

'I don't really see it as just a job,' her mother replied. 'I remember the matron who trained me calling it a vocation rather than a job. Perhaps it's a little of both,' added Orla.

'What age were you when you decided you wanted to be a nurse?' Clara asked, realising she had given any thought to her mother's aspirations as a young woman.

Orla stared out into the distance as if trying to recall some distant memory. 'I remember having my appendix removed when I was ten. My bed faced the nurses' station just outside the children's ward and I remember deciding then that I wanted to be a nurse.'

Clara was curious now about her mother's life before she was born. 'Why didn't you do your training in Ireland?'

'I applied to several hospitals in Dublin, but the waiting list was three years.'

Orla had forgotten much of the details, but she remembered writing to at least a dozen hospitals in England. Gloucester Royal Infirmary was the first to accept her application. She trained as a general nurse for three years before specialising in palliative care.

'Did you know I met your father at the Royal Infirmary in 1981?' Orla turned to look at Clara with a smile.

Clara shook her head. She had never thought about how or where her parents met. Rufus tugged on the lead as he tried to follow a golden retriever puppy. The owner pulled on the lead, dragging the golden puppy away. Rufus started whining and Orla picked him up and placed him on the bench beside her. She stroked his back to calm him. She looked at Clara blankly; she had lost her train of thought.

Clara prompted her, 'You were telling me how you met Dad...'

'Oh yes,' Orla smiled. 'He played rugby with a team in Monmouthshire. They came to play a match against Gloucester Old Boys. He fractured his wrist during the game match and was taken to the Royal Infirmary. I was working in A&E that Sunday evening because it was especially busy. He made me laugh despite the fact he was in pain and I knew I wanted to see him again. Lucky for me, he wanted to see me again too,' Orla laughed. 'And lucky for me,' Clara winked at her mother.

'He called me the next evening to thank me for taking care of him. The following weekend, he arrived on the train from Abergavenny to meet me. Once his wrist had healed, he drove to Gloucester two or three times a week to see me.'

'How long were you dating before you got married'? Clara asked, trying to get the full story of her parents' history before she and Cormac were born.

'We waited until I qualified as an RGN, which was fifteen months after we first met. When we got married, we bought a house in Monmouth, half-way between Tony's work in Abergavenny and my work in Gloucester.'

'When did you move to the Cotswolds?' asked Clara.

'Your father got a job as a rugby coach in Cheltenham College when Cormac was a year old, then we sold the house and bought the house in Winchcombe in 1985, the year you were born.'

'Didn't you give up working after Cormac was born?' The details of her mother's career were sketchy for Clara.

'I finished my training as a palliative care nurse in the Royal Infirmary when Cormac was six-months old. I left the Infirmary and took a part-time role in a nursing home on Malvern Road.

Clara rubbed her forehead, feeling a sensation of pins and needles crossing her brow. Something was niggling at her. She had become accustomed to the sensation, but usually, it involved her connection to David Perry.

Rufus was getting uneasy and wanted to carry on with his walk. Orla put him down on the ground and stood up to obey his command. She continued chatting to Clara about how she and Tony restored the house in Winchcombe. Clara nodded absent-mindedly as she climbed the steps to the Cobb. What was she missing? Suddenly, it hit her. The nursing home David Perry stayed in before his death was on Malvern Road. Surely it was too much of a coincidence that her mother also worked in a nursing home on Malvern Road. Clara was about to ask her when she realised she had fallen behind. Rufus was straining on his lead, pulling Orla in his wake as he tried to sniff two approaching dachshunds. Clara caught up and took the lead from her mother. They continued walking to the end of the Cobb, where the famous scene from *The French Lieutenant's Woman* was filmed in the 1980's. Looking out to sea, Clara felt the irony of standing on the same spot as the heroine who waited forlornly for her lover.

Orla served up one of her daughter's favourite meals, Thai curry, while Clara opened a bottle of Riesling. They clinked glasses and toasted each other's good health. They finished it with a bowl of Purbeck ice-cream purchased in one of the colourful huts on the seafront. They sat outside on the balcony, which overlooked the sea to catch the evening sun. Clara was in a pensive mood. Orla sensed something was bothering her. She sat quietly, waiting for her daughter to speak. From experience, she knew asking questions would only make her clam up. Finally, Clara cleared her throat and asked, 'Did you nurse a man called David Perry?'

Orla was quiet for a moment as she reflected on her daughter's question. She recalled her encounter with him almost thirty-three years earlier. It was a strange question for Clara to ask, yet oddly she had expected it. 'Why do you ask?' Orla's eyes searched her daughter's face for some sort of clue.

'I came across him in my research for my thesis,' Clara replied casually. She knew her mother well enough to recognise when she was stalling, or searching for a way to edit the truth. Clara's tone was brusque. 'Did you meet him?'

'Yes, yes, several years ago. I'm trying to remember when.'

Orla paused for a few moments to let the atmosphere settle before continuing. Somehow, the mention of David Perry caused a powerful reaction in Clara. 'He was a patient where I worked, in a nursing home on Malvern Road.'

Orla was unsure if she should reveal everything she remembered about him. She sipped her wine, aware of her daughter's intense attention focused on her. She proceeded with vague details about the building as she refilled both their glasses.

'David Perry owned the building and turned it into a nursing home. Did you know his father was Viscount Maybury?' Orla asked.

Clara nodded, and Orla sensed her impatience. She wanted more intimate details about him than that. Orla continued in the same vein, 'They own several properties in Cheltenham.' Clara moved uneasily in her chair. Her mother was deliberately stalling.

'To be honest, I didn't know him very well because he had his own private nurse,' Orla said, as if to put an end to the matter. She wasn't giving away any more information until Clara told her the real reason she was interested in him.

They were both silent for a few minutes. Orla glanced at Clara, who had put on her sunglasses to shield her eyes from the low sun. A tear slid down her cheek, which she quickly brushed away, but not before her mother saw it. Orla's suspicions were correct. Somehow, the old man had known something about her unborn child. His last words to her had made her deeply uneasy, he knew she was pregnant weeks before Orla had it confirmed. She let out a heavy sigh.

Perhaps Clara deserved to know what happened on the night David Perry died. About to continue her story, she looked at Clara who was pushing her sunglasses onto her forehead. She saw something that for a long time afterwards she tried to make sense of. Perhaps it was the wine, or the golden hues from the evening sun, but a transformation had come over her daughter. She looked primal, almost like an Egyptian Priestess that decorate a pharaoh's tomb. Clara, fixed her with a steady gaze and sent goose bumps up Orla's spine, spellbinding her until she revealed every detail about David Perry's last night on earth.

'I was on duty the night David Perry died,' Orla recalled the night now, as if she was in the building on Malvern Road. 'It was my third month working in the care home. They asked me to replace his private nurse who had called in sick.' She paused as she retraced her steps along the landing leading to his bedroom. 'I went to his bedroom to check on him around nine. He was sitting in an armchair by a window overlooking Christ Church.'

Orla recalled the scene vividly as if it had happened the previous night.

'I introduced myself and asked if he needed anything. He shook his head and ignored me while he continued engrossed in his book.' Orla smiled as she recalled, 'I put his haughty behaviour down to him being an aristocrat. I turned down his bed and refreshed the water on his bedside table. At nine-thirty exactly, his usual bedtime, he asked me for his nightly medicine. When I returned, I propped him up in bed with extra pillows and he continued to read his book. I remember the Celtic symbol on the front cover because it was similar to the triple spiral on the entrance stone at Newgrange.'

Orla was amazed by the sharp detail she recalled from events that had happened thirty-three years before. 'I handed him a glass of water to take his pills. When he took the glass from my hand, he looked at me with eyes that had seen worlds far beyond mine. He told me I was expecting a child. At first, I thought he was being insensitive. I was still carrying extra weight since giving birth to Cormac. He took my hand and told me I would give birth to a very special girl. I wasn't sure what to make of him,' Orla recalled. 'I thought he was crazy. But then, a month later I found out I was pregnant with you.'

Orla realised she must only have been a week or so pregnant when he gave her a message for the child. Until now, she had never thought about it again.

'What was the message?' Clara asked.

Orla recalled word-for-word David Perry's last words. 'Look for me and I shall lead you back to the dawning of our lifetime.'

When Orla came to check on him an hour later, he was dead. She blinked a few times as if waking from a trance. Never in her life had she recalled anything with such clarity. It was as if she had returned to the nursing home at the moment David Perry passed away. He was reminding her of her promise to relay his dying message.

Clara touched her mother's hand and thanked her. She went into her bedroom to get a shawl; the sun had set and the temperature had dropped. Clara recalled her mother telling her many years ago that she was born three weeks prematurely during a family visit to County Meath. Orla reading her mind, recalled the day Clara was born. She had tripped and fell, which brought on early labour. There wasn't enough time to reach a hospital. A local woman who was a retired midwife came to help with the birth. Clara arrived ninety minutes after the contractions started, making it a swift delivery into the world. Orla remembered cradling her baby daughter as she looked out the window of her childhood room. The sunlight shimmered on the River Boyne, and she felt immense relief and gratitude for her healthy baby girl. She didn't realise that a hundred yards downstream, Tom Perry and his family solemnly stood by the riverbank as they scattered David Perry's ashes in the river.

14

When the doors between the cosmos and the human mind are closed, the dream becomes confused with Reality. Man turns against his fellow man and chaos replaces cosmos. Man must learn to forgive himself and forgive others, after all everyone is just fleeing from their own damning thoughts.

On a cool September morning, David Perry found himself a stranger standing at the front door of his town house in Cheltenham. Tom had returned to boarding school for the autumn term and so only Gertrude would be there to greet him. There was a flicker of relief on her face when she saw her husband standing in the front hallway. She kissed him on the cheek as she would greet any acquaintance who entered their home. She handed him the Cheltenham Post. His name jumped out on the headlines: '*Local Explorer Returns after Evading Russian Capture*'.

David followed his wife into the sitting room and threw the newspaper on the coffee table. She called the housekeeper to make tea. She nodded politely at David's brief explanation of his delayed homecoming, all the while gazing out the window to Imperial Square. David wondered if she was expecting someone else to call. He picked up the paper and read the article about his return to Cheltenham. He knew the newspapers used his story as propaganda to fuel the cold war between Russia and the West. A similar report, featuring the return of Dr Biddulph and Professor Tony Higgins, was published in the national press two weeks earlier. The report omitted the facts that they were on Russian territory when they were captured. The article read the Russians arrested them in Mongolia, intimating they were prisoners of the cold war. David had no sympathies for Russian ideologies, but he abhorred dishonesty and blatant propaganda, whether it was Whitehall or the Kremlin.

Gertrude handed her husband a bundle of correspondence from well-wishers and reporters. She had informed immediate family and close friends of his expected date of arrival. She suggested to David that they hold an informal gathering in a few days to thank everyone for their well wishes. David nodded, already feeling a chill of boredom creep through his spine. He changed the subject. 'Is the car in good driving order?'

'That old thing? It's gone. Henry suggested we replace it with a newer model,' replied Gertrude, with a wave of her hand. She seemed flushed when she mentioned her brother-in-law.

Henry charmed several society ladies but had yet to get married. David wondered if, in his absence, his older brother had cuckolded him. Gertrude certainly would have been flattered by his attention. David rubbed his forehead. He needed to get out and clear his head. He put down his teacup and asked Gertrude for the car keys. Gertrude stood up and fetched her purse from the hallway. She coolly dropped the keys in David's lap before resuming her position by the large Georgian window.

The new Ford sped through the large wrought-iron gates down the avenue to Maybury Manor. David pulled up at the front steps of his ancestral home. He ran up the steps two at a time and pressed the doorbell. The housekeeper, Mrs Parsons opened the door. Her arms opened wide when she saw who was standing there. 'It's you, Master George, we thought we'd lost you.'

David stepped inside and planted a kiss on her cheek, making her blush. 'Your mother is in the drawing-room,' said Mrs Parsons, shooing him to the door as if he was still ten-years old.

'And my father?' asked David.

'Lord Maybury is out, sir,' said Mrs Parsons as she retreated to the library carrying a bundle of correspondence.

Lady Isabel rose gracefully to greet her younger son. Tears stung her eyes as she held his face in her hands for a few moments.

'You seem sad, my dear,' she said as she took his hand and led him to the large sofa.

David was most like her. He was kind and the most sensitive of her three children. Both she and her husband despaired of Henry and his refusal to settle down and get married at age forty-two. Lydia, the youngest of her three children, lived on the French Riviera with her husband and young daughter. She searched David's face for some clue to his melancholy. Lady Isabel suspected David's wife was partly to blame for his growing sadness. Lady Gertrude Newnam was a society beauty who dazzled her younger son into a marriage proposal just three months after they met. Lady Isabel had her suspicions that her real quarry was Henry and his title. But Henry was smitten with an American heiress who, after toying with him for fourteen months, broke off their engagement to marry the recently widowed Duke of Yarmouth.

'Let me look at you', Lady Isabel said as she looked her younger son up and down. 'My, my, you are skin and bone, and brown as a chestnut.'

Lady Isabel knew that Gertrude and Henry had become close in recent months. She had observed them on a number of occasions at Maybury Hall in intimate conversation. She was aware of the gossip that was already circulating in the town. It would cause a scandal if Gertrude left one brother for the other.

'Was Gertrude happy to see you?' Lady Isabel asked with a sarcastic tone.

David slumped back on the sofa and sighed. 'Get to your point, Mother.'

Lady Isabel pursed her lips as she always did when she had something unpleasant to say. 'She and your brother are way too close for my liking.'

She studied her son. On seeing a blank expression on his face, she proceeded with candour. 'We need to handle this situation carefully, David. Your father has taken steps to ensure the liaison comes to nothing. He has spoken to Henry and told him in no uncertain terms that if he pursues the affair with Gertrude, he shall not receive the lands or title.'

David was momentarily stung by his mother's direct accusations about his wife and Henry. Gertrude was in love with his brother. He felt his fingers curl around the jade amulet in his pocket, giving him strength.

'And what does he plan to do with the lands and title if he disinherits Henry?' asked David, raising an eyebrow.

'They will pass to you, naturally,' replied Lady Isabel.

'Nonsense, I don't want the title or estate, Mother,' David replied wearily.

'I'm sure it won't come to that if your brother mends his ways but unless he produces a bonafide heir for Maybury, it will pass to Thomas,' said Lady Maybury as if it was already decided. She called for tea, wanting to put an end to the distasteful discourse.

David hardly knew how to reply to such a blatant assumption about his son's future. By the time he recovered enough to reply, Lady Maybury had changed the subject to her brother, Lord Hargreaves. She had spoken to him on the telephone earlier and she was eager to visit him at the family home in Hampshire.

David had many childhood memories of holidays spent on his grandfather's estate in the Test Valley. Lord Hargreaves left India two days after David and arrived home last night. Lady Isabel had arranged a two-day visit to Hampshire to see her brother. She asked David if he would accompany her. David hesitated for a few moments, it sounded more like a command than a request. He would like to spend some time with his uncle since he saw him only briefly in Delhi. However, he didn't want to get into an argument with his mother over his son's future. He had planned to visit Tom at Winchester College in the next few days which was only ten miles from his uncle's house. He reluctantly agreed to accompany his mother, making a mental note to telephone the college and arrange for Tom to stay with them for a night.

As David drove out of the gates of Maybury Hall, he had a moment of clarity. Until now, the women in his life treated him like a pawn, something to be controlled and manipulated. Both his wife and his mother were subtly trying to control him by deciding his future and sealing his son's fate. His mother was seeking to control him, and Gertrude was trying to hurt him. With this awareness, it occurred to David that both women represented his relationship with his inner feminine. He had fallen a long way from the harmonious relationship that had once existed between the Priest and Priestess of the Altay Mountains. Since his discovery of the Jade Mummy, the feminine was growing in strength. The Priestess was the archetypal feminine who lived within him. He would die for her.

Frank Jones looked up from his desk to see a tall, fair-haired man looking through the window at the photographs on display. He recognised his profile from the newspapers. It was Viscount Maybury's younger son, the explorer who evaded capture by the Russians. Frank Jones watched discreetly while the gentleman seemed to make up his mind whether or not to enter. Finally, he turned the door handle and ducked down to enter the seventeenth-century doorway. Frank Jones had a chance to observe him while he scrutinised some photographs hanging on the wall. He would make an interesting profile to photograph, with his curling mop of hair that looked as if it hadn't seen a pair of scissors in months, and a slightly hooked nose which gave him an air of sophistication. He looked every inch the explorer that he was. Frank came out from behind his desk and introduced himself. The explorer shook his proffered hand.

Those in the know highly recommended Frank Jones' photography studio. David needed someone to develop the rolls of film from his trip. Frank Jones listened as the explorer impressed upon him the secrecy surrounding the film. Under no circumstances did he want the Press getting hold of his negatives. Frank, always the professional, produced a privacy document for such situations, which he and David Perry signed. David handed over the film from his camera, feeling confident it was in safe hands. He said he would return to Tewkesbury in a few days to collect the photographs.

Tom Perry hadn't seen his father since the previous February. The disappointment of his father's absence during summer holidays faded away when he saw his father pull up outside the school in a brand new Jaguar. David traded in the Ford chosen by Henry and Gertrude. Tom's eyes lit up as he slid into the leather upholstered passenger seat beside his father. He ran his hands over the wooden panelling on the front dashboard. Tom waved at his friends as they drove under the college arch. They sped past the cathedral towards

Stockbridge road. Tom thought the car was so much sleeker and faster than the Ford his mother drove. Tom let down the window to feel the wind blow through his hair as he watched the countryside flash past. They pulled up at the Grosvenor Hotel in Stockbridge and passers-by slowed down to look at the shiny burgundy car. David put his arm around his son and took him inside for cake and lemonade. Tom tucked into a large slice of Victoria sponge and swung his legs happily in the large leather armchair. David Perry smiled at his nine-year-old son as he licked jam off his fingers and drained his glass. No doubt Gertrude would admonish him for such manners, but his son's unaffected manner delighted David. He was an easy-going young boy and clever, too. David wanted him to have opportunities outside the stifling world of privilege and title. He insisted Tom should attend Winchester College rather than Harrow, where he and countless other generations of Maybury boys had gone. Things were transforming in Britain. The old social orders were crumbling.

David purchased a property in Cheltenham to secure his son's future. He had also put in an offer on an old country manor house in the Vale of Evesham. The late owner had bequeathed the lion's share of the land to the National Trust as part of the Cotswolds conservation scheme, leaving one-hundred-and-fifty acres with the manor. David hoped to move there as soon as the deeds were in his possession. Gertrude could have the house in Imperial Square. The house would be a refuge for him away from the confines of tedious society gatherings in London and Cheltenham. He hoped to be settled in by Christmas, in time for Tom's school holidays. They could escape there for a few days to fish in the nearby river. For now, he decided not to tell his plans to anyone. The deal could easily fall through if Lord Maybury caught wind of it. David's father liked to control both his sons' dealings, and he would oppose David leading a separate life to his wife. David saw the irony of the situation; his father had several infidelities and thought nothing of it. As long as a man was discreet, it was acceptable in society. Lord Maybury considered divorce a scandal and was unperturbed by the double-standards. For him it was black-and-white. David must keep up appearances with Gertrude, and Henry must find a suitable wife to produce an heir.

David hadn't seen his older brother since his return. Henry was visiting their sister Lydia in France, no doubt wanting to avoid him and a scandal. David wasn't angry with Henry, in fact he felt nothing. Henry lived in a perpetual state of dissatisfaction, and David knew that brought its own retribution. He would soon move on from Gertrude leaving her heartbroken, especially when he realised David didn't care. He had seen the pattern play out too many times; Henry was only interested in the chase. Once a woman succumbed to his charms, he got bored, setting his sights on another clandestine prize. David and Gertrude's marriage was over long before he left for Mongolia, but he stayed for Tom's sake. Looking at his son digging into a bowl of ice-cream, he realised he had used him as an excuse to avoid confronting the situation. Since his expedition, everything had changed. He was no longer the pliable husband and dutiful son. He was his own man, even if he wasn't entirely sure who that was.

The following evening, after a successful afternoon of trout fishing on the Test, David dropped Tom at Winchester College. Tom pulled him close and gave him a tight squeeze before returning to his dormitory. David collected his mother and they set off for home. He tuned out as she insisted on sharing the latest drawing-room gossip on the two-hour drive to Cheltenham.

David leafed through the correspondence in his study looking for a letter from the estate agent. They had accepted the offer on the Evesham property. The agent asked him to drop by their office at his earliest convenience to complete the transfer. Once he had the deeds to the property, he would inform Gertrude of his plans. She was upstairs getting ready to attend a charity event at the Municipal Library. She stopped briefly by his study to ask about Tom before leaving in the waiting car. She glanced at the documents on his desk, but if she had any suspicions, she didn't voice them.

David wanted to wrap up the sale before telling his parents. First thing the following morning, he was in the office of Fenchurch & Lyle Solicitors, eager to close the deal on the manor house in Evesham. He dropped the title deeds off at the bank before driving out to his new house. He had already arranged for a builder, electrician, and plumber to meet him at the property to give him estimates for any repairs. An engineer was coming to connect the telephone that afternoon and a furniture delivery van was due to arrive with new beds, sofas, a table and chairs. By four o'clock in the afternoon, he was satisfied that his land agent had everything in hand. He drove to Tewkesbury to collect the photographs from his travels.

The shop bell tinkled as David pushed the heavy oak door. He glanced at the clock; it was five minutes before closing time. The photographer emerged from the darkroom and handed David an envelope containing the negatives and printed photos. The photos had enthralled him but his professionalism stopped him from asking questions. There was one photo above all else that David was dying to see. He paid Frank Jones and apologised for his late arrival. Not wishing to delay him any further, David left the shop, hoping to find a quiet place to examine the contents of the envelope.

David strode down the side street to the banks of the river Avon and sat on a bench. He opened the envelope and flicked through the contents until he found what he was looking for, the photo of the Jade Mummy. He felt the Priestess calling him, closing the portal of time. A mist rose above the river as the sun dipped in the west. David stared off into a distant world, one he had inhabited in another lifetime. He held her memories with his own. Her rebirth was approaching, as was his inevitable death.

15

The sun lights the pathway to the two doors. That which throws shadow is an illusion. Light has no shadow, only form has shadow. The ego is perfect for a mind addicted to worry and fear. However, it is superfluous for the simplicity of the cosmic mind.

The tradition of May Day celebrations stretched back several centuries at the Maybury Estate. Every year, the parkland was transformed into a child's paradise with colourful stalls selling candy-floss, ice-creams, candy sticks and lemonade. A merry-go-round, swing-boat and donkey rides all had queues of children waiting a turn. In the centre of it all, there stood a giant maypole.

In the evening, there was a procession, lit by lanterns, leading to a ring fort where once stood a stone circle. A few stones remained with the rest pilfered long ago. Local folklore said it had been the site of a great battle between the Celts and the Romans. The May Queen resplendent in a golden gown wore a headdress made of newly unfurled leaves. She made her way to the hill fort just before sunset to reclaim her throne from the Old Man of Winter.

Clara arrived just as the pageant was about to begin. Low clouds covered up the evening sun and lanterns lining the path of the procession seemed to glow brighter. A hush descended on the crowd as the May Queen emerged from her horse-drawn carriage. Local children dressed as wood nymphs scattered leaves and petals in her wake. Squeals of delight pierced the hushed atmosphere as young and old alike delighted in the spectacle. The May Queen led the procession to the hill fort as the crowd pressed forward to watch the combat between winter and summer.

The Old Man of Winter emerged like Pan from a copse of trees, dancing around the remaining standing stones, claiming all the seasons for himself. There were gasps from the crowd and children held their breath, hoping the fairy princess would not die. Old Man Winter reached a large wooden throne decorated with garlands just as the May Queen climbed to the top of the fort. A fire eater danced around them, adding to the drama and spectacle. He blew fire above their heads as they locked arms in a battle for the Throne of Summer. A troop of dancers emerged from the copse, breaking into two groups to represent summer and winter. They joined in the mock battle for the throne until finally a crescendo of music saw the Old Man of Winter fall to his knees and renounce the throne. The May Queen took her rightful place on the Throne of Summer amid much applause and shouting. And just as she seated herself on the throne, the setting sun broke through clouds as if nature itself had liberated summer from the grip of winter.

Clara wandered back down the slope, stopping to greet Imogen and her excited children. It was the first year Imogen had taken them to see the pageant. She leaned in to whisper to Clara, 'Do you really think it derived from Celtic traditions? It seems to me they have reimagined the Greek legend of Persephone.'

Clara smiled at her friend's classical reference and replied, 'Most cultures have their own legends of winter and summer.'

They walked down the hill towards Maybury Manor. All the rooms were lit up and she took in the beautiful Georgian architecture. Clara wondered who the current Viscount was. He must be a great-nephew of David Perry, she thought. His elder brother inherited the title, which would make his son or grandson the current owner of Maybury. When they reached the playground, Imogen's children made a beeline for the merry-go-round, which was lit up with twinkling lights. Clara spotted the familiar figure of Tom Perry speaking to a group of stewards. She broke into a smile and waved to him. He saluted her just as someone came to speak with him. Clara recognised him, it was the architect she had met on Malvern Road. Clara said goodbye to Imogen and made her way towards the exit. A steward tapped her on the shoulder. 'Miss Lewis, can you come with me, please?'

Clara looked startled, and the steward quickly assured her she wasn't in any trouble. 'Viscount Maybury requests your presence at the reception.'

Clara looked dumbfounded. She finally managed to say a few words, 'I'm not dressed for an occasion.'

'It's a casual affair,' offered the steward as he led her past the barrier separating the playground from the driveway to the manor house.

Clara gathered her thoughts and asked, 'Which one is Viscount Maybury?'

Before the steward could reply, she found herself standing beside Tom Perry. 'Welcome to my home, Clara.'

'I did not know you were Viscount Maybury. I thought your cousin ...,' she trailed of feeling embarrassed.

'I inherited the title when my uncle died. He had no direct heir,' Tom said as he led her through the double fronted doorway into a magnificent hallway. He made a few introductions before politely taking his leave to speak to more guests. Tom Perry's son, the architect, came over and formally introduced himself as James Hargreaves-Perry.

Clara replied rather stiffly, 'Clara Jane Lewis.'

She felt a blush creeping over her cheeks when she used her full name. Luckily, a jocund younger man joined them, relieving her embarrassment. James introduced him as his younger brother, Walter. He looked familiar to her, but she couldn't quite place where she had seen him.

'Miss Lewis, aren't you a history student?' asked James Hargreaves-Perry, remembering their encounter a few weeks ago.

Clara's mouth was dry. Walter Hargreaves-Perry called over a waiter and handed Clara a glass of champagne. She took a few sips to regain her composure. She had told him a few white lies in order to find out about the building on Malvern Road. Her mind was racing trying to remember what she had told him. Her only option was to tell him the truth.

'I'm a student of history at the University of Gloucester. I'm doing a research PhD.' Clara felt herself flush as she held his gaze.

'Didn't you say you were interested in the architectural heritage of Cheltenham when you came to visit?' asked James Hargreaves with a raised eyebrow.

'Uh, yes, and I um, was researching your grandfather, um, David Perry to authenticate some theories in my thesis.' Clara felt his intense gaze boring through her.

'So you lied about your historical interest in the building?'

Clara almost felt offended by his remark. She stood up straight and said, 'Your father has helped me with my research into your grandfather's travels and his discoveries.'

She hoped that would put an end to his questions, but it seemed to make him even more suspicious.

'Why such a personal interest in my grandfather? Surely information about his expeditions is on file at the Municipal Library or the British Museum?'

He made a valid point, and Clara was at a loss how to reply until she felt a deep calm come over her. Like the May Queen, she exerted her right to freedom.

'I admire the courage shown by David Perry and the lengths he went to discover ancient cultures. He didn't just see a pile of bones or mummified remains, but actual lives, ancestors who gave us a rich tapestry of culture, tradition and spiritual beliefs. He never exploited or profiteered from his discoveries. Rather, he used these discoveries to enlighten people about the scourge of modern religions and the lack of spirituality. He believed in self-governance and how nations can thrive given a shared philosophy and respect for their fellow men.'

Clara heard the words roll off her tongue as if someone else was speaking. She had both the Hargreaves-Perry brothers' attention.

James put down his glass and said, 'They discarded his work as the ramblings of a madman, but it was this world that drove him crazy, with its social classes and inability to see the power of the human mind.'

His words were unexpected and almost moved Clara to tears.

'Thank you, Ms Lewis,' he said, clearing his throat. 'I agree. My grandfather was an exceptional man ahead of his time.'

James wished her a pleasant evening and went to join his colleagues from the world of architecture, who were in deep discussion in the library. Walter remained by her side for a few moments longer and said, 'I never really knew my grandfather. He died when I was four. Apparently he was quite a legend even if he went a little potty in the end...' he trailed off as he looked over Clara's shoulder, spotting some friends who had arrived. He excused himself and went over to greet them.

Clara finished her glass of champagne and went to find Tom Perry. It was time to leave. Passing a row of photographs on the stairwell, she stopped to read the inscriptions. One photo needed no introduction; it was a colour photograph of a young David Perry looking handsome in his riding gear and holding the reins of a horse. He was tall for that era, over six foot, with fair hair bleached by the sun and hazel eyes looking out under dark eyelashes. He was smiling at her from across the timelines. She wanted to go back in time to meet him. In her heart, she was sure they had spent many lifetimes together, but her mind could make no sense of it. As she was grappling with her feelings for a man long since gone, his son appeared by her side and placed his hand on her arm. He noticed her eyes were moist with tears. It seemed improbable, but somehow he thought there must be a connection between this young woman and his late father. Before Clara had time to say goodbye, he told her to wait a moment while he went to fetch something. Clara dabbed her eyes as she stood at the foot of the carved wooden staircase. Finally, Tom emerged from his study holding a small green object and held it out to her. She picked up the jade amulet from the palm of his hand and marvelled at its intricate carving. 'This belonged to my father. It held great significance for him. I want you to have it.'

Clara shook her head as she felt the tears welling up again. She couldn't speak. Tom Perry closed her hand on the amulet and put his finger to his lips. Clara put it in her handbag without saying a word, nodding her head in gratitude.

Clara turned the lock on her front door, relieved to be home. She sat down at her study table and switched on her laptop. Taking out the jade amulet Tom Perry had given her, she placed it on the windowsill in front of her table. It was highly polished with carvings of what looked like ancient deer. She wondered how David Perry possessed such a wonderful object. Perhaps he found it in the tomb with the Jade Mummy. She closed her eyes picturing David Perry in the Altay Mountains. Suddenly, she saw an image of him in a desert town among traders and travellers. She was sure that she, too, was in this place several lifetimes ago. It was a town on the Silk Road in China.

Clara opened a book on the old Silk Road between East and West. The deadline for her thesis was approaching. Her workload had increased since she added the confluence of cultures in southern Xinjiang to her thesis. However, she felt it necessary because it influenced and shaped Celtic culture in Europe. The discovery of the Tarim Mummies proved Europeans travelled between East and West for thousands of years. Clara's believed that they didn't just trade in silk, jade, horses and metal, but in spiritual ideas and practices. They formed a cultural group of tribes living within the region. These ideas travelled with nomads to central Europe, laying the foundations for the Celtic culture.

She had never in her wildest imaginings thought her thesis would lead her on such a rich and varied journey to discover the roots of Celtic spirituality. It was archaeology of the Celtic spirit as much as its culture, an excavation of stories and faces to reveal the sacred energies behind the early settlers. Somewhere along the way, the pure connection between the ancient spiritual leaders and the priests was corrupted by power and greed, leading to ritual sacrifice and questionable practices. This instilled fear in the people and led to the demise of their culture. In the absence of true spiritual leaders, Celtic society became undone, and the people were subdued. The Romans amalgamated them into their culture by killing the Druids in Anglesey.

Was all this religious and cultural upheaval down to man's inner battle to quell and suppress his spirit? wondered Clara. The ego of man didn't want to believe in mortality or be held accountable for his actions. Ancient Kings, Queens, Pharaohs and Emperors all took their treasures into the tomb for use after death. Some of them killed their entire household to take with them to the afterlife. Clara wondered if the druids had abused their role as ego took over. Such abuse of power would have left the people vulnerable to attack from the Romans and the Vikings.

Her eyes grew heavy with sleep. Clara switched off her laptop and called it a night. Theories and narratives for her thesis swirled around in her head, preventing her from drifting off to sleep. She put on some calming music and concentrated on the sensations in her body rather than the incessant noise in her head. After a few minutes, her mind emptied and her body relaxed. She felt tingles up and down her body as she drifted to another dimension beyond time.

A spectrum of a light seemed to split in two and move towards two doors. They emerged as a man and a woman dressed in long robes. Each carried a sceptre, one labelled Truth, and the other Wisdom. They descended separate stairways, opening onto a tiered landscape. As they stepped onto the first tier, their image doubled to two men and two women. At the next tier, their image doubled again to eight people. This repeated through several tiers until there were multitudes of men and women in the landscape. Clara woke from the dream. She realised she had seen this vision several times in her dreams. She took a pen and notebook from her night stand to jot down a few words to help her remember the dream. Closing her eyes to sleep, the vision emerged once again in the same format, except it had a different outcome. A woman stepped out from the multitudes of men and woman onto a staircase to resume her journey down the staircase. The steps were coming towards Clara, as though the last one stopped just behind her eyelids. As the woman reached the last step, she raised her head to look across at a staircase to her left. The scene was a perfect mirror image, but for one exception, the man on the other stairway was at a different level than the woman. Her face came into sharp focus and Clara recognised her as the Priestess, the archetypal feminine from her vision in Maybury chapel. The man's head was bowed and shadow obscured his face.

Clara opened her eyes. She sat up in bed and looked around. Taking a deep breath, she wrote down what she could recall of the dream. Suddenly, she understood its meaning. She was both the woman and the man on the symmetrical staircases. She was here to balance both masculine and feminine energies. She identified with being solely a woman, rejecting the male aspect of her being. Her relationship with her ex-husband reflected this. David Perry represented her search for the perfect male energy. In truth, the journey to wholeness started and ended within her.

16

Life is a continuous experience. Everything that was will be again. The spiral of life ascends or descends according to one's perspective. The dreamer who remains conscious controls the dream. The dreamer, who believes the dream is real, loses touch with reality. He stumbles from dream to dream, birth to death, until he learns to take control of his experience.

Altay Mountains
Fourth Millennium BCE

A Siberian wind blew its icy breath through the Ob valley. The Dahaean tribe rounded up their sheep and goats, taking them to shelter in the south-facing caves. Zarun, the Priest, dispatched a group of riders to gather up the wild horses grazing down in the plains and bring them to the shelter. For the past several years, icy winds and snow blizzards prolonged the winters. Zarun wondered how much longer his tribe could live in such freezing conditions. Several families of the Dahaean tribe had migrated. They followed the mountains westward in search of a more temperate climate.

Every year, the families who remained lost newborn children, and many elders didn't make it through the freezing winters. It was time for the tribe to make a decision about their future. They had remained in the Altay Mountains, their home for generations, hoping that the winters would return to normal, but it appeared they were only getting worse. The climate was changing, prolonging winter by several weeks, and reducing summer dramatically.

Once they safely sheltered the animals, Zarun the Priest sent out a call for everyone to gather at the temple in the centre of the subterranean cave system. Ayzik, the Priestess, took an alabaster jug and dipped it in the waters of the sacred pool. She raised the vessel high above her head as she recited a chant to begin the ritual. Men, women, and children gathered around the pool while Ayzik circled it, sprinkling water on the feet of everyone gathered there. Zarun the Priest spoke to the tribe about the change in weather patterns and how it was affecting the growing season. He pointed to a small opening in the cave above the sacred pool. Every year, the rising sun illuminated the pool for three days, showing the end of one cycle and the beginning of another. Using this event as the apex of their year, the tribe marked the days until the growing season began, when they brought the animals down to the plains to graze. It was the time they planted seeds for harvest. During the time of Zarun's father, the period between midwinter and rogation measured sixty days. However, in recent years, it had almost doubled, marking a severe change in the climate pattern. The Dahaeans were all agreed that something must be done.

Zarun and Ayzik had previously travelled south beyond the Tien Shan Mountains to the desert plains. There, they had met people from several other tribes, nomads who travelled across continents to find new cultures and discover new practices. Zarun and Ayzik traded wool and horses for new grains, grass seeds, and fine objects made from alabaster and jade. They drew patterns in the sand, showing the nomads where they had come from and the type of animals they hunted and tamed. What interested Zarun the most were the people from far away in the West. Their ways intrigued him, and they spoke of fertile land beyond the long spine of mountains running from east to west. In his heart, he had long felt a move westward would benefit his people. Ayzik agreed they must move their tribe away from the hard living conditions of the Altay Mountains.

The journey that Ayzik and Zarun made to the Tien Shan Mountains had taken one whole year to complete. The journey west could take two or three years. Zarun put the proposal of moving west to the Dahaean tribe. He explained that the move would be permanent. They would set about finding unknown lands for future generations of their people. In the end, they agreed that the weather was forcing them to leave. By the spring equinox, which was in twenty-one days, they would be ready to leave their beloved mountains.

Ayzik and Zarun were expecting their first child. The birth was imminent. The baby would be a couple of weeks old when they left their homeland to seek a new land. The women of the tribe were busy preparing a birthing chamber for the new arrival. Zarun sat in the cave where his young wife lay on a mound of animal skins. The women were tending to her and encouraging her to push through the pains that gripped her every few moments. Although it was cold tendrils of hair clung to Ayzik's forehead that was covered in beads of sweat. Reaching out, she took her husband's hand. She tried to speak, but Zarun placed his fingers on her lips to silence her.

'You must save your strength for the little one,' he said, trying to hide the anxiety he felt.

He looked around at the women's faces; his wife's light was fading fast. He grasped her hand in his, willing her to live. A tear slid down Ayzik's cheek.

'Husband, listen to me. You must provide a new beginning for our child and our people. Never forget we came from one light. One day, we shall return to our true being beyond the two doors.'

Zarun nodded his head, unable to speak. His dear wife was about to depart this world. She raised her hand, placed it on his head and said, 'One day I will return to the land where you will make our new home.'

The elder woman of the tribe gently pushed on Ayzik's swollen stomach to help the baby out. Ayzik howled in pain, using what little strength she had left to push her baby into the world. When the elder held up her newborn son, she closed her eyes for the last time.

Zarun placed the last stone on his wife's kurgan. Because of inclement weather, the burial mound had taken almost three weeks to complete even with the help of ten men. They could not reach the higher plateau where the elders were buried. Instead, they built a separate burial mound halfway up the mountain for their beloved Priestess, placing all her valuable items in the tomb, as was their tradition. Zarun made her a promise to lead the Dahaean tribe safely to a new home in the west, where future generations would live harmoniously with nature.

His great-grandfather, Dahae, had brought the tribe together from several nomadic families who roamed the regions surrounding the Altay Mountains. It was Dahae's idea to bring stability to the tribe by herding wild horses and goats. Rather than continuing the old practice of chasing wild herds, he rounded them up and corralled them using the natural fortress of the mountains. When word spread about their new methods, several new families came to join the tribe of Dahae. The Dahaeans worked together to feed all families and collectively took care of their animals and crops. Their farming practice worked for several decades until the climate changed, now forcing them to leave their homeland. The Dahaeans looked to Dahae's great-grandson to offer them guidance in all matters. After the death of his wife, Zarun found it difficult to focus on the migration of his people. The only small light in his life was the fact that his son was thriving thanks to a young mother who nursed the infant along with her own. The tribe trusted Zarun to lead them to an unknown land, a land where their children and children's children would live longer and healthier lives. He had made a promise; he would not let them down.

Zarun and the elders mapped their route along the corridor of mountains stretching from east to west, a series of mountain ranges known as the Steppes. At the far west of the Steppes was the river Danube. Zarun had met a man from this region on his travels. He explained to Zarun that to reach the fertile lands of the west, he must follow the Danube from where it emptied its waters into the Black Sea, back to its source. He told Zarun to follow the river past dense forests to the plains further north. The knowledgeable traveller drew a map for Zarun showing islands off the mainland which had a temperate climate, ideal for growing crops. These islands were mystical and spiritual. The traveller said that at one time, a chalk land bridge had connected them to Europe, but it had eroded over the past few centuries, and cut the islands off from the mainland. Zarun had felt his spine tingle on hearing about these islands, a sure sign that this was the new home of the Dahaeans. There, they would raise their children and adapt new farming methods to suit the climate.

It was fourteen days after the spring equinox when the tribe left their home in the Altay Mountains, two weeks longer than they had planned. It gave Zarun enough time to bury his wife and allow his son to grow strong enough for the journey. Zarun put his son, whom he named Dahae after his ancestor, in a papoose slung over his back. Taking one last look at Ayzik's resting place halfway up the mountain, he vowed to return for her in another lifetime. He would perform the sacred ritual to invoke her return to her new home on the western islands.

17

Human life is a borrowing of skin and bones. All matter is subject to mortal law. Spirit is governed by universal law and is eternal. To excavate the truth beneath the overlay of belief and superstition is the work of many lifetimes.

Arthur Lewis looked through Professor Berkeley's notes. She had secured a permit to conduct a dig with her students at Bryn Celli Ddu on the island of Anglesey during the summer. She attached a letter to her notes, asking him if he would compile a geophysical profile of the site. Grace Berkeley lectured with Arthur at Bangor University. She had long been fascinated by the druids and had written books on their ancient practices. This dig would form the basis for her next publication. Arthur picked up the phone to call her. He needed more information before he committed to the project. If he was to do this favour for Grace Berkeley, then he would require one in return. His niece, Clara, had recently completed a research PhD at Gloucester University. She had asked him to keep his ear to the ground for any archaeological projects. Grace Berkeley would have to consider his niece for the research assistant job if she was to secure Arthur's expertise. She read over Clara's résumé and agreed to his terms. In fact, she knew she would have chosen Clara anyway over any of the other candidates given her qualifications.

Clara punched the air as she finished the call to Professor Berkeley. She had secured her first job in the field as a research assistant on Celtic druid practices. She phoned her uncle Arthur to thank him for putting her name forward for the job. He invited her to stay with him and his family for the duration of the three-month dig. Clara had given no thought to accommodation during her time on the island and therefore readily accepted his invitation. The dig was starting in four weeks. Clara had research work to complete before joining Professor Berkeley and her team on site. Two weeks earlier, Clara had presented her thesis to the faculty at Gloucester University. She had come directly to Dorset afterwards to spend time by the sea at her mother's house in Lyme Regis. Imogen and her two children rented a mobile home in a nearby caravan park. Both of them were relieved to finish their studies. Clara wrote a list of things she needed to do before the July start date on Anglesey. Top of the list was a trip to the British Museum in London. She picked up the phone to call her brother.

The train from Gloucester pulled in at Paddington Station at four-thirty in the afternoon, twenty minutes later than scheduled. Clara disembarked and made her way through the ticket barriers to the London Underground. She checked her route on the District Line before buying a ticket for the journey to Richmond. She looked at the enormous face of the station clock. It would be another hour before Cormac returned home from work. She went down to the Underground and checked the platform information. The tube to Richmond was due in two minutes. Clara glanced at her watch, it was five o'clock. She had hoped to avoid rush hour but the train delay outside Reading meant she arrived at the busiest commuter time. Clara squeezed through the doors and into the crush of passengers on the District Line. She gripped the extended handle of her hard-shell case while using her free hand to cling to the upright bar. There was no fear she would fall over as she was pinned between a swell of commuters. When the train pulled out of Earl's Court station, a few seats became available. Clara sat down and looked out the window as it emerged from dark underground tunnels to cross the River Thames. An automated voice announced the next stop was Kew Gardens. Steel, metal and glass gleamed in the afternoon sun and the River Thames meandered by like an old man on his journey to the sea. The last stop was Richmond, and Clara stood up as the remaining passengers stood by the doors, eager to get off the tube. Cormac's flat was near Richmond Park, a brisk ten-minute walk from the tube station. Clara crossed the road at St. Matthias' Church and rolled her case down the leafy street to her brother's flat. Cormac was in a convenient location to commute to his office in south London and as a bonus, he was within walking distance of Twickenham Stadium, home to English Rugby.

Just as she turned the corner onto Park Road, Clara heard a car horn beep behind her. Cormac pulled into the underground car park. Clara waited for him at the steps to open the front door of the Victorian building. He carried her case up the flight of stairs to his first-floor apartment and left the suitcase in the hallway. Clara followed him into the living area. She glanced around the open-plan kitchen, dining and living area, noting that Cormac had attempted to tidy up before she arrived. He smiled at her, reading her mind. She wheeled her case into the guest bedroom as Cormac took fresh towels from the airing cupboard and handed them to her.

Cormac's culinary skills had improved little since his days in Gloucestershire so they chose dinner from one of the many take-away menus pinned to a notice board in the kitchen. Cormac took a bottle of sparkling wine from the fridge to toast Clara's academic triumph while waiting for the local Thai food restaurant to deliver dinner. Clara was glad they were staying in tonight. She could see Cormac was tired after a busy weekend. Monday was his evening to kick back and relax. He seemed happier than when she saw him in March. She was about to ask him about his love life when his phone rang. By the tone of his voice, she knew that he had met someone. He stepped out onto the small balcony in the living area gesturing to Clara he would be just a couple of minutes. Clara raised her eyebrow with a knowing grin, and Cormac knew she had guessed he was speaking to a woman. When he returned, Clara was busy plating up their Thai food, which had just been delivered. Cormac refilled their glasses, and they laid all the cartons on the round glass table.

'Her name is Gwyn,' said Cormac, pre-empting his sister's question. 'She's a nurse in Richmond Hospital.'

Clara took a bite from her prawn tempura, letting her brother tell her as much, or as little, as he wished to. She playfully slapped away his hand as he tried to snatch tempura from her plate.

'You should have ordered your own!'

Cormac ignored her and tossed a prawn into his mouth.

'How did you meet her?' Clara asked.

'One of my teammates was in hospital with a burst appendix. Gwyn was on the ward when I went to visit him. He introduced us and the rest, as they say, is history.'

'Or history repeating itself,' Clara said.

'What do you mean?' asked Cormac, piling noodles onto his plate.

'Mum and Dad met at a hospital. She bandaged his fractured wrist after a rugby injury.'

Cormac raised his eyebrows in response since his mouth was full of food. 'With a name like Gwyn she must have some Welsh connections,' Clara continued trying to prise more information out of her brother.

'She's from Chepstow.' Cormac got stuck into his Pad Thai, and Clara asked no more questions.

More than once, she had cautioned her brother about his rash behaviour in the early stages of relationships. He had been engaged twice, both times within a couple of months of meeting his girlfriends. A few years ago, he stopped speaking to her for several months when Clara said she didn't trust his girlfriend, Jenna. Cormac told her to keep her opinions to herself, and maybe she should focus on the problems in her own relationship. The truth of this hit home with Clara because her marriage was falling apart. She didn't realise anyone else had noticed. It caused tension between the siblings for several months. When Cormac heard Clara was leaving her husband, he drove to Cambridge to collect her and take her home. He stayed with her and their mother for five days until she told him to go back to London. The irony was that when he returned unexpectedly to his flat in London, he found his fiancée, Jenna, cosied up with her ex-boyfriend.

The following morning, Cormac woke Clara before he left for his nine o'clock meeting in Guildford. She looked at her watch. It was two minutes past eight. She had an appointment with the curator of Celtic artefacts and sacred objects at ten o'clock at the British Museum. Clara showered quickly and got dressed. She absently buttered a slice of toast while checking messages on her phone. She estimated it would take forty-five minutes to reach central London. By the time she reached Richmond Underground, the morning rush hour was over. She changed trains in Earl's Court for the Piccadilly Line to Holborn station. Although it was June, the weather was quite overcast, making it humid on the Underground. Clara ascended several elevators to reach street level. She glanced at the murals adorning walls of the station referencing the Roman and Egyptian antiquities displayed at the British Museum. Clara remembered hearing on a documentary that they used Holborn Underground as an air-raid shelter during the bombings in the Second World War. The tunnels were also used to protect the precious artefacts from the museum including the Parthenon Marbles, more famously known as the Elgin Marbles. Clara finally reached the street level from the underground labyrinth. She turned onto High Holborn and made her way to the British Museum.

The curator, Sophie Rhys Phelps, took Clara through the collection of artefacts discovered around the British Isles. She produced maps and studies from a previous excavation at Bryn Celli Ddu, where Professor Berkeley's dig was based. Sophie led her through an exhibition area to a quiet room where she could study the files from the last dig at the site in 1929. Clara read the introduction; 'the monument originated as a stone circle; they remodelled the stones into a passage tomb during the late Neolithic. At dawn on midsummer solstice, shafts of light from the rising sun penetrate the passageway to light the inner burial chamber'.

Clara made notes from the 1929 excavation before moving back in time to the Mesolithic era. She wanted to find out when man first came to Anglesey. People returned to the British Isles after the Ice Age, between 11000 and 9000 BCE. These early inhabitants were hunter-gatherers and would remain so until farming practices were developed in the Neolithic Age. The Neolithic period ushered in the widespread practices of agriculture across the British Isles, with a new lifestyle change from hunter-gatherers to a settled lifestyle of farming. With the change in practices came new settlements and the population increased rapidly. Farmers studied weather patterns and the seasons of the year. Although many people believed henges, which were stone and wooden circles, were erected as places of worship, they may have simply been intended as a seasonal calendar to know when to sow crops.

As was often the case, Clara found her research yielded more questions than answers, such as, where did the first farmers find grains of wheat, or grass seed? Where did they learn to domesticate and breed wild cattle and horses?

The majesty of the stone circle created during the Neolithic would have been impressive. Clara thought the Avebury stone circle and Stonehenge must have invoked awe in the communities. Perhaps the combined effort required to build these giant structures also fulfilled a spiritual need. This may have led to the sites serving a dual function, as a farming calendar and a ceremonial site to honour the ancestors.

The twentieth and twenty-first centuries saw agriculture bulldozing its way through several rare habitats leading to wide-scale deforestation on the planet. In Britain alone, this had led to the extinction of hundreds of species of plants and animals as large-scale farming destroyed their habitats. Nature was paying a high price for man's progress. Man, in turn would pay a high price for destroying his natural habitat.

Clara lost track of time in the world of the Neolithic. It was almost closing time and Sophie came to gather up the research material. Clara thanked her and gathered up her things. She had half an hour to make it across town to meet Cormac. When she arrived at the station, he was waiting for her. He explained Gwyn would join them for dinner when she got off work at eight o'clock. First, they had to visit their aunt Cerys, who lived near Kew Gardens. Cerys Lewis was

BEYOND THE TWO DOORS

the eldest of their father's siblings. As young adults, if Clara or Cormac had any reason to stay overnight in London, they stayed on the sofa bed in their aunt's one-bedroom apartment overlooking the Thames. Cerys Lewis had worked in publishing all her working life. Now retired, she still read manuscripts sent to her by the publishing house. Cerys had a warm welcome for her nephew and a more reserved greeting for her niece. Clara was aware that she met Cormac for coffee once a month, but she hadn't seen Clara since her wedding to Charles. Clara immediately felt her aunt's shrewd eyes watching her, remembering that her dad used to joke that Cerys could see around corners. It made her feel uneasy. Cormac's phone rang. It was a call from the office. He apologised to Cerys and said he must take it. She pointed him towards the bedroom to speak in private. With Cormac out of the way, Cerys zoned in on Clara. 'So, my dear, how are you feeling?'

Clara put down her teacup and said, 'I'm very well, thank you.'

'But that business with your husband, dear, was unfortunate. Imagine claiming you were possessed!' Cerys tut-tutted as she peered at Clara over the rim of her cup.

Clara went pale. No one had ever mentioned the incident in such a forthright manner. She hoped everyone had dismissed Charles' claims as wild accusations.

'Soon to be ex-husband,' was Clara's terse reply.

'Never mind dear, demons have a way of working through all of us at some point or another.' Cerys leaned forward and in a confidential tone said, 'Sleepwalking isn't a crime, you know.' She sat back and chuckled, 'Not unless you tried to kill him.'

Clara gritted her teeth. She wanted to hurl the cup of tepid tea in her aunt's face, but she smiled sweetly and said, 'I save that kind of behaviour for anyone who interferes in my business.'

The pub beside the restaurant was unusually busy. Clara sat at a table tucked behind a low beam, waiting for Cormac to return from the bar with drinks. She hadn't mentioned her conversation with their aunt. She was still fuming at her audacity to pry into her personal life. Clara had found it hard to discuss events that led to the end of her marriage even with her counsellor and she certainly wasn't going to tell Cerys. Having a few moments alone gave her the opportunity to compose herself. Her anger subsided, and she acknowledged it was her aunt's manner to be direct, if somewhat interfering.

Cormac returned from the bar with the drinks, with Gwyn by his side. Clara stood up to greet her and banged her head on the beam. The impact temporarily stunned her, and she quickly sat down to regain her balance. Gwyn checked her over and asked Cormac to get a tea towel and a glass of ice from the bar. Gwyn wrapped the ice in the towel and placed it on Clara's head telling her she would probably have a bump on her head for the next few days. Clara assured her she was fine and took a sip from her gin & tonic.

Clara could see Cormac and Gwyn were smitten with each other. When they finished their drinks, they went to a restaurant nearby where Cormac had made reservations.

Gwyn announced she had secured a nursing post in Bristol. Cormac ordered a bottle of champagne to celebrate and added that he had landed a position as manager in his firm's new office in Bristol also. Clara clapped her hands in delight and joined in a toast to their new jobs. Cormac explained they would rent a house somewhere in south Gloucestershire. His new position started in two weeks. Gwyn had to work out a month's notice in Richmond Hospital.

Clara had a wonderful idea and said, 'You can stay at my house in Tewkesbury. I'm going to Bangor for three months to work on an excavation. It will give you time to find a suitable place.'

Cormac looked at Gwyn, who nodded excitedly. 'That would be great. Thanks.'

'Here's to new beginnings,' Clara said, as she clinked glasses with Cormac and Gwyn.

18

The greatest achievement of man has been to harness the natural elements such as fire, water, air and soil. In as much as it has helped his progress, it has also led to his undoing. In the circle of life, the balance of giving and receiving is law.

The Dahaean tribe were gathered by the river Danube. They had made a two-thousand-mile journey to reach the end of the Steppes. They found thriving farming communities living by the Danube on land cleared from forests. These were not hunter-gatherer tribes but people with a new purpose to tame their environment. They had learned how to produce yearly crops and fatten livestock. They welcomed the Dahaeans, impressed by their riding skill on the wild horses that they rode. These European people wanted to learn this skill from the strangers. They offered the tribe knowledge and grain in exchange for instruction from them on how to break in wild horses. The Dahaeans taught them how to ride, and the Europeans showed them how to cultivate the soil to produce new crops every year.

Zarun the Priest observed the practices of their hosts. They traded tools and grain for the knowledge of horse breeding. He would take these skills to the western islands of the far west of Europe. It had been an exceptional year for harvest and Zarun gave thanks to the cosmic intelligence beyond the two doors for the bountiful season bestowed upon his hosts.

Time moved on and Zarun gathered his people to plan their departure for the western islands. Some of the Dahaean families had become accustomed to life in the settlement and were reluctant to leave. They asked Zarun if he could promise the same opportunities that they had here on the settlement. He shook his head. It was not in his power to make such promises. He reminded them of the pact they made before they left their home in the Altays to stick together until they found a new homeland for the entire tribe. Zarun knew that many of them were weary from travel. They had a taste of a new, settled way of life and wanted to embrace it. He felt defeated. His intention was to keep the tribe united in their search for a new homeland. He felt he had no choice but to bless them and wished them well in their new home by the Danube.

Zarun held his son's hand as they climbed into the hide and skin-covered boats that would take them across the water to the high white cliffs that gleamed in the sun. He tested the sturdiness of the boats before taking the horses on board. Their number was now reduced to fifty-six men, women, and children. Zarun was torn leaving almost half his tribe behind. He wrestled with his conscience. His wanted to stay at the Danube with his kinsfolk, but his inner guidance was too strong to ignore. He gathered the rest of the tribe and charted a course for the western islands.

His son, Dahae, had grown into a strong young boy with eyes like his mother. Zarun felt her presence with them, guiding them and alerting them to dangers. Her presence was strongest when he prayed to the cosmic intelligence beyond the two doors. He was certain that she was there, waiting for him to return. He was determined to find the portal to facilitate their reunion at the end of their time on earth.

Zarun and Dahae stood on top of a high chalk cliff, waiting for the rest of their people. They had safely made it across the channel of water from the mainland on boats fashioned from wood, bark and animal skin. The hard part had been calming the horses they had taken with them. When all the Dahaeans had safely crossed, they found shelter in a thickly wooded valley on the chalky downland. There, wild boar and deer were abundant, similar to those in the Altay Mountains. They hunted and roasted a boar on a spit for their first tribal meal in this unknown land, giving thanks for their bounty.

The Dahaeans lived as hunter-gatherers, just like the rest of the sparse population who called these islands home. They travelled along the coastline, a novel landscape for a tribe from the deep interior of the Asian landmass. Occasionally, they came across lone fishermen or small groups of hunters. They observed how the natives speared fish and how they cooked it over an open fire. The local hunters used rudimentary tools of flint to slit the fish and remove the gut and bones. It took the Dahaeans some time to adjust to a diet of fish. They caught deer and boar when they camped inland, but mostly they moved along the coastline, following the sea, hoping to find another island to the west. Zarun felt sure the portal for renewal and rebirth was on that mystical isle.

One night, in a dream, Zarun's great-grandfather came to visit. He showed him a river travelling eastward through a fertile vale; a life-giving river, a sacred river. Zarun and the Dahaeans would sail across the sea to the mouth of this river.

The next morning, Zarun walked to a high cliff edge to survey the weather out at sea. He could see land shimmering in the far distance. A ripple of energy flowed through him, telling him that this was the mystical isle, the land where his tribe would call home.

It was nearing mid-summer, and the days were long. It was the best time to cross the sea that separated the islands. He spotted a small cove where there were some fishing boats. He gathered his men and rode down to the fishermen's camp. There were now sixty members in the tribe and six horses, including two young foals. They required sturdy vessels to transport them safely across the sea. Trading one of their horses for four boats, they planned their voyage. They camped by the coast while they waited for the fishermen to make the boats seaworthy for the voyage. Zarun received another blow when four more families of their tribe refused to travel. Their children had been terrified and suffered acute sea-sickness on the last voyage. Zarun pointed across the sea and said if they should ever change their minds to look for them in the valley of the east-flowing river. They would erect two tall poles at the entrance to their land, showing that it was Dahaean territory.

The fishermen made rudimentary sails to keep the Dahaeans on course in high winds. Young Dahae was frightened of the sea monsters, believing they might eat him just like the drawings on the rock face where the fishermen camped. Zarun reassured him there were no monsters, explaining that the drawings represented the often turbulent and hungry sea. Zarun and his son felt nauseous from the constant motion of the waves. The sea-sickness continued for several hours until at last the mist cleared and the winds died down. Young Dahae cried out excitedly, 'Land!'

The crying and wailing of the children stopped, and suddenly there was utter calm. Zarun saw a beach near a large inlet. It was the place his great-grandfather had shown him in the dream. Zarun bowed his head and thanked the cosmic intelligence for guiding him and his people to their new home. Dragging the vessels ashore, the Dahaeans walked along the beach with their horses and few belongings. Zarun carried the seeds from the farmers of the Danube in cloth tied around his waist. He had wrapped them in sealskin to prevent seawater from destroying them. For now, his people would have to feed themselves by foraging and hunting until the seeds yielded crops. Making their way up the coast, they spotted a band of hunters watching them from a hill behind the dunes. Zarun mounted his horse. He beckoned to four of the men to follow and they rode towards them. He wanted to ask the hunters' permission to stay in their territory for a day or two. As they drew closer to the hill, the men fled in terror. Never had they seen such tall warriors flying on air with swift, four-legged creatures. Zarun slowed his horse to a trot, careful not to frighten them further. When he drew level with them, he dismounted the horse. They scoured the ground for sticks and stones, which they raised in fear. Zarun crossed his arms in front of his chest as a sign of peace. When the natives had lowered their rudimentary weapons, he opened his arm in a sweeping gesture to take in the rest of his tribe and said, 'Dahaean.'

They spoke in whispers among themselves until one stepped forward and also crossed his hands across his chest. His companions backed away as Zarun's horse whinnied. She reared up on her hind legs, scaring the natives and sent them running. Zarun pulled on her rein to calm her. This sent the natives scampering down the hill towards the river. Zarun stood and watched them wade through the water to the opposite side. He wondered what kind of impression they had made on them. Surely the native tribes would spread the word that strangers had arrived on their shores. One day, far into the future, the Dahaeans would form the basis for the legend of the Tuatha de Danann; tribe of the Gods.

The Dahaeans followed the river for three days until it curved southwards. Zarun knew he had arrived at the location shown to him in the dream. Many of the tribe, weary from several years of travel, wept when they realised they had finally reached the land promised to them by the ancestors. It was late summer, more than three full years since they had left the Altay Mountains. The sun was high in the sky as they set about lighting fires to cook the fish they caught. Zarun wandered a little distance through the forest until he came to a natural clearing. He lay on the ground, feeling his heartbeat become one with the earth. On this spot, he would build a monument for rebirth and renewal. At the next winter solstice, he would mark the spot when one yearly cycle ended and a new one began. Not only would the monument mark the passing of time, but also serve as a reminder of life as a unified whole.

The Dahaeans worked toward a shared vision to create a circular monument to mark the passage of time of the year and in the cosmos. They erected a circle of small wooden poles before midwinter. This would help to pin-point the exact angle of the rising sun. Local tribes, curious about the wooden circle, observed the Dahaeans from the edge of the forest. Zarun beckoned them to come closer until one by one, they joined the building project. Every winter, local tribes gathered at the site. The construction of the monument became a focal point for their communities. The natives had a rudimentary knowledge of the solar and lunar movements. Together with the Dahaeans, they worked to erect a large wooden henge. When it was complete, it would measure the seasons. Using the wooden henge, they could predict when it was time to sow and time to harvest.

The Dahaeans shared seeds from their crops with the native tribes, showing them how to place it in the soil. The skill and legend of the Dahaean tribe grew on the island. Several bands of hunter-gatherers came seeking knowledge of how to grow crops. Each year, the winter gatherings grew greater and Zarun harnessed their power to build an even greater monument, one which would mark the passage of time. This would harness the energy of above and below, to create a portal to the cosmos beyond the two doors.

Stories of the skilled farmers from foreign lands spread with travellers who crossed the sea and eventually reached the Dahaeans who had stayed on the chalk lands of the larger island to the east. Ten years had passed since their tribe had set sail to the western isle. Five Dahaean men made the journey across the sea to find their people, remembering the instructions Zarun gave to them on his departure. When they reached the shore, the natives recognised the similarities to Zarun and his tribe. They pointed them towards the Dahaean settlement on the river Boyne. Zarun, seeing the familiar sight of his people approaching the settlement, dropped his tools and ran to greet them. Over dinner, the reunited tribe exchanged stories of their life on each island. Many of the children, who set out on the journey from the Altay Mountains, were now young men and women and had children of their own. Zarun and Ayzik's son Dahae was twenty-one years old. He had a young wife named Bruin. She was the daughter of a local chieftain who provided labour and tools to construct the new monument at Newgrange. Several families settled in the area to help in the construction.

The visiting Dahaeans spoke of life on their island. They had little success growing grain by the coast where they had settled after Zarun and the others had left. Moving south and inland, they came to chalk lands where they successfully grew crops year after year. Some years the weather was better than others, producing a high yield of grain. Other years they relied on a subsistence of berries and fruit to get them through the winter. Zarun told them that the key to a good crop was not only weather, but judging the perfect time to sow the seeds. He showed them the circular wooden henge that measured the movements of the sun. Knowledge of the solar and lunar movements would allow them to plant seeds at the best time to achieve a bountiful yield. Zarun stood at the point where the sun rose in midwinter and then walked around to where it rose at midsummer. He retraced his steps about halfway between the two points and called his tribal brothers to join him. This marked the spot when it was time to sow grain. The five men picked up some sticks and arranged them in a circle, and with Zarun's guidance they practised erecting a similar solar calendar to help them achieve good yields. Once they had mastered the construction of a wooden henge, they returned to their families across the sea, bringing with them the knowledge of the cosmos and how to harness its energy in the temporary world.

Zarun waited for the midwinter sun to rise and cast its rays through the roof box in the monument to mark the passage of time. A beam of light lit up the chamber heralding the end of one year and the start of another. This was the focal point of the solar cycle when the sun aligned with the greatest force in the universe. He was satisfied that the roof box was perfectly aligned with the midwinter sun. He lay down beneath the beam of light and squinted at the rays from the winter sun. He saw the image of Ayzik beckoning him.

His time had come to leave this world and return to his beloved beyond the two doors.

19

Man's understanding of the cosmos is hampered by the conditioned mind. Limited thought patterns work similar to gravity; they are useful to keep man stuck in a world of his making, but not so helpful when he wishes to escape. What often appears as madness in the mind can indicate the dismantling of the dream world.

The ferry sounded its horn as it pulled out from the island of Anglesey. The Holyhead to Dun Laoghaire Ferry sailed twice daily across the Irish sea between Britain and Ireland. David Perry left his car below deck and climbed the stairs to the lounge area. He gripped the armrests of his seat and stared out the large window at the choppy sea. He braced himself for a rocky voyage. He had taken the ferry for the convenience of taking all his journals and photographs in the boot of his car. Looking at the conditions made him regret not taking a flight to Dublin. It was his first trip to Ireland in his sixty-six years. He had come to visit his old friend and colleague, John Biddulph.

Dr John Biddulph caught the bus to Dun Laoghaire to meet his friend, whom he hadn't seen in over a decade. He had recently retired from the British Museum and was a guest lecturer at Trinity College, Dublin, for the autumn term. Twenty-six years had passed since he, Perry and Higgins had gone on their expedition to the Altay Mountains. He needed Perry's help with details of their trip to Asia. Biddulph was writing his autobiography, which included his explorations and work for the British Museum. Perry kept several journals on his expeditions and Biddulph hoped he could help him fill in a few blanks.

David clutched his satchel under his arm as the boat came into dock. In it, he had photographs and journals of his travels. There were photos of an exploration on the Nile and the Valley of the Kings that included a photo of John Biddulph emerging from the Great Pyramid of Giza. He wanted it for the cover of his new book. He also included a photo of Biddulph, Higgins and himself on the plateau of the Altay Mountains, taken by the guide who had sold them out to the Russian authorities. The following year, a team of Russian archaeologists claimed the discovery of the kurgans on the plateau as their own. It was a condition of Higgins and Biddulph's release that Russians claimed the discovery of the ancient site. However, the photograph David held in his hand proved otherwise. He and his colleagues were the first to discover the burial mounds.

David Perry never disclosed his discovery of the Jade Mummy in a separate kurgan further down the mountain. He trusted she remained undiscovered in her resting place. David kept the photo of the Jade Mummy in his safe in Evesham. He wanted to keep her whereabouts secret until she was set free. David felt tears sting the back of his eyes. The discovery had changed him profoundly. He was at a loss to explain how the Priestess from several centuries ago affected him so. He lived with an inner struggle between his own personality and the mind of the ancient Priest. Late at night, he often went jogging on the hills around his estate, trying to outrun the shadows of madness that darkened his mood. David carried the jade amulet given to him by the old healer in Hotan. He ran his thumb and forefinger along the smooth surface and relaxed a little. The ship's horn sounded, and he got into the driving seat of his car. David glimpsed the shoreline as the cargo doors opened. He looked in the rear-view mirror and a trick of light revealed an image of the Priest. David knew the sign; the Priest recognised this place. David had several of these flashbacks in Mongolia and China, and once on the south coast in Dorset, which had deeply puzzled him. After two decades, he knew the unerring feeling that accompanied the Priest's appearance. Somehow, he had arrived on English shores and sailed across the sea to Ireland. It must have taken him several years to travel the thousands of miles across the Steppes and mainland Europe. David opened the glove compartment and popped a couple of aspirin. The thought of it gave him a headache. He started up the engine of his Jaguar XJ6 and drove onto Irish soil.

John Biddulph had his lodgings on campus at Trinity College. He had arranged for David to have a private viewing of the oldest written manuscript discovered on the British Isles; The Book of Kells. It contained the four gospels in elaborate design, on leaves of vellum. John explained they named the book after the place it lay for centuries, Kells in

County Meath. David felt a shiver up his spine. Maybe it was the dull lighting or the cool air in the room that made him feel an atmosphere of reverence and truth. He watched as the curator carefully turned some pages, David realised it must have taken several years in a scriptorium before a manuscript of this exquisite detail emerged. He could almost sense the reverence as novice monks perfected their craft to work on this masterpiece of the medieval world. The craftsmanship and attention to detail left him speechless. Each letter unfurled as a gift to God.

The following morning at six, David and Biddulph set off for the passage tomb at Newgrange, thirty miles north of Dublin. John explained that the burial chamber lit up at sunrise from the eighteenth to the twenty-third of December. Today was the twentieth, and signs were good for a clear sky at sunrise. David listened as Biddulph filled him in on facts about the site. It dated back to the fourth millennium BCE, predating the Pyramids in Egypt. It was constructed before Stonehenge and Avebury stone circles in Britain. Biddulph explained that a team of archaeologists had recently completed restoration of the site. It now sported a shiny white quartz facade and a dome which they covered in grass. He added that there were two impressive monuments close by, known as 'Knowth' and 'Dowth'. These appeared to have a similar function to the bigger monument of Newgrange, although no one could say with absolute certainty what they originally intended the monuments for. David felt he was sliding into an alternate world, a place where time folded into a nanosecond and space expanded into the infinite. The change was imperceptible to his colleague, who continued to relay facts and dates but for David, all mental activity had momentarily ceased as he felt a deep connection to the Boyne Valley. John Biddulph parked the car as first light appeared on the eastern horizon. Biddulph opened the boot of his car and pulled out a large torch to light their way to the monument. David didn't need the light. He felt surefooted, as if he knew the terrain like the back of his hand. When they reached the entrance stone of the tomb, a handful of people had already gathered. Biddulph looked at his watch. Another forty-three minutes until the sun rose at eight fifty-eight am. He shone his torch on the entrance stone to get a closer look at the carvings. Biddulph explained the triskele pattern to David, a carving of three interlocking circles representing the three tombs in the Boyne Valley. David regarded the carving for a few moments before commenting, 'Explanation objectifies it, draining life and energy from the source.'

Biddulph looked quizzically at him. Perry often displayed signs of eccentricity, which had led him to ignore the rumours about his friend's mental health. In the dim light, Biddulph saw the curator coming to lead them into the chamber. A hush fell over the group as he stood before them and introduced himself. He explained how the first rays of sunlight would enter the roof box above the passage approximately four minutes after sunrise. He explained calculations based on the movement of the Earth's tilt proved that first light would have entered at the precise moment when the sun rose four thousand years ago, the time of construction. The small group followed the Curator into the tomb, and he pointed out the cruciform shape of the passage containing three alcoves. He glanced at his watch and put his index finger to his lips. It was time. Outside the tomb, in the distance, someone was playing a bodhrán, a handheld drum used in traditional Irish music. The steady beat matched the beat of David's heart. A vision of the Priestess appeared before him, rising from the earth to greet the new solar year. Her eyes burnt like fire, piercing David with her light. The Priestess shimmered brightly, before finally merging with the morning light. David heard a chanting sound like an echo from the distant past. Biddulph tugged sharply at the sleeve of his coat and David realised it was he who was chanting. He blinked a few times to adjust to the darkness. The solstice sun had come and gone, and everyone had left the tomb.

Biddulph stopped to talk to a colleague from the British Museum. David walked past them, mindful he had embarrassed his friend. A few side glances were cast in his direction. David stood near Biddulph, but he made no attempt to introduce him to his colleague.

John Biddulph had ignored rumours that his esteemed friend, the Hon. David Hargreaves Perry was losing his mind. He discounted any claims as professional envy, or perhaps class envy, given Perry's privileged background. It wasn't until Tony Higgins mentioned Perry seemed 'away with the fairies' that Biddulph took notice. Higgins visited Perry last March during the Cheltenham racing festival. When they discussed their expedition to Mongolia, Perry chanted in a strange voice. At first, Higgins thought his friend had one too many glasses of port and thought no more of it until the following night, when he claimed he was a priest from the Altay Mountains. The whole thing left Higgins feeling unsettled. He phoned Biddulph when he returned to London. The conversation passed through his mind like a flash. He could no longer ignore Perry's state of mind. This latest incident had happened publicly in Newgrange, in view of reputable archaeologists and historians. It could very well ruin David Perry's reputation as a great explorer. Biddulph realised Perry's journals were of no use to him now. He couldn't authenticate his work as a reliable source in his upcoming autobiography. Perry's New Age nonsense could tarnish his own reputation by association.

'No, I didn't take any drugs or smoke pot,' replied David, slightly bemused by his friend's question.

'So what was that chanting in the tomb about?' Dr Biddulph retorted, trying to suppress his annoyance.

'I'm not sure. I didn't know I was doing it until you shook my arm,' replied David, sensing Biddulph's chagrin.

'Are you seriously telling me you don't know what happened in there?' Biddulph turned towards him with an incredulous look on his face.

'No, I don't know what happened. It's all a blur.'

John Biddulph regarded his friend for a few moments and realised he was telling the truth. Recalling Tony Higgins' story, Biddulph wondered if the trigger for David Perry's mental disturbance had begun in the Altay Mountains. Other explorers had reported strange happenings in the Altays. One report to the British Museum described strange experiences after taking part in shamanic practices. The explorer claimed the experience warped time and messed with his head. John Biddulph let out a deep sigh. He must ensure that David Perry's archaeological and geographical notes were removed from the research library at the British Museum and other notable libraries.

David drove his car onto the ferry that was to sail from Dublin to Holyhead. He had promised his son and grandchildren before leaving that he would be home for Christmas. Gertrude was also spending Christmas Day at Tom's house, and although they had lived apart for decades, they had never officially divorced. Gertrude's affair with David's brother, Henry, had ended when he married an American heiress twenty years previously. Daphne's tight rein on the finances curbed Henry's excesses and saved the estate from ruin. David hoped they would have an heir so that his son could live his life without the shackles of duty that came with a title. However, Henry and his wife Daphne didn't have children, and the family agreed that Tom was to inherit the title and estate.

David looked out at the swell of the Irish Sea. He felt nausea creep upon him and he shut his eyes and gripped the armrests of his seat. He focused on his breathing to drown out the noise of seasick passengers. David saw an image dancing like a firefly behind his eyelids. Then he saw her: The Priestess, radiant and full of life. She ascended a flight of steps, slowly turning around to look at him. She gestured for him to ascend a set of stairs to her right. Her robes trailed on the steps behind her as she gracefully made her way towards a door. As she slowly turned the handle, David saw white light streaming through. She was waiting there for him. David's eyes fluttered open with the brightness of the light. This was the same vision he had in the passage tomb at Newgrange. She arrived with the morning sun and floated into the chamber. David let out a brief gasp; the Priestess was waking up and coming back to life. All at once, he felt elated and confused, knowing that her rebirth meant his death.

The sound of the ship's horn startled David. Looking out, he saw the headland of Anglesey emerge through sea fog. He made his way below deck to his car. David started up the engine, and a thought went over and over in his mind, 'I must die if she is to live.'

David's mind was racing. As he motored through Wales towards England, he had to check his speed several times. He pulled over to take a break just past Shrewsbury. He looked out over the River Severn as it wound its way south through the Shropshire countryside. David got out of his car to stretch his legs. It was almost dark except for the lights of a few passing vehicles. He walked to the bridge, leaning over to watch the River Severn flowing past. His mind raced with thoughts of the Priest and Priestess. Over and over, one thought tossed around like a branch in the fast-flowing river; 'I must die if she is to live.'

He climbed onto the bridge and stared at the river. It pulled him in like a portal to another world. He was falling. Falling through time, falling through memories, falling through the cosmos to another place, a place where the Priest and Priestess stemmed from the same root. He saw two doors. He reached out his hand towards the light, just one more step. Suddenly, a hand grabbed him and pulled him away from the doorway. Someone was dragging him away from the light. He flailed his arms in vain, but he had no strength left. He surrendered to the force dragging him from the water. The last thing he heard before he blacked out was the sound of sirens.

20

*The battle of good and evil rests in the mind of man.
Similarly, fear and desire are bedfellows that govern the
self-activity of ego. Desire is the motivating force, and fear is
the destructive force. The primary purpose of the human
journey is to derail the forces that propel the ego dream of
separateness and allow the spirit to emerge as a true child of
the Cosmos.*

Viscount Maybury sat in his study, turning over his father's
book in his hands. The green cover had a triskele symbol
denoting the Celtic content. The title read; *'Newgrange:
Archaeology, Art and Legend'*. It was written by the
archaeologist who had overseen the restoration of the
monument at Newgrange. His father had made several notes
in the margins, referencing how the original construction
would have taken place. How he had come into possession of
such detailed knowledge was a mystery to Tom. Perhaps the
young woman who researched his father's papers might have
some ideas. The more he delved into his father's past, the
more mysterious it became.

The island breeze offset the warm summer sun shining
down on the site at Llyn Cerrig Bach on the island of

Anglesea. Clara took a quick break from the dig to drink some water. So far, they had uncovered evidence of the Beaker people from the early Bronze Age. There were also signs of Iron Age and Roman-occupied Britain. Previously, they found evidence of Neolithic dwellers nearby. Looking skyward, Clara wondered what a Neolithic man might make of the site today with the constant hum of traffic from the A55 taking passengers to the nearby port of Holyhead, and the criss-cross plumes of jet trails in the sky. The primary interest of the dig, directed by Professor Berkeley, was to uncover evidence of Druids on the Island. According to the Roman historian Tacitus the isle of Mona, now known as Anglesey, was the stronghold of the druids. The druids were the priestly class of the Celtic World. The power they wielded over the population prompted an attack by the Roman Governor, Paulinus, in 60 CE. The Romans knew that those who controlled the spiritual welfare of the country controlled the people, and according to Tacitus, the Roman Legion found the Druids near the oak groves in Anglesey.

The team were gathering the following morning at sunrise to witness the midsummer solstice at the site. The small tomb at Bryn Celli Ddu was aligned with the rising sun at midsummer. This year, Clara's world revolved around the lives of the Neolithic people. Not only did her research but also the solar year. She was about to experience the midsummer solstice on Anglesey and in exactly six months, she would be in the passage tomb in Newgrange. She felt goose bumps despite the warm summer sun. A shiver went down her spine and something primordial ran through her like cosmic dust. It was similar to the feeling that preceded her vision at Maybury chapel that happened exactly three months ago on the day of the Spring Equinox. Clara's instincts told her both experiences were connected. The Priestess was awakening on the eve of the summer solstice. She was regaining her power.

Clara felt dizzy and sat down on a grassy mound. She was fearful of the consequences with the resurgence of the Priestess. She reached for her phone in the pocket of her backpack to distract her from her current thread of thought. There were a few missed calls, one from her mother, one from her uncle Arthur, and another from Tom Perry. She listened to her voice messages. Her mother hadn't left a message. Arthur called to say he was on his way to the site if she'd like a sandwich from the nearby deli. Tom Perry's message was brief; 'I found something of interest belonging to my father. Call me when it's convenient. Thank you.'

Clara, intrigued, pressed dial and waited for Tom to answer, but it went to voice message. She was about to leave a message when she spotted her uncle crossing the field clutching a brown paper bag. She put away her phone and tucked into the freshly made sandwiches.

Arthur and Clara discussed what they discovered at the site so far. Clara reasoned that whoever built this monument on Anglesey was aware of the passage tomb at Newgrange. Arthur argued that the entrance at Bryn Celli Ddu was aligned to capture the rays of the sunrise at the summer solstice, whereas the Newgrange monument aligned with the winter solstice sunrise. Clara picked up a stick and scratched the alignments as they would appear within a circular henge. Arthur mused on the drawing for a bit and saw the obvious criss-cross shape the tombs made. A stone circle was erected on the site before the passage tomb on Anglesey was constructed. This allowed the builders of the summer monument to follow the direction of the sun, the same method that was used in Newgrange to orientate the roof box with the winter sun. Arthur asked Clara if she had any theories on how stone circles, or henges, developed into passage tombs. He pointed out a few examples of Megalithic sites that were developed or replaced during the Neolithic. On a purely logical level, Clara agreed with him, but she knew there were deeper spiritual reasons behind the progression.

She reflected on Arthur's question for a few moments before answering, 'I believe that at one time, man had an intimate relationship with the cosmos. Humanity was connected by one mind, the cosmic intelligence that guides a flock of birds or shoals of fish. At some point, human minds exerted freewill to separate from the cosmic mind. The human mind gathered knowledge and became identified with a false narrative leading to mortality and death. When all ties became severed with the cosmic mind, humans became separated from each another.'

Clara popped the ring on her cold can of cola and took a mouthful before concluding, 'Of course, this is an ongoing part of the evolutionary process.'

Arthur chewed on a stick of liquorice while mulling over Clara's theory. She spoke with such authority that she could convince the most stoic of doubters.

'Many passages from the Bible would substantiate your theory. But what were the spiritual beliefs of these first dwellers?' asked Arthur, trying to probe further into her theory.

'If there was no separation from the cosmos, then there were no false beliefs,' Clara replied simply. 'A separate deity, or pantheon of gods, came later with separation of consciousness. They needed a shared belief to unite them. The focal point for people of the Megalithic era was the sun. Its energy moved through them to create a world of form and colour. To them, it was entirely natural to follow the movements of the solar year, given that this too was the pattern of their mind.'

'Why do you think the winter solstice continued to be of such significance to Megalithic and Neolithic Man?' Arthur asked, intrigued.

Clara's pupils dilated, despite the bright afternoon sun. 'During the short days at winter solstice, the sun aligns with the central intelligence that rules the cosmos: the primary sun of the whole cosmos. It was a time of death and rebirth.'

Clara inhaled deeply. She had spoken the words so rapidly that she was out of breath. She quickly added, 'As a disclaimer, I don't have an astronomical background to support this conclusion.'

Both Arthur and Clara fell silent for a few minutes. The site seemed more sacred somehow after Clara's words.

Finally, after a long pause, Clara spoke, but somehow Arthur already knew what she was going to say. 'The next step for humanity is the evolution of the mind. We must rise above the fragmented thinking that separates us if we want to save ourselves and the natural world.'

Arthur nodded in agreement. 'It is difficult to give up knowledge and beliefs. We like to think if we sufficiently research a subject, we are experts in our field. We construct our entire education system this way.'

'It takes a critical mass to take an evolutionary step,' Clara replied.

'Perhaps Adam and Eve were the original Hunter-Gatherers,' Arthur mused, 'and their offspring, Cain and Abel, were the first farmers. Their competitiveness caused one to rise against the other.'

Clara smiled at Arthur's analogy before adding to the Genesis theme, 'Perhaps Noah was the first environmentalist. His mission was to protect endangered species from human pollution.'

'I guess all the ancient texts from Homer's Odyssey to the Bible tried to convey the perils of the human mind. As a species, we have fallen a long way from our original glory.' Arthur pushed himself up into a standing position and surveyed the surrounding area. Extending a hand, he pulled Clara to her feet.

Suddenly, there was an atmosphere in the place, almost as if a ritual had just taken place. He looked at Clara. He could tell she felt it, too. Dark clouds scudded in from the sea, covering the clear blue sky.

'I think we may have brewed up a storm,' Arthur said, half joking.

Clara stood motionless for a few moments and Arthur watched her walk towards the tomb. He wanted to follow her, but something rooted him to the spot. Visitors to the site seemed to have vanished, as if scattered by the thunderous clouds. A faint sound of metal on clay echoed across the field where two archaeology students were working on the excavation site. There was no birdsong or insect noise. It was as if the world had stopped breathing. Clara stooped to enter the tomb. To Arthur, she appeared different, almost ethereal. He heard the first rumblings of thunder over the Irish Sea. The rain fell in heavy droplets, a prelude to the coming deluge. Arthur wanted to run for shelter, but he couldn't move. He was under some kind of spell. A bolt of lightning ripped through the dark clouds, followed by loud crashes of thunder. He called out to Clara, but he heard no reply from the burial mound.

Arthur heard someone calling from across the field and he woke from his trance. He turned to see one of the archaeology students beckon him to shelter under a tarpaulin protecting the dig site. When the downpour arrived, it seemed to melt the stony grip that held him like a statue in the field. He ran towards the shelter and took a position where he could still see the burial chamber. Perhaps it was a trick of the light, but through the torrential rain, he saw a group of figures in long white garments on top of the monument. He patted his pockets for his glasses, but remembered he had left them in the car. Arthur blinked a few times, but the image remained. He asked the students if they saw anything. They squinted, trying to see past the heavy rain, and shook their heads. The deluge continued for a further ten minutes before abating. The image vanished with the rain, leaving Arthur to wonder if it had been a trick of the light. He walked across the sodden field towards the tomb and watched Clara emerge.

'Are you okay? That was quite a storm.'

'Yes, I'm fine,' replied Clara, climbing to the top of the burial mound. 'It's quite refreshing to die and be reborn in an afternoon.'

Arthur looked up at her, slightly blinded by the sun emerging from behind the clouds. From the glow on Clara's face, he didn't doubt her.

21

One can never truly point to the beginning or end of a circle. Endings and beginnings are the same. They flow seamlessly one to the other like revolutions of a wheel, each revolution marking another phase in the continual life experience of the universe.

Sunlight streamed through the long sash windows, illuminating the old drawing room in the west wing. The honey colour stone, a trademark of Cotswold houses, came alive with the golden rays of the evening sun. David Perry squinted as he looked through the collection of photographs he had taken with his old Leica camera. Memories came flooding back of adventures through Europe, Asia, Africa and the Americas. He carefully studied the photos he had taken in the Altay Mountains during his 1948 expedition. He picked up the photo of the Jade Mummy and pressed it to his chest. Life had changed utterly since that fateful moment when he first discovered her kurgan.

David survived the fall from a bridge over the River Severn. If it hadn't been for a truck driver, he would have drowned. To this day, he had no clear recollection of why it had happened. During his convalescence, he was assigned a psychiatrist to figure out why he 'jumped' off the bridge. David assured the doctor that he had no suicidal tendencies. He remained on the psychiatric ward for three weeks before being discharged into the care of his son.

Henry had asked Tom frequently to move into Maybury Hall. David noticed he seemed relieved to have a valid reason not to move in with Henry and Daphne. He told his uncle that he needed to be close to his father in Evesham. David moved out of the manor house into a stone cottage on his farm. Tom and his family moved into the big house. David pondered what might have been had he remained in Cheltenham with Gertrude and Tom during that fateful summer of 1948. Gertrude came to take care of him after his release from the hospital. David was grateful for her help, but he was glad when she finally returned to her house in Cheltenham.

David gathered his papers and threw them into a barrel at the gable end of the cottage. Striking a match, he set fire to any private documents. He looked at the photo of the Jade Mummy one last time before consigning it to the flames. A gust of air threw sparks into the air, and the photo flew up and landed a few feet away on the ground. David was temporarily transfixed by the figure that had once held the spirit of the Priestess. Like a flash of light, his mind sparkled with the remembrance; the Priest and Priestess were dual aspects of his true being. The power that entwined them lay beyond the two doors in the cosmos. David finally understood that he encompassed both male and female. He finally remembered his confused thinking that day on the

218

Severn Bridge. He thought that he must die to allow the rebirth of the Priestess.

A spark from the fire caught hold of a gauze curtain billowing through the gable end window. David, lost in his reverie, sprang into action. He ran to the back door of the cottage and down the passageway to the scullery, where the blaze was catching hold. The door was jammed. He rattled the doorknob, trying to push it in when it occurred to him that his housekeeper must have locked it to keep the dogs out. David saw plumes of smoke seeping out from under the closed door. He dashed across the hall into the kitchen and grabbed the keys. He tried several keys before one finally clicked in the lock. David opened the door to a blazing inferno. The flames had taken hold of the curtains and were licking the wooden table and chairs. A pile of logs crackled beside a small tin of gasoline used to light the stove. David grabbed a bucket of water from the kitchen and threw it on the burning logs, trying to quench the flames. He tried to grab the tin of gasoline before it added fuel to the flames but it was too late. The room exploded with flames.

David escaped into the hallway and shut the door behind him, hoping to contain the blaze. He picked up the telephone receiver and dialled 999 for the fire brigade. The dogs were whining behind the living room door. David ran down the hallway to let them out. He whistled or them to follow him out the back door. David turned to see if the fire was progressing further through the house when a lintel collapsed in the living room doorway, blocking his way out. The fire had already spread to the attic, causing the roof to partially collapse. The dogs leapt over the falling beams and out into the backyard. Their barking and the smell of smoke alerted Tom, who came running from the Manor house to the cottage. Calling out to his father, he heard a faint reply from inside the burning house. He tied a handkerchief over his mouth and nose and ran to the back door where he discovered his father trapped under a fallen lintel. He tugged at his father's jacket, tearing and ripping the fabric, until finally he managed to pull him free. He threw David's arm around his neck and dragged him outside. Just as he sat his father down on a bench in the yard, the roof of the cottage caved in. Tom shuddered to think what would have happened had he not heard the dogs making a tremendous racket. They had saved their master's life.

The sound of sirens echoed some way off. Tom jumped up on the wall to see if they were coming in this direction. He spotted a fire brigade on the way towards the farm. His father must have called them. Tom jumped down off the wall and heard choking sounds coming from his father. He was gasping for air. Tom was frantic. He didn't know what to do. His father pointed towards the shed, Tom looked up and spotted his father's old oxygen mask, which he used in high altitudes. He yanked it free from its hook and placed it over his father's face. The fire engine pulled up on the road, and a medic hopped out and ran towards Tom and his father. Looking at Tom he said, 'He's a lucky man. You saved his life.'

The hospital discharged David with minor cuts and burns. The blaze completely gutted the house along with all his possessions. The only thing that survived was a stack of photos and half a dozen paper files containing papers he was about to burn. David smiled at the irony of it all. Most of what he wanted to incinerate had survived, and what he needed had been destroyed.

He moved back into the manor house until he secured new accommodation. He would stay with Tom as a temporary measure until one of his rental properties in Cheltenham became vacant. His eyesight was failing, which made it difficult for him to drive particularly at night. It would be easier for him to live in town rather than out in the countryside. He discussed plans to turn his extensive property on Malvern Road into a retirement home. Tom thought it was a great idea. There were only a handful of decently run care homes in a fifty-mile radius. Tom said he would help him convert the property and ensure the staff was properly trained.

Four months after the fire, David Perry moved onto the top floor of the retirement home on Malvern Road. He had planned to stay for three to four months until the project was up and running. However, one week after his seventy-fifth birthday, he had a stroke which left him partially paralysed. Two full-time nurses were assigned to him, covering day and night shifts. With the help of a physiotherapist, he walked with the aid of a cane. Tom had a lift installed so his father could easily access the top-floor apartment. David Perry was wise enough to know he hadn't much time left on the planet. He felt his energy gain momentum as it prepared to leave the body and return to the two doors. The death of the masculine acted like a coiled spring, releasing the door of the feminine. This was the yin and yang of existence. He opened a new book his son had bought him; '*Monuments of the Boyne Valley*'. He made several notes about the excavation of the passage tomb in the margins, and on pieces of notepaper that he tucked between the pages. There was no way to explain it satisfactorily to anyone without sounding daft, but he had lived in Newgrange at the time of its construction. A mind soaked in judgement and identified with gender could never comprehend the simplicity of the universe. One day the feminine, the dual aspect of his being, would come to find it. He scribbled the notes, symbols and diagrams that he knew one day would make sense to her.

The nurse on night duty arrived with his medicine. David hadn't seen her before. She beamed a smile at him while she prepared his medicine. Her eyes shone with an inner radiance. She was in the early stages of pregnancy. David and his alter ego the Priest bowed to the feminine. The nurse was carrying her into the world.

David closed his book and put it on the nightstand. He took his medicine and whispered a few words to the nurse and her unborn child. It was time to return to the two doors. He would keep watch over the feminine, just as she had guided him for the past seventy-seven years.

22

In a world of temporary things, search for the eternal. Thoughts are seeds that are planted in the mind. You can plant conscious seeds that sprout kindness and gratitude, or unconscious seeds that sprout self-interest, competitiveness and greed. Either way, you reap what you sow.

Flopping onto her sofa, Clara leafed through her mail. A letter from Bath University stood out among the junk mail and regular household bills. She tore it open to read an acknowledgement of her application for a research fellowship. She checked the heading of the letter, dated ten days ago. Since Cormac and Gwen had moved into their house in the Forest of Dean two weeks previously, Clara's post had been lying unopened on her front mat under the letterbox. She glanced at the clock; it was too late to call their office. She would call them first thing in the morning.

Cormac had stacked a few letters and packages on the study table in the guest bedroom. Among them was a package stamped with a seal. It was from the Maybury Estate. It was the book Tom Perry had promised to send her. According to Tom, David Perry was reading it during the weeks before his death. He said it contained diagrams and notes that may interest her. Clara flicked through it. There were several notes in David Perry's small handwriting, along with pieces of notepaper containing maps and diagrams. She set it down on the coffee table to read later. She was tired after the three-and-a-half-hour drive from Anglesey. An accident on the M5 closed two lanes on the motorway, bringing traffic to a near standstill four miles north of Tewkesbury. She lay back on the couch, staring at the ceiling, contemplating her future. She wanted to travel more, perhaps work on archaeological digs in Europe and Asia. She had applied to be part of an archaeology team going to Gobekli Tepe in Turkey, but the competition was fierce. Gobekli Tepi changed almost every assumption made about civilization over the past twelve thousand years. Until the discovery of Gobekli Tepi, archaeologists assumed that the stone circles and passage tombs of the Celtic world were the oldest places of organised worship in the world. However, they discovered megaliths at Gobekli Tepi dating to the tenth millennium BCE. This predated Stonehenge by seven thousand years.

Clara stared at the letter which came from the Archaeology Society, and unsurprisingly, she didn't get a place on the expedition. They said she hadn't enough work experience. There had been thousands of applicants from all over the world. Clara considered her options. She must work for at least a year to pay off her student bills and pay the instalments on her new car. Clara decided to accept the research fellowship at Bath University, if it was still available. She was only an hour's commute from

Tewkesbury to Bath. She had applied to Worcester and Warwick universities and she was still awaiting their response. In the meantime, she had a couple of weeks to enjoy a study free September.

Orla Lewis met her daughter in the square adjoining Bath Abbey after she finished her interview at Bath University. She sat on a bench enjoying the street performers who entertained the crowds of tourists flocking to the city for its Georgian architecture. Currently, a string quartet was playing Chopin's Largo from Violin Sonata in D Major. It was one of Orla's favourite pieces. The late September sunshine cast a glow on the honeyed Bath stone, bathing the cathedral in an ethereal glow. She recalled as newly-weds, she and her husband spent two nights here before continuing to Cornwall for their honeymoon. It was thirty-eight years ago, but to Orla it seemed like only yesterday that they set off in his Ford Capri. She had a photo of Tony standing proudly beside his car in blue jeans and his wild mop of fair hair glinting in the sunlight. He taught her how to drive in that car, which was an indication of the love and trust he had for her. That Ford Capri was Tony's prized possession.

A tap on the shoulder startled Orla. She turned around to see Clara smiling. 'Oh sorry love, I was miles away. How are you? Did the interview go well?'

Clara hugged her mother and replied, 'I will start in two weeks. Someone pulled out last minute, so they offered me the fellowship. So Mum, what planet were you on before I arrived?' Clara asked cheerily.

Orla grinned, 'I was on planet honeymoon. Your father and I came here after our wedding.'

Orla rummaged for pound coins in her purse. She went over to the musicians and dropped the coins into an open violin case. She linked her daughter's arm and they left the square.

'Cormac is leaving work early to join us. He'll send a message when he arrives.'

Clara responded, 'We're only forty minutes from his office. Isn't it great we can get together like this?'

Orla nodded. She was especially happy to meet both her children together. They hadn't been together for several months.

Clara looked at her watch. It was one-thirty, and she was famished. They weaved their way through the crowd towards a cafe by the weir. They ordered food and went outside to sit on the terrace to enjoy the pleasant September afternoon. The sound of tumbling water on the weir soothed Clara. She visibly relaxed, and Orla asked her about her new position at Bath University. Just as she was about to reply, Clara noticed a familiar figure coming their way from the cafe. Orla had her back turned and looked around to see who had caught her daughter's attention. Orla shielded her eyes from the sun trying to see his face. She suppressed a look of surprise when she realised it was Viscount Maybury.

Clara pulled back her chair to stand up but Tom's swift wave of the hand indicated that she remained seated. 'Will you join us?' Clara asked.

Tom nodded his head as the server placed a third chair at the table. 'This is my mother; Orla Lewis,' Clara made the formal introductions. 'Mum, this is Tom..., Viscount Maybury.' Clara still hadn't got used to using his formal title.

'Tom, please', he said diffidently.

'Pleased to meet you,' replied Orla, unaware her daughter was on friendly terms with Viscount Maybury.

'Have we met before?' asked Tom Perry with a quizzical look as he tried to place Orla.

'I met you several years ago,' she replied. 'I worked in the care home your father owned.'

'Yes, of course,' Tom recollected. 'It's very nice to meet you again. 'If I recall correctly, the last time we met was the morning after he died?'

Orla nodded her head and gave a slight side glance at her daughter. Tom turned his attention to Clara. Fate seemed continually to prove there was a link between her and his late father. Clara thanked him for sending her the book his father was reading when he died. She explained to her mother that it was a book on the monuments at Newgrange and David Perry had made several interesting notes. Orla looked thoughtful for a moment and said, 'I remember the book. My father also had a copy.'

She proceeded to tell Viscount Maybury that she grew up on a farm in the Boyne Valley. She remembered the excavation of the site when she was a child. Her father had helped with the excavation in his spare time. The history of the site fascinated him and he was fortunate enough to be present when they discovered the roof box. He spoke of little else for weeks. The monument was officially dated to the fourth millennium BCE in the years following the excavation. Orla remembered how her father marvelled at the precision of the people who constructed the tomb, and how the roof box was perfectly aligned with sunrise at the winter solstice.

Tom encouraged Orla to tell him more about her father's interest in Newgrange and Irish Folklore. She recalled that her father maintained that they were part of a lineage of farmers descended from the earliest known farmers to settle in the Boyne valley. These early settlers introduced farming by observing the movement of the sun and the stars. The passage tomb at Newgrange honoured the sun, proving to her father that the people of the Boyne Valley were descendants of the early settlers who first introduced farming in Ireland. Orla stopped and took a sip of water, giving Tom Perry time to digest her recollections.

'There was one more thing,' she said, as if it had just dawned on her after several years. 'He maintained the passage tomb at Newgrange had a strong link to the archetypal feminine.'

Tom and Clara both shifted in the seats. 'Why?' they chimed simultaneously.

Orla shrugged. 'I don't know. He said it was a tradition that predated Christianity and the Celts.'

Clara mused over her mother's reply. She wondered, by any chance, if her grandfather had kept notes about his observations of Newgrange. It seemed Tom was already ahead of her.

'Do you think it possible that your father kept diaries that may give a clue to why the Boyne Valley was a place of Feminine worship?'

'He kept farming journals, but I'm not sure if they'll contain anything useful.' Orla looked bemused that he should show such an interest in her father's work. She looked at her daughter and her face looked as keen as the Viscount's.

'I can ask my brother John, who lives on the farm, if he's ever come across anything,' added Orla, not wanting to disappoint her eager audience.

'I can have a look when I go over there for the Winter Solstice,' Clara said. 'That's if Uncle John doesn't mind.'

Orla, ever the nurse, noticed Viscount Maybury turn as pale as a ghost. She whispered, 'Can I get you anything?'

He shook his head and patted her on the hand. 'No, thank you, I'm fine.'

Taking a sip of water, he said he must go. His driver was waiting for him. Clara stood up and walked him up the steps to street level, where his chauffeur had parked the car.

'Be careful, my dear. Digging about in the past can cause us to lose all sense of perspective. It was my father's downfall,' said Tom. 'This life is a culmination of many lives, but remember, this is the most important one,' he added as he reached his car.

Clara wrinkled her brow. 'How do you know this life is the most important?'

Tom took both her hands in his. 'Because this is the one you are living.'

Orla noticed her daughter was contemplative for the rest of their lunch. They both noticed a change come over Viscount Maybury when Clara mentioned her visit to Newgrange at the Winter Solstice. Why it should affect him was a mystery to Orla. She tried broaching the subject with Clara.

'Do you think Viscount Maybury is okay? He seemed like he'd seen a ghost when you mentioned your visit to Newgrange.'

Clara was only digesting the incident herself and could offer no insight. 'I'm sure it's nothing to worry about, Mum. He's seemed fine when he drove off.'

Orla let the subject drop, sensing Clara's reticence to discuss the subject. Clara wondered if Tom Perry's reaction had more to do with his father's experience at Newgrange than her upcoming visit. She had read David Perry's notes on Newgrange. He had recounted an episode within the chamber where he felt transported to another lifetime, where he had been a priest overseeing the construction of the Newgrange monument in memory of his wife. The Jade Mummy had once been his wife, the Priestess. It was entirely conceivable that Tom Perry had read his father's notes and wondered if Clara was the Priestess.

Tom Perry looked out the window at the rolling hills of the Cotswolds. He reflected on Clara's revelation about her visit to the passage tomb in Newgrange for the Winter Solstice. This was the event which had driven his father to insanity. Tom never realised what was going on in his father's mind until he read his notes in his book '*Monuments of the Boyne Valley*. Tom had wondered for years why his father had returned a different man from Mongolia in 1948. He seemed to live in the past, cut off from everyone around him and those who loved him. Reading over his notes in the margins, he realised his father had developed a personality disorder. He was living two lives: one as a Priest of the ancient world, another as an explorer, a confused man lost the twentieth century.

Traffic was moving slowly outside Cheltenham. Viscount Maybury instructed his driver to take the exit for Evesham Vale. He wanted to visit his father's old house. Tom sold the Manor house when he inherited Maybury Hall. He needed the money to modernise the plumbing and electrics. The Evesham house was now in the hands of a surgeon, Daniel Patterson, and his wife. He had heard his wife say Mrs Patterson was a formidable lady. They were both trustees on the literary arts council. As the car approached the driveway, he considered what he might say to the current occupants. The gravel drive crunched under the wheels of the Bentley, prompting a young man lounging on the front lawn to look up from his book. Tom rolled down the window and inquired if the owners were home. The young man replied that his mother was inside.

Tom looked up at the newly constructed entrance. Balustrades lined the steps to the front door and continued out to each side of the house. Tom thought it was an attempt to give the house more grandeur than it deserved. A wide terrace stretched the width of the facade, with steps sweeping down to the left and right of the entrance. They had widened the doorway to facilitate two carved oak doors. As he approached the steps of the terrace, an adolescent girl came running outside, narrowly avoiding a collision with Tom. A few moments later, a middle-aged woman came out to the terrace calling after her, 'Annabel, get back here this instant!'

The young girl had already swept down the steps and onto the lawn. She pretended to be out of earshot. Mrs Patterson was about to follow her down the steps when she realised a stranger was standing at the entrance. Annoyed that he witnessed her shrill reprimands, she said in a clipped tone, 'How may I help you?'

Mrs Patterson cast her eyes to the driveway and spotted a Bentley parked there. She altered her tone to a more civil pitch. 'Are you looking for Mr Patterson?'

Tom recognised her from her regular appearance on a gardening programme on television. There were some of her books sitting on a shelf in his wife's potting shed.

'Sorry to trouble you without calling first,' Tom said courteously. 'I am the former owner of the Manor. I was visiting the area and came on impulse. If this is an inconvenient time, I can arrange to call another day.'

'Of course, I didn't recognise you, Sir', Mrs Patterson said almost purring. 'Please, come in.'

'Julia Patterson.' She put out her hand to shake his, 'Pleased to make your acquaintance.'

Tom tried to stifle a grin as he followed her through to the drawing-room at the front of the house. After some banal small talk, Tom got to the point of his visit. He had endured enough of Mrs Patterson's false charms. 'I think I may have left behind some books belonging to my late father when we moved to Maybury Hall.'

'Well, let me see,' Julia said, picking up her laptop. 'We have an inventory of all the books in the library on file.'

Tom noticed how she emphasised the word *library*, giving the impression that it was filled with rare and magnificent books. The study, as his father called it, contained just one wall of bookshelves.

'What are the titles?' Julia Patterson's voice cut across his straying thoughts. Tom didn't know the titles. With affected patience, she inquired in a patronising tone what category they belonged to.

Tom replied, 'Archaeology and History.' He watched as she scrolled through a list of titles.

'Well, we appear to have rather a lot of history books. Come with me to the library and see if you recognise if any books belong to your father.'

Tom heard her emphasis on the word '*if*'. It was clear she thought he was mistaken. Tom followed her to the room where his father spent most of his time during his life here. Luckily, when he moved to the cottage, he left several volumes of valuable books behind in the manor house because there wasn't room at the cottage. Mrs Patterson swept into the room as if it was the library at Oxford. To Tom, it seemed smaller than he had remembered. With a sweeping hand gesture, she showed him the shelves containing the history and travel books. She stepped aside to let him look at the titles. She placed her hand on a shelf containing a series of her gardening books, as if to demonstrate her celebrity status. Tom, shrewdly aware of her intent, ignored the invite to stroke her ego and focused on finding his father's books. He recognised a series of books bound in red leather. Many times, he came to visit his father and found him poring over their contents. Tom turned to Mrs Patterson, firstly making a polite inquiry if she or her husband owned the books. She stepped forward and pulled down one volume. On the inner leaf someone had written the initial DP 'Well, that should solve it,' her voice belying her growing impatience. 'DP are my husband's initials, Daniel Patterson.'

Tom nodded politely. He was wondering how to approach ownership issue when they heard the crunch of gravel outside as a car pulled up. It would seem that the other 'DP' had arrived home. A look of surprise crossed Daniel Patterson's face to see Viscount Maybury standing in his study. His eyes darted to the red leather-bound book in his wife's hands and the mystery was at once solved.

'Ah, I see you came to reclaim your father's old books,' he said genially. 'He was a great explorer.'

Mrs Patterson flushed, 'but your initials are on the inside.'

Her mouth gaped open as she stared at her husband. She looked from her husband to Viscount Maybury.

Tom smiled, 'David Perry, my father's initials.'

Mr Patterson pulled another volume from the shelves. 'I found a photo of him and two colleagues on an expedition, tucked inside this book.'

Tom's driver carefully put David Perry's books in the car. Mrs Patterson said very little, embarrassed by her faux pax. Tom, sensing her discomfort, thanked her for her cooperation. He refused the polite offer of afternoon tea and descended the steps towards the car. As the driver crunched down the gravel driveway, Tom spotted the daughter with another adolescent girl propped up against a tree smoking a cigarette. He hoped that one day she would escape her stifling environment. She might find that there was a vast world beyond the confines of the class system.

Tom placed the red leather-bound books on the bookshelf in Maybury Manor. They might offer some clue why his father obsessed over passage tombs. His instincts told him that his father was exploring the role of the archetypal feminine in Celtic Society. He looked at the calendar on his desk. It was the twenty-first of September. He had three months to present his evidence to Clara Lewis.

23

Hurt can transform people in two ways; the first is by constructing a fortress to keep out potential attacks and trapping pain. The second, by widening the crack inflicted by hurt to escape the hard shell of reason that imprisons the soul.

Charles Embrey missed the exit for Tewkesbury. He slammed his palm on the steering wheel in frustration. The drive from Cambridge had already taken forty minutes longer than his sat-nav had calculated. He continued to the next motorway exit, adding a further ten minutes to his journey. He was going to meet his estranged wife whom he hadn't seen for over two years. His solicitor could have easily handled the divorce papers but he felt he needed closure, or so he had concluded in psychotherapy. It had seemed like a good idea, but now, with all his turbulent emotions arising, he wanted to turn the car around and drive back to Cambridge. He pulled up at the next exit to gather his thoughts. It seemed ironic to him it was he who ended up in therapy when it was his wife who displayed signs of a personality disorder. Sometimes, he wasn't sure who she was. In the last few months of his marriage, he felt he was living with a stranger. Sometimes he awoke to hear her chanting in her sleep. When he shook her awake, he noticed how her blue-green eyes would dilate and turn a darker shade, almost as if she were someone else.

Charles shuddered. He turned the ignition in his car and turned up the heating. He recalled, with vivid alacrity, the winter's night that he woke up to find her pounding the front garden with her bare feet. She went round and round in circular movements, making it look like some kind of shamanic ritual. He was almost afraid to approach her; her wild apparel looked like it belonged to prehistoric Britain rather than the twenty-first century. The frost was thick on the ground and when he called her name and she looked through him as if he wasn't even there. He stood in the doorway calling her name until finally she turned to look at him; the look sent chills down his spine, even now. Finally, she came out of the trance and strolled into the house. She lay on the sofa, her teeth chattering from the cold. Charles fetched a blanket and a hot-water bottle to place at her ice-cold feet. He stared out the front window. The mid-winter sun was rising for the shortest day of the year. Opening his laptop, he typed *'sleepwalking'* in the search engine. After reading a few paragraphs on the NHS website, he concluded it was a temporary condition. Later that day, when she woke up, he told her what had happened. She looked at him in disbelief and thought he was exaggerating. He realised she had absolutely no recollection of the event, and this worried him. Several weeks passed without incident until one morning in March he found her lying in a foetal position outside the house. Fortunately, he found her before the neighbours left for work. She was clutching a large pitcher in her right hand.

Despite Charles' best efforts to convince her to see a psychiatrist, his wife refused to acknowledge there was a problem. He asked a colleague who lectured in psychological and behavioural sciences to call around one evening. She politely answered his questions, assuring him she didn't feel stressed or anxious. Once the professor had left, she calmly went upstairs, packed a bag, and informed Charles that she was leaving. By the end of the week, she had handed in her notice at the university and moved out all her belongings.

Now, two years on, Charles pulled up outside her house. He clutched an envelope containing the papers that would sever legal ties between them. Charles hoped it would cut emotional ties, too. Clara, despite her odd behaviour, was a special woman. He naively thought he could replace her but as time went on he realised he missed her deeply. His therapist asked him if Clara measured up to his ideal woman.

Charles retorted, 'What kind of nonsense is that?'

He was only going to counselling sessions to appease the Head Dean at the college. He insisted Charles seek professional help when his emotional state continually affected his performance.

Charles stepped out of the car and stretched after the long car journey. Suddenly, he felt self-conscious and awkward. He did not know how to approach his wife after a two-year separation. Before he had time to compose himself, the front door opened, and there she stood, a vision of health and happiness, almost as if she had never broken his heart.

'Would you like some tea?' she asked as Charles followed her through to the kitchen.

'Tea would be fine,' he replied.

He took in the open-plan kitchen and living room. She had done alright for herself, he noted as he looked around. He pulled a book down from the bookshelf and flipped through it distractedly, trying to recover momentum. He hadn't expected such waves of emotion to sweep over him. He had missed her. His head was throbbing and his throat felt dry. He helped himself to a glass of water from the filter jug by the kitchen sink. Clara placed a mug of tea on the kitchen counter and a selection of biscuits. She pulled out a high stool from underneath the counter and waited for him to sit down. Charles noted a transformation in her. He couldn't quite put his finger on it. She was so confident, in control of her emotions. The old Clara was always unsure, relying on him to make decisions. He always felt that he was the stronger, mentally and emotionally of the two. Now he wasn't so sure. He tried to regain control by throwing her off balance.

'Do you still have the blackouts? You know the sleepwalking episodes?'

Clara coolly met his eyes. 'I am in very good health, thank you.' Clara put down her mug. 'I am sure you didn't drive all this way to discuss the past when you want to get on with your future. Do you have the papers?'

Charles looked at her steady expression. There wasn't a flicker of the indecisive woman he married. He pulled the envelope out of his coat pocket and left it on the counter between them. While Clara flipped through the pages, it suddenly occurred to him what was different about her. She was more like the woman that emerged during her blackouts. The old Clara had disappeared, and in her place was the shamanic woman he had seen that frosty morning in the front garden.

Clara looked over the pages as a mere formality. She had already received an email from her solicitor with the document attached.

'Freedom at the stroke of a pen,' Charles' inane comment met with no response from her.

Clara picked up a pen and signed her name beside the post-it strip. Glancing at her ex-husband, her eyes flashed and Charles realised she had always been free. The woman he married had disappeared on that winter morning over two years ago. He couldn't explain it, but it seemed like the Clara he'd known had died. Charles didn't know how close he was to the truth, and that in six weeks his ex-wife would face death, in circumstances not even he could have predicted.

As he reversed out of the driveway, Charles Embrey was feeling a little unnerved. He wasn't ready to drive the three-hour return journey to Cambridge. He pulled up at a petrol station, giving him time to consider his options. He could drive to Shropshire to see his Aunt Clarissa. She had generously taken guardianship of him and his brother after their parents died in a boating accident. He dialled the house phone, but there was no answer. It was pointless calling her mobile phone; she always had it switched off. He tried to think if he knew anyone else in the region. There was an old friend from Winchester College; his family had a country pile somewhere near Cheltenham. Scrolling through his contacts, he found the number. Walter Perry picked up his mobile phone and saw the name of an old school friend on the screen. 'Embrey, you old rascal, long time no hear.'

Charles let out a deep sigh. It was good to hear a friendly voice. Charles took the next exit to Cheltenham.

'I'm fine, old chap. By the way, I'm on the way to see you, Perry.'

A message from Walter popped up on the screen with the postcode and directions. Driving through Charlton Kings, he recognised the village; he was close to the Maybury estate. He visited when he was sixteen, over twenty years ago, for a wacky pageant in May, which celebrated the start of summer. Walter, ever the naughty scoundrel, nicked a bottle of scotch and a couple of bottles of wine. He, Walter, and three others scarpered across the fields to the woodland on the edge of the Cotswold Hills. The combination of alcohol and chain-smoking made Charles violently sick. Blacking out, his school friends had to drag him back to the Manor house. Viscount Maybury, Walter's father, gave them a severe dressing down. Walter always veered to the wild side, unlike his brother, James. Walter Perry would have been expelled twice over if it wasn't for his family's influence in Winchester College. He lost touch with Walter for several years after he moved to New Delhi to work with the British

High Commission. The Hargreaves-Perry family had a long history in India that stretched back to the British Raj and the East India Company.

Walter Perry had changed little over the years. He filled out a bit, which was no bad thing, Charles thought, remembering the skinny, long-limbed boy fearless in the face of adversity. Walter quickly summarised his current circumstances in brief sentences between puffs on his cigarette. He spent his time between the Maybury Estate and London, in an apartment he owned in St. Catherine's Dock, near Tower Bridge. He was vague about his work, said it was government-related, giving Charles a distinct impression that it was top-secret.

'So Embrey, what brings you to Gloucestershire on this grey November day?' asked Walter, stubbing out his cigarette.

'I was signing divorce papers,' Charles replied. 'I'm officially a free man,' Charles injected a note of cheeriness, which he didn't feel.

Walter let out a low whistle. 'Join the club mate. Any children?'

'No, you?'

'No. Two dogs. They live in Melbourne.' Walter lit another cigarette. 'We met in Delhi. After we got married, we moved to Australia. It lasted twelve months and then I came home. And you?' Walter asked as he poured them both a drink.

'After two years, I realised I'd married a madwoman.'

'Mr Rochester, I presume,' Walter chuckled as he made a mock bow. 'Did she set your castle on fire, then?'

Charles grinned and took the proffered scotch. 'Just the one. I'm driving.'

'Why don't you stay tonight? It's raining cats and dogs out there now. You can make an early start of it in the morning.'

Walter had a point. Charles swirled the whiskey around his glass while pondering Walter's invitation. 'Are you certain I'm not putting anyone out?'

'Of course not, I'll see that one of the guest rooms is ready.'

Walter poured them both another scotch before leaving to find the housekeeper. Charles threw back his drink and settled back into the armchair. He stared into the smouldering fire, dwarfed by the large marble fireplace. He relaxed with every mouthful of the golden liquor. After a few minutes, footsteps approached. He looked around, expecting to see Walter. Viscount Maybury came to a halt in the centre of the large living room when he realised a stranger was sitting in his armchair. Charles immediately stood up to introduce himself, adding that he was an old school friend of Walter's.

Viscount Maybury regarded him for a few moments before saying, 'You're the boy who got alcohol poisoning. You caused quite a stir at the May Festival, if I remember.'

Charles nodded, feeling like a chastised sixteen-year-old again. It seemed it was a day for retribution, first Clara and now Viscount Maybury.

'Are you married?' he asked, sensing Charles' uneasiness.

'Yes Sir. I mean no Sir, well, eh, not anymore.'

Charles fumbled to find words. The elderly gentleman intimidated him. 'I live in Cambridge. I'm a don at the university,' Charles said, trying to regain composure.

'What brings you to Gloucestershire?' Viscount Maybury asked.

'I was in Tewkesbury visiting my wife... ex-wife... divorce papers.'

Charles wanted another drink. His tongue seemed to be too big for his mouth, causing him to stutter, a condition he developed after his parents died suddenly. He had overcome it years ago by attending speech therapy, but every so often in stressful situations, it returned. Viscount Maybury pointed to the armchair and Charles resumed his seat by the fire. The Viscount stood by the window looking out over the deer park. He said nothing for several minutes making Charles feel uneasy. He heard words tumbling out of his mouth.

'My ex-wife is from near here. I met her in Cambridge where she worked in the archives at the University. I'm a professor of economics.'

Charles continued his speech unguarded. The whiskey had loosened his tongue. 'Unfortunately, she became a little unhinged. I found her performing a strange ritual in the depths of winter. Although, of course, she denied it and made me feel I was the crazy one.'

Charles wanted to clamp his hand over his mouth to stop himself from speaking. For a minute it seemed as if Viscount

Maybury hadn't heard a word he said. He stepped away from his position at the window. Charles felt relieved. He was leaving the room without saying as a word. His relief was short-lived.

Viscount Maybury retraced his steps to the doorway and said, 'What was your wife's name?'

Charles turned around and for a split second, he thought about telling him to mind his own business, but he was a guest in his house. 'Clara Lewis.' The name tasted bitter on his tongue.

24

It is necessary in life to develop one's unique language, aside from the native tongue. The soul has a unique sound and rhythm, which is expressed through art, poetry, and dance. Creativity is the gateway to the soul. It leads to a deeper understanding of the light that permeates all lives, all beings.

It was the week before Christmas and all flights were completely booked out, except for a few at a sky-high price. Clara opted to take the car ferry from Holyhead to Dublin. She secured a morning crossing for the eighteenth of December, two days before her planned visit to Newgrange. Her return sailing was on the twenty-second, giving her enough time to catch up with her relatives in Ireland and to return in time to spend Christmas with her mother in Lyme Regis.

Clara reflected on the phone call she received from Tom Perry. He had tried to warn her about the peril of visiting Newgrange for the Winter Solstice. He based his fear on his father's experience there several years earlier. Tom backed up his argument from his father's notes, citing the death and rebirth of the Feminine in ancient Celtic texts. But Clara wouldn't be deterred. This was her destiny, come what may. Her intuition told her that the archetypal male had taken his place at the time of alignment at the Winter Solstice. Now it was the turn of the feminine, the sacred energy burning within her.

The ferry crossing was smooth enough, considering the time of year. Driving off the ferry at Dun Laoghaire port, she set her sat-nav for Jenny's house in the pretty town of Slane. The drive to Jenny's house would give her time to gather her thoughts on the days ahead. Jenny invited her to stay when she heard she was coming for the winter solstice in Newgrange. She lived three miles from the family homestead on the River Boyne. Clara had fond memories of visits to Slane as a child and later, going to outdoor rock concerts at Slane Castle. She recalled how excited she was going to her first ever gig with Cormac and Jenny in the grounds of the castle.

Letting down her window, cold, fresh air hit her face. Memories seemed to fill the car with stale air. This wasn't a time for nostalgia. Something new was emerging, something that stirred when she found David Perry's photo of the Jade Mummy. Sometimes, it felt as if she was living two lives. She realised she had never understood this dichotomy. Charles didn't understand it either. She hoped it would help them both if she unravelled the mystery of the masculine and feminine inside her.

The scent of truth was intoxicating, awaking a keen sense that this life was a dream, a story arising from her thoughts and actions. Most of these thoughts arose from the conditioned self, a mental stream of thoughts created from learned beliefs. Beyond this conditioned self, she was eternal. The pure energy of her eternal-self resurfaced, with scintillating accuracy, to remind her of this truth. It was difficult for her to put into words how this affected her. Charles had thought she was mentally unstable, and perhaps for a time she was. When she stopped ignoring her intuition everything improved. Her truest self was emerging through long-held beliefs and conditions. Looking for outside validation from her ex-husband had caused conflict and pain, leading to their eventual split. Clara realised that her split from Charles was inevitable. It wasn't his fault. She had outgrown her conditioned-self, and this made them incompatible. Clara's thoughts came to a standstill along with the traffic on the M50, Dublin's orbital motorway. She turned on the radio to get the latest traffic report. There was a collision at the junction with the M1. She checked her phone for an alternative route, but she had already passed the exit. She had no choice but to sit in traffic until all lanes reopened. Clara checked her rear-view mirror. There was at least half a mile of traffic behind her. She proceeded toward the M1 exit at a snail's pace.

Her thoughts drifted to her Celtic heritage, a gift that had fascinated her since she first heard her grandfather's stories. It also provided her with a PhD and not only that, she believed it brought her healing and understanding. It also provided an insight into past rituals that showed unity between man and nature. She felt blessed to have opportunities to revisit times and places charting humanity's long and varied evolution on earth. Her research of the Celts led to a discovery of both her spiritual and cultural ancestry. Both converged at a point before the written word, a time when people communicated not only with language but by transmitting ideas. Instead of using libraries, they tapped into the unknown, some central source uniting all life in the cosmos. Clara was ready to step into the unknown, into the place where all life had emerged in a myriad of forms.

Clara reached the picturesque village of Slane later than expected. Jenny and her husband were keeping watch for her car to pull into the drive. They came out to greet her, followed eagerly by their two-year-old spaniel, Buster. Clive took Clara's suitcase and brought it inside. Jenny gave her cousin a hug, then catching both her hands, she stepped back to look at her. She thought that she looked much better than when she saw her the previous spring in Cheltenham. She congratulated Clara her on her PhD and new position at Bath University. She linked her arm and led her into the house, with Buster following on their heels. Jenny had picked up an array of delicious treats on her way home from work. As was the custom in Ireland, tea was made as soon as a visitor stepped through the door. Clive drained his mug and said he had to return to the farm. He was head groom at his uncle's stud farm outside the village. Jenny proudly told Clara that they'd recently had two winners at Fairyhouse racecourse.

Clara yawned. She had left Tewkesbury at four in the morning to reach the ferry port at Holyhead. Jenny saw her fatigue and suggested she take a nap before dinner. Clara was so tired that she agreed and followed Jenny to the guest bedroom. Almost as soon as her head hit the pillow, she was asleep.

Jenny crept downstairs where Buster was sitting by the back door waiting for his evening walk. Jenny fastened on his collar and pulled on a reflective vest before setting off along the banks of the Boyne for a stroll. At the shortest days of the year, light faded at four-thirty. When she reached the riverbank, she let Buster off lead to sniff and scamper along the footpath. Her thoughts turned to Clara. She had known her since they were toddlers. They loved listening to their Grandad's stories about Irish legends such as Cú Chulainn, Fionn Mac Cumhaill, and the supernatural race known as the Tuatha de Danann. Clara sent her a copy of her finished thesis, which she dedicated to their grandfather, Jack Flaherty. Jenny thought it was an intriguing read and enjoyed the references to the mythical Irish heroes they had grown up with in song and legend.

As a child, Jenny adored her English cousins who came to visit during school holidays. Clara became more like a sister, given that they both were the only girls in their respective families. As teenagers, they spent hours texting each other about their latest crush, exchanging music tastes or discussing the latest cinema release. Somewhere in their early twenties, they lost touch, both following separate paths and making plans with their new circle of friends. Jenny didn't see Clara for three years, and then one day she received an invitation to her wedding. Jenny had never met Charles Embrey. She hoped they would be happy but when she saw them together before the wedding, her hopes faded for a happy union. Clara seemed different, less carefree. She was moulding her life to suit Charles and his lifestyle. She felt that somewhere underneath, her childhood friend was suffocating. On the night before the wedding after one too many glasses of wine, Jenny summoned the courage to ask Clara if she was happy. Clara replied tersely, 'Yes, of course I am.'

Jenny took another gulp of wine and probed a little deeper, 'Do you remember when we were kids and we would wear mum's lace curtains to pretend we were getting married?' Clara cracked a smile.

Jenny continued, 'I wanted to marry Joe O' Brien, and you wanted to marry the king of the Tuatha de Danann!' They both erupted in laughter.

Finally, Clara caved in and said with a sigh, 'Oh Jenny, I don't know who I am anymore. Night time is the worst. I close my eyes and see shadows, ghosts of people I used to be.'

'What do you mean, people you used to be?' Jenny lowered her voice, trying to hide her alarm. She poured them both another glass of wine. 'Have you spoken to Charles about it?'

'No, he'd think I'm crazy,' Clara replied. Seeing the look on Jenny's face, she added, 'You think I'm crazy?'

She tried to stand up and stumbled, knocking a glass of red wine onto the cream rug in her parent's living room. Jenny sprang to her feet to help clean the mess. The moment passed, and neither friend mentioned it again.

Jenny returned from the dog walk and unlocked the back door. She put Buster into the adjoining garage with his doggy treat. She went upstairs to change into a clean pair of jeans and noticed Clara's door slightly ajar. She peeped in to see she was fast asleep, with the woollen throw pulled up to her chin. Jenny felt protective of Clara and she was glad they saw more of each other now. She closed over the door and tiptoed along the landing to her bedroom. Taking out an old photo album, she looked at the strip of photos she and Clara had taken in a photo booth when they were twelve. They looked so happy and carefree, Jenny with her tongue out, Clara in fits of giggles as she did bunny ears with her fingers. Jenny felt a pang of remorse. She had judged Clara for her unusual admission the night before her wedding. Jenny did not stay in touch with her afterwards, justifying it by thinking that Clara had a new life and new friends. She remembered a family gathering a couple of years back where she overheard a conversation between her cousin Linda and a friend that Clara's marriage was in trouble. Jenny recalled, to her shame that she asked Linda to expand on the story. She said that Charles wanted to admit Clara to a psychiatric ward. Jenny was about to dismiss the rumours as total nonsense when Orla came in and said, 'Please get your facts straight before spreading pernicious rumours.'

Jenny was mortified. She had no idea Orla was there, and seeing the look of hurt and disbelief on her aunt's face, she knew she had crossed the line. She apologised to Orla before when she got her on her own and although she accepted her profuse apology, Jenny knew she wouldn't forget it. She said she wouldn't tell Clara about the incident, not for Jenny's sake, but because it would upset Clara. It taught her a lesson she would never forget.

When Clara finally appeared with tousled hair and crumpled clothes, Jenny was in the kitchen reading an equine magazine to help take her mind off things.

'I'm so sorry, Jenny, I slept longer than I wanted to. Weren't we supposed to be at your parents an hour ago?'

Jenny patted the seat beside her at the table and shook her head. 'We'll go tomorrow. Here, you must be famished. There's stew on the stove.'

Clara forgot how good Irish stew tasted. It reminded her of cold winter evenings when she and Cormac came home from school. Their mother would have a pot of stew ready for them on the stove. She took down a bowl from the plate rack and filled it with stew. When she had finished, she and Jenny sat on a couch in the kitchen chatting about their fond memories of their grandfather. Clive popped his head in to say goodnight before going upstairs. Jenny offered Clara a nightcap, but she shook her head and opted for a cup of herbal tea. She sat sipping her peppermint tea without saying a word. Jenny felt vulnerable, almost as if her recollection of her previous betrayal showed on her face.

She felt tears sting her eyes and reached out. Placing her hand on Clara's arm, she said, 'I'm sorry I wasn't there for you when you left Charles...' her voice tapered off as she choked back tears.

Clara remained silent, her eyes conveying an understanding. Jenny reached for a tissue to dry her eyes.

Clara reached out and placed her hand on her arm. Jenny looked her in the eye for the first time in years. She saw a woman rooted in her power, sure of her place in the world.

When Clara finally spoke, her voice was clear and strong. Jenny listened as she revealed her reasons for coming to Newgrange at the winter solstice. She explained that all the voices in her head, of which she spoke of on the eve of her wedding, were the female ancestors, a line of female suffering that stretched back to the beginning of time. Jenny hung on her every word; they had power and truth in them. Clara explained how the journey through the ancient Celtic world had led to a journey within. It led to a source where masculine and feminine energies were equal. This source directed the path of each sentient being that inhabited the earth. Clara said she realised why the Celts hadn't documented their history. History wasn't part of the psyche of ancient man. They kept no tablets or documents of the past because they integrated knowledge and purpose as part of the present.

It was after midnight when Clara and Jenny went upstairs to their rooms. Jenny quietly opened the door and crept into bed, trying not to wake Clive. Lying on her pillow, she felt tears slide from the corner of her eyes. She, too, felt the pain of the feminine, present in every woman since the dawn of time.

25

Love is the ruler of the Cosmos and of all of its particles. In the depth of winter, it pours liquid light through the darkened chamber of death. To the guests of the earth, it marks the end of the solar year and hopes for the year to come. For the sacred few who feel the grass grow through their feet, water flow from their fingers and flowers budding on their lips; all life rushes toward them, crowning them as kings and queens of the earth.

Driving up the lane to the Flaherty farm gave Clara goose bumps. She remembered as a child how she trembled in anticipation of adventures and stories that were awaiting her. Jack, striding across the farmyard to the stables, gave her a wave. Gavin, Jenny's younger brother followed behind, carrying a saddle. Jenny stopped the car and Clara jumped out to greet them. Amid the joviality and hugs came a booming voice from the back door of the farmhouse. John Flaherty came out to greet his niece and ushered everyone into the kitchen, where Tilly produced a tray of freshly baked scones from the Aga. Gavin, unable to resist the smell, pinched one from the cooling rack. Tilly playfully flicked a tea towel at him. They all gathered around the large oak table in the kitchen. Clara asked what time was lunch as she reached for her second scone. At this rate, she wouldn't be able to eat until tomorrow.

Jack replied with a grin, 'Don't worry, Clara. I've tacked up a mare for you. You can work off that extra scone,' he added cheekily.

Clara's mouth was full. Jack took advantage and retreated to the back door to pull on his riding boots. Clara swallowed a mouthful of scone and jam, shouting after him, 'Hope you're ready for a real challenge.'

She laughed, remembering all the times she had outstripped him when he was a young boy, spurring on his competitive streak. But by the age of ten, not one of them could compete with him on the track.

John Flaherty asked Clara about her work at Bath University. He inherited his father's enthusiasm for the Neolithic. He had worked at stables in the Wiltshire Downs in his early twenties, only a few miles from the stone circle of Avebury. John had met Tilly, who grew up in Marlborough, on a night out with friends in Salisbury. A year later, they were married.

John sensed Clara's eagerness to get out to the stables, and he asked Gavin to tack the horses. Clara thanked Tilly for the tea and scones. Feeling like a young girl again, she excitedly skipped outside and followed Gavin to the stables.

Jack held the reins as Clara pulled herself up onto the chestnut mare. She fastened the riding helmet underneath her chin before Jack handed her the reins. Gavin had farm work to get on with and he drove the tractor to the higher fields behind the farmyard. Clara's horse trotted behind Jack's, through the yard and onto the farm track. Turning through an open gate, Jack's horse broke into a canter. Clara followed suit, exhilarated by a sense of freedom as the wind whipped tendrils of hair across her face. She was flying through the landscape, utterly wild and free...

Ayzik the Priestess rode like the wind over the plains on her trusted mare that led to the foothills of the Altay Mountains. The passing clouds threw shadows over the hills and the morning sun transformed the land with a golden glow. They were people of the sun; it was their ritual to greet the sun each morning and give thanks for another day on earth. She looked at her arms gripping the rein. Tattoos covered her arms from wrist to elbow, denoting creatures of the Altays. She loosened her grip on the reins and dug her heels into the horse's flank to go faster, her hair flying behind her as she soared at full gallop through the landscape...

'Clara, Clara, pull up. PULL UP!' Someone was screaming at her. It was too late. Clara came to a sudden halt at the precipice of a large pond. The horse bolted, throwing her down the bank. Jack heard the loud splash from 50 yards away.

Clara struggled for air. She couldn't move. She was deep in mud and silt at the bottom of the pond. Clara stopped struggling and let go. She saw two doors opening before her. There was utter peace.

She stood at the entrance to two doors. She reached out her hand to open the door filled with light.

Jack pulled up at the pond and dismounted his horse. Slipping and sliding down the bank, he saw Clara lying face down in the water. He tugged at her clothes, trying to pull her out of the silt and mud. He cursed himself for not clearing the pond earlier that year. He pulled and tugged against the suction until finally, he dragged her lifeless body onto the embankment. He wiped the mud off her face and cleared any silt from her mouth. Frantically, he tried to resuscitate her, but he couldn't feel a pulse. He pulled out his phone and called the emergency services before calling Gavin. A few minutes later, he heard the tractor coming at breakneck speed down the field. The horses were spooked and ran back towards the farmyard. Jack wouldn't give up. He kept breathing air into her mouth and performing chest compressions hoping to revive her. Gavin knelt beside him and took over while Jack felt for a pulse. He looked at his brother and shook his head. Clara was dead.

A few minutes later a medic arrived on the scene, followed ten minutes later by an ambulance. The paramedic knelt beside Clara. She felt for a pulse but found none. She was about to declare time of death when Jack shouted, 'Her hand moved!'

The medic put her ear close to Clara's heart. 'She has a pulse, but it's very faint', she said, her eyes wide in amazement.

Jack sat in the back of the ambulance, praying for Clara to pull through. She looked so vulnerable hooked up to the breathing apparatus. A paramedic asked him questions about Clara's fall, which he tried to answer as accurately as possible. How long she had been underwater until he pulled her out? When did he begin CPR? They reached the hospital in thirty minutes and they wheeled Clara to an emergency room. Jack sat in the waiting room feeling helpless. He pulled his phone from his pocket; he had ten missed calls. Jack phoned Gavin, who was shutting in the horses in the stables. He handed the phone to their father, who was sick with worry. Jack told him what happened and he nodded gravely.

'She's in a critical condition. They're not saying much, but it's not looking good...' Jack's voice trailed off. John Flaherty heard the desperation in his son's voice. There was little hope.

John Flaherty didn't know how to tell his sister the terrible news. He took a deep breath before making the dreaded call to Orla. He relayed what happened trying to sound calm and reassure her, they were waiting for an update from the hospital. Orla Lewis immediately understood that her daughter was in a critical condition. It was not what her brother said that alarmed her, but what he didn't say. She hung up and called Cormac. They needed to get on the next flight to Dublin.

John and Tilly made their way to the emergency room, where they found Jack pacing up and down. As soon as a nurse came through the double doors, Jack rushed over to get an update on Clara's condition. She asked him to wait for the A&E doctor, saying he would be along shortly. It seemed an interminable few minutes until a young doctor emerged and asked for John Flaherty. John, Tilly and Jack gathered round to hear what he had to say. Jack leaned on a chair, not trusting his legs to hold him up. The doctor said he had performed a tracheotomy to help her breathe. She was being transferred to ICU where she would be aided by a respiratory machine.

John and Jack asked questions simultaneously; 'Is there brain damage?' 'Will she breathe on her own again?'

The doctor replied that the next twenty-four hours were critical. John, shaking the hand of the young doctor, suddenly felt ancient. The doctor introduced himself as Dr Altan. John regarded the doctor's kind eyes. He looked of Asian descent, perhaps from China or Mongolia.

'You look so young,' said John absently as he focused on the doctor's features, trying to suspend any bad news he might impart.

Dr Altan smiled. 'I've been an A&E doctor for five years,' he said to reassure him. 'I'll send someone for you when your daughter is settled in ICU.'

John was about to tell him she was his niece but realised she felt like a daughter to him. He went out into the hospital grounds to get some fresh air. He felt so grateful for the simple act of breathing. Jenny came running across the car park towards him, waving frantically. He told her what the doctor had said and that it would be an hour before they had an update on her condition.

'It's my fault, Jenny.' Jack felt tears sting his eyes. 'I shouldn't have let her take off at a full gallop.'

Jenny put her arm around her brother. 'You can't blame yourself, you did everything you could,' she said, trying to reassure him. 'Clara wouldn't want you to think like that.'

Jenny's phone buzzed. It was Cormac. She passed on what the doctor had said. Clara was out of the operating theatre and on her way to ICU. He and Orla were waiting to board a flight from Bristol Airport. Jenny volunteered Clive to collect them at Dublin Airport. Cormac replied that there was no need as they had a hire car. They hoped to reach the hospital by ten pm.

Tilly picked up a few things for Clara in a department store near the hospital. She was unsure whether to get a nightdress or pyjamas, so she picked up one of each. She went to the check-out and hurried back to the car. She pulled in at a deli to pick up food and drink in case anyone felt like eating later. No one had an appetite at the moment. She received a text from Jenny asking her to pick up a brush and dry shampoo. She double-parked outside the pharmacy and ran in to get them and any other toiletries Clara might need. As she hopped back into her car, her phone buzzed. It was John; Dr Altan was with Clara in ICU. She threw the things on the front seat and drove back to the hospital.

Ayzik, the Priestess, drifted into a peaceful sleep. Dreaming of her home country in the mountains, she could smell juniper berries and the waft of pine needles after the rain. She stepped closer to a wild apple tree to pluck its ripe fruit; she tripped and tumbled into a deep hole beneath the earth. An enormous pile of stones entombed her. She felt suffocated; she tried to breathe, but there was no air.

Someone was coming. He lifted one eyelid and then the other, shining a bright light into her eyes. She saw his brown eyes shining like sunlight; it was Zarun; he had found her. He had come to take her home.

Jack Flaherty stood up every time he heard the door open from ICU. The doctor, followed by two others, had rushed in almost twenty minutes ago. Jenny tried to calm him, despite her overwhelming anxiety. Eventually, Dr Altan emerged and came to speak to them.

'What happened?' asked Jenny, almost afraid to hear his answer.

'She is regaining consciousness.' Dr Altan began with the positive news before adding, 'However, it's too soon to say if she'll make a full recovery. We should have a clearer picture by tomorrow morning.'

Jack looked at Jenny and let out a deep sigh. She responded with a sigh of her own. They were in for a long night.

Ayzik, the Priestess, tried to open her mouth to speak to Zarun. She heard his voice clearly as he tried to soothe her. He was waiting for her. She must wake up. The revolving door of life and death had separated them for far too long.

Jenny asked the nurse if she could take a few things to Clara. She asked her to wait while she paged Dr Altan. She smiled at Jenny. Opening the door to ICU, she said, 'The doctor said you can see her for a few minutes.'

Jack jumped up to go with them, but the nurse raised her hand and said 'only one visitor at a time.'

Cormac and Orla landed in Dublin Airport at ten-past-eight. They had a twenty-minute delay on the runway in Bristol waiting for take-off. There was much joviality among the passengers who were already in a festive Christmas mood. Cormac thought his mother would pass out with anxiety. Just before take-off, he received a text from Jenny to say Clara was stable. As soon as they touched down on the runway in Dublin, Cormac sprang out of his seat and grabbed their bags from the overhead lockers. There was a long queue for the automated passport control. Cormac beckoned to a supervisor to tell her they had an emergency. They unhooked the security strip and rushed them through. Cormac linked Orla's arm and led her to the car hire office. They were on the M1 within ten minutes. Cormac checked the best route on his phone and pressed 'start'. They should reach the hospital at ten pm.

John checked his phone and told Tilly that Orla and Cormac had landed in Dublin and were on the way to the hospital. He checked the time; it was after nine. He went to join Tilly, Jack and Gavin in the canteen. Jenny was in ICU with Clara.

Jenny gasped when she saw how frail Clara looked. She had a drip and a tube from her neck hooked up to a breathing apparatus. Tears stung her eyes, and she needed a moment to compose herself. A nurse at the station placed a stool beside the bed and said, 'Ten minutes.'

Jenny placed her palm on Clara's hand. Dr Altan arrived at the nurses' station and flipped through some charts. He briefly smiled at Jenny as he placed a cuff around Clara's right arm to check her blood pressure; all the time, he held her hand to reassure her. Jenny thought it was an enormous responsibility to be an A&E doctor. Dr Altan looked the same age as she was or perhaps even younger. He had a very gentle manner and his brown eyes brimmed with kindness. She observed how he spoke to Clara as if she were fully conscious, giving Jenny fresh hope that she would recover. Perhaps if anyone could rescue her from her coma, thought Jenny, it was this kind man. Dr Altan nodded to Jenny as he was leaving. His shift was over. He asked her to speak to Clara just as she would normally. When he left, Jenny leaned closer to Clara.

'Our friendship means the world to me. I hope that wherever you are, you can find a way home.'

Ayzik's eyes fluttered open, recognising the voice of her sister, Nasif. She tried to speak but no sound came out. She drifted back into a deep sleep...

Jenny called the ICU nurse to come over. 'I saw her eyelids flutter open,' she said breathlessly.

She stepped aside as the nurse leaned over her and checked her pulse before returning to the nurses' station.

Jenny thought she was ignoring her. 'I know what I saw,' she said, trying to lower her voice.

The nurse was on the phone. Unbelievable, thought Jenny. The nurse returned and in a low voice said, 'I have paged Dr Altan. I'm sorry, but you must leave now.'

Jenny reluctantly left ICU and waited outside for Dr Altan to return. She wanted to tell him exactly what she saw. There was no doubt in her mind that Clara had tried to open her eyes. Jack tried to keep pace with her as she grew tired of waiting and charged towards the main desk. She asked them to page Dr Altan. They took the details and said they would try to reach him, but he was officially off duty. The nurse gave her the name of the doctor on night duty and asked Jenny to wait in the ICU waiting room until he came.

Jenny turned back toward ICU when she saw Dr Altan in the hallway speaking to another consultant. He looked at her and saw her face flushed with anxiety. He asked her to take a few deep breaths and then tell him what had happened. She told him that Clara had tried to open her eyes. Dr Altan turned to his colleague who was coming on for the night shift and after a brief discussion, they both went into ICU. Jenny sat outside, wondering what was going on.

Ayzik listened carefully. She heard a wheezing sound, something she had never heard before. Zarun had returned. He hadn't abandoned her.

Orla and Cormac arrived close to ten. John and Tilly were waiting anxiously in reception for them.

'Clara attempted to open her eyes,' John said. 'It's a good sign,' he added, trying to ease his sister's anxiety.

On the way to ICU John explained to them that the doctor who operated on Clara had gone off-duty but he would be back in the morning at eight. The night duty doctor had been to check on her. Cormac patted his uncle on the back, thanking him for staying with Clara. He told them to go home and get some rest. He promised he would call him if there was any change.

When they reached ICU, only one visitor was allowed in. Tears streamed down Orla's face as she took her daughter's hand in hers. She spoke softly, 'You are my angel. I hope you find your wings and come back to us.'

The nurse on night-duty looked over briefly before bowing her head to hide a tear. There was something heartbreaking about a parent watching their child struggling to live, or in some cases, struggling to die.

Cormac and Orla took turns through the night to spend an allocated ten minutes every hour by Clara's side. John, Tilly and Jack left the hospital at midnight. Jack wanted to stay, but Cormac insisted he go home to get some rest. He blamed himself for Clara's accident and was emotionally drained. Jenny insisted on staying until Dr Altan returned in the morning. She briefly dozed off. When she woke up, she was stretched out on a row of chairs with Cormac's heavy winter coat thrown over her. She looked up at the clock on the wall. Five hours until the day shift began.

Ayzik, the Priestess, saw images of a man and a woman entering through two doors. She had entered this world at precisely the same moment as Zarun. Beyond the two doors, they were one light source. Here, in the physical world, they were two; experiencing life in a male and female body. Over several lifetimes as man and woman, they fell out of step with each other. When she entered a door, he left through the other. The number of times she had to live in the physical world without Zarun distressed Ayzik. She felt his hand in hers. He had returned to her side. He was waiting for her to wake up. She summoned the power of the rising sun, the power that guided her people to open her eyes...

Orla Lewis stood by the window in ICU waiting for Dr Altan to complete his check-up. He was a capable young doctor. Being a nurse, she wanted to know a little of his background training. His parents were killed in a car accident when he was nine and he came to Britain to live with his mother's family in Oxfordshire. He studied at Oxford University and did his internship here at Tallaght hospital in Dublin.

Orla glanced at her watch; it was ten minutes before nine. The sun was about to rise on the shortest day of the year. This morning, Clara should have been standing in the passage tomb at Newgrange, watching the sunrise light up the burial chamber. She glanced at the bed where a machine was keeping her beautiful daughter alive. Rays of sun shone through the window, falling across Clara's face. Dr Altan seemed to murmur something in her ear. Orla couldn't quite make out what he was saying until she realised he was speaking his native Mongolian language.

Suddenly Clara's eyes opened. They looked piercingly blue in the first light of day. Orla couldn't move, she felt rooted to the spot. Clara's lips curved into a smile at the young doctor leaning over her. He said, 'Welcome back.'

Orla felt emotion crash around her as she watched her daughter reach out to touch his face.

Cormac and Jenny jumped to their feet when they saw a team of consultants go through the doors of ICU. Before they could ask what was going on, Orla emerged to tell them

Clara had regained consciousness. They were removing the tube so she could breathe normally. It was a tense few minutes while they waited outside the operating theatre for news of Clara. Jack arrived just as Dr Altan came out with a look of relief on his face. Clara was breathing normally and her vital signs were normal. They were optimistic that she would make a full recovery.

Clara opened her eyes as the doctor explained he was going to remove the tube from her oesophagus. She winced as she felt a needle in her hip. The nurse placed a reassuring hand on her arm, telling her it was an injection to help her relax. Dr Altan applied pressure to her chest. A deep breath filled her lungs, activating the most powerful alchemy on the planet, the force that brought life into all sentient beings.

Zarun, the Priest, looked into Ayzik's eyes and said, 'Welcome back.'

She watched him leave with his medical team. Finally, they had returned to earth at the same time and place. The circle was complete.

EPILOGUE

The spiral of events happened rapidly. I waited, in anticipation, beyond the two doors for the conscious return of masculine and feminine energy. I am the union of masculine and feminine. It matters not what gender each form takes on earth. I am the consciousness from which both energies emerge into the physical world. As the cycle of evolution completes a revolution, both doors open to receive twin aspects of consciousness. I can see with equanimity the simultaneous unfolding of both aspects of my energy field; Masculine and Feminine. One is luminous, filled with colour, the other glows with inner heat.

In each human, both masculine and feminine energy are equal. How the energies separate, and how they reunite, is down to each pairing. They are free to experience the physical world separately, yet they must always remember that they are one. If they forget this truth, they will suffer a loss that causes a chasm deep in the psyche. This chasm causes them to identify with their physical gender as a man or as a woman, thus forgetting their highest consciousness as both Masculine and Feminine energy. True pairings of masculine and feminine can manifest as same gender or opposite gender. True pairings require no outer confirmation, nor are they attached to ritual and ceremony to cement what is already whole. This awareness keeps both doors open so that I, the source and unity of both their parts, have a complete view of the physical world beyond the two doors.

About the Author

Collette O'Mahony is the author of many publications, including the Matrix of Light series. Her writings explore the evolution of human consciousness and authentic living. Harmony and wellbeing are themes running through all of Collette's books, offering the reader practical techniques to release stress and anxiety. Her writing is pragmatic and grounded in her experience of dealing with life's challenges. Collette lives in England.

www.colletteomahony.com